ALSO BY KRISTEN PROBY

LOVING
Cara

KRISTEN PROBY

POCKET BOOKS

New York London Toronto Sydney New Delhi

Pocket Books
A Division of Simon & Schuster, Inc.
1230 Avenue of the Americas
New York, NY 10020

First Pocket Books paperback edition February 2014

POCKET and colophon are registered trademarks of Simon & Schuster, Inc.

For information about special discounts for bulk purchases, please contact Simon & Schuster Special Sales at 1-866-506-1949 or business@simonandschuster.com.

The Simon & Schuster Speakers Bureau can bring authors to your live event. For more information or to book an event, contact the Simon & Schuster Speakers Bureau at 1-866-248-3049 or visit our website at www.simonspeakers.com.

Interior design by Kyle Kabel
Cover illustration by Alan Ayers

Manufactured in the United States of America

10   9   8   7   6   5   4   3   2   1

ISBN 978-1-4767-5900-5
ISBN 978-1-4767-5899-2 (ebook)

For Gram

Acknowledgments

I would like to thank my editor, Abby Zidle, for her patience and good humor while working with me on our first project together.

To my agent, Kevan Lyon, for your endless hard work and dedication, and for believing in me.

To my publicist, K. P. Simmon of Inkslinger PR, for ALL THE THINGS!

A big thank-you goes out to Kent Laudon, northwest Montana's wolf management specialist for Montana Fish, Wildlife & Parks. Thanks, Kent, for spending time explaining wolf habits to me. Any mistakes in this story are my own.

And to you, the reader. Without you, there would be no stories. Thank you from the bottom of my heart.

Prologue

The cell phone on my belt vibrates against my hip, and I pull it from its holster, register my dad's name on the caller ID, and answer.

"What's up, Dad?"

"Where are you, Josh?" His voice is hard but calm, and all the hairs on my body immediately stand on end.

"I'm checking fence on the far-west pasture, about fifteen minutes from the house."

"We need you here, Son."

"Is Mom okay?" My voice is calm, and just as hard as Dad's. We're nothing if not calm in a crisis.

"She's fine, but we have a situation."

"I'm on my way."

Holstering the phone, I kick Magic gently and

she immediately sets off in a gallop toward the house.

What the fuck is going on?

The last time Dad called with that tone in his voice, my brother, Zack, had been hurt in Afghanistan.

He's in Afghanistan now.

Before long, the old, sprawling house comes into view. Although mostly retired, Mom and Dad still live in the big house, and I rebuilt one of the old farmhand houses on the opposite side of the property a few years ago. I'm in charge of the Lazy K Ranch now, and I love every minute of it.

Mom and Dad step out onto the porch as I dismount, and suddenly I hear tires on the gravel driveway.

"What's going on?" I demand, scowling as I watch my dad's eyes go hard. A blue rental pulls to a stop in front of us.

"Kensie called," he mutters.

"How could she do this to him?" Mom whispers with tears in her eyes. "To both of them?"

"Would someone like to tell me what in the hell is going on?"

"Get out of the car, Seth."

I know that voice. Ice instantly runs through my veins as I turn to see Zack's wife, Kensie, pull herself out of the passenger seat, open the back door, and pull my nephew, Seth, out of the car, along with a duffel bag, which she throws without care onto the dirt.

"What's this about?"

"Seth's your problem now," she replies coldly.

My eyes immediately fall on the boy, who's looking down and drawing circles in the gravel with the toe of his worn shoe. His jeans are a size too small, the hem riding above his ankles, and his T-shirt is stained and dirty.

"Seth isn't a problem," Mom replies, and flies down the stairs to pull Seth into her arms. He stiffens, but doesn't pull away. He also doesn't hug her back.

Jesus, he was here two years ago, bright-eyed and interested in all of the ranch animals. Now his eyes are dull and tired.

"He is for me," Kensie replies with a shrug. Her clothes are impeccable, and I assume purposefully a size too small. Her hair and nails are polished and perfect. She winks over at me and my stomach rolls in revulsion. "How are you, handsome?"

"What is this about?"

"Zack made noise about wanting a divorce the last time he called from BFE, so I beat him to the punch. Cole"—she gestures toward the car and the man sitting impatiently inside—"doesn't want a kid around, and frankly, I'm tired of being a full-time mom."

"You're *tired* of being a full-time mom?" I yell. Dad shakes his head and my mom tries to pull Seth away and into the house, but Dad puts his hand on her shoulder, stopping her.

Seth shouldn't hear this bullshit.

"Twelve years I have been alone with him," she sneers, and points her finger at her son. "While Zack spent more time in a desert or in a plane with the army, leaving us in a different city every two years, I stayed because Zack's paychecks were nice, and I didn't have to work, but I'm done. I sold his car." Dad gasps and I want to wrap my hands around her little neck and squeeze. Zack loves that damn car. "I gave the rest of his shit to charity and I'm giving you the kid. If Zack wants to traipse around the world every year and ignore his family, fine, but I'm done! I deserve more than this!"

She's screaming now, carrying on about what is owed to her, but I can't take my eyes off Seth. His face hasn't shown one bit of emotion. Most kids would be in tears, horrified by their mother's behavior.

How long has this been going on?

"Seth is always welcome here," I begin, and take a few steps toward Kensie, satisfied when she shuts her foul mouth and her eyes go round as I get closer.

I've never enjoyed scaring women. It's easy for me to do with my size and is something I've always been careful of.

But I'm going to scare the shit out of her.

"But *you* are not. Seth will stay with us until Zack is back in the States in a few months. You are never to come back here." I step closer and loom over her. "If you ever show your face here again, I'll have you arrested for trespassing and I will ruin your pathetic life."

Her eyes widen and her jaw drops in surprise as she takes half a step away from me, but she quickly pulls herself together and squares her shoulders, pulling her painted-on eyebrows into a scowl.

"Why would I ever come back here? There's nothing here I want." She raises her chin defiantly and, without a look at Seth, climbs in the car, which peels out of the driveway.

"Oh, honey," Mom whispers, and kisses Seth's hair. He shrugs and pulls away, grabs his bag, and looks up at me for the first time since they drove up.

"Can I stay here, Uncle Josh?" His eyes flick over to Magic and back to me. He always loved the horses.

"Of course, buddy, you always have a place here."

He nods soberly and looks back down at the ground, waiting to be told what to do. Mom is openly crying now, and Dad just shakes his head, wipes his hand down his face, and sighs. "Come on, Seth. Grandpa will show you to your room. You can have your dad's old room."

"I don't want anything of his," Seth spits out, his hands in fists. "I'd rather sleep in the barn."

Dad blinks in surprise, glances to both Mom and me, then frowns. "Okay, the spare room it is then."

"Come on, honey, let's get you settled and I'll fix you some lunch." Mom smiles at Seth through her tears and wraps an arm around his thin shoulders. "We've missed you so much. There are some fish out in the creek that need to be caught, you know. . . ." Her voice fades away as the three of them walk into the house, and all I can do is stand here, my hands on my hips, and wonder what the fuck just happened, and what are we going to do with a twelve-year-old boy?

CHAPTER

— EARLY SUMMER —
CARA

"Cara, do you have a minute?" My boss, Kyle Reardon, pokes his head in my open classroom door and offers me a warm smile.

"Sure, what's up?"

He saunters in and takes a long look around my empty classroom. The breeze from the open windows ruffles his hair, and he runs his hand through it as he leans against my desk. "Looks like you're ready to get out of here for a few months." He gazes down at me warmly. "Remember last week when you mentioned that you'd be up for a tutoring job this summer?" I roll back in my chair and look up at him. He's handsome, with short copper hair and blue eyes, a nice build.

He's also married with four children.

"I do," I confirm.

"Well, I have one for you."

"Who?"

"You know the King family, right? They run that big ranch just outside of town."

"Of course, I grew up here, Kyle," I reply dryly. In a town the size of Cunningham Falls, Montana, we pretty much all know each other, especially those of us who grew up here, just as our parents did, and their parents before them.

"Zack's boy, Seth, needs a tutor this summer."

"Zack's back in town?" I ask, my eyebrows raised in surprise.

"I don't think so." Kyle shakes his head and shrugs. "I can't tell you their business, small town or not. Seth is staying with Jeff and Nancy, and Josh is helping too."

"Oh," I mutter, surprised. "So for whom would I be working, exactly?"

"So proper," Kyle teases me, and grins. "You'll be working for Josh. You can go straight to his place on Monday morning. They'd like you to come Monday through Friday, about nine until noon."

"Geez, he must need a lot of tutoring."

The laughter leaves Kyle's eyes and he sighs. "He's a really smart kid, but he's stubborn and has a bit of an attitude. I'm warning you, he's not an easy kid to work with. He's only been here for three months. He refuses to do the work or hand it in."

"Does he start trouble?" I steeple my fingers in front of me, thinking.

"No, he just keeps to himself. Doesn't say much to anyone."

I'll have to work with Josh King, which won't be difficult. He was always nice to me in high school, smiles at me in passing when I see him around town. He and his brother are nice guys.

Rumor has it he's a womanizer, but nice nonetheless.

And I'd be lying if I said I hadn't had a crush on him for as long as I can remember.

But I can be professional and teach Josh's nephew. I didn't really want to paint my entire house this summer, anyway.

"Okay, I'll give it a go."

"Great, thanks, Cara." Kyle stands and turns to leave my classroom. "Have a good summer!"

"You too!" I call after him as he goes whistling down the dark, deserted hallway.

Cool, I have a summer job.

I love my town. Like, wholeheartedly, never want to move away, love it. I don't understand how Jillian, my best friend since kindergarten, can stand living so far away in California. Our town is small, only about six thousand full-time residents, but the population doubles in the peak of summer and the heart of winter with tourists here for skiing, hiking, swimming, and all the other fun outdoor activities that the brochures brag about.

We sit in a valley surrounded by tall mountains,

and when it's sunny, the sky is so big and blue it almost hurts the eyes.

I pull into the long gravel driveway off the highway just outside town and follow it past the large, white main house to the back of the property where Josh's house sits. It's not as big as the main house, but it's still large, bigger than my house in town, and is surrounded by tall evergreen trees and long lines of white wooden fences.

I do not envy the poor sap who has to paint the fences every few years.

The butterflies I've kept at bay come back with a vengeance, fluttering in my belly as I come to a stop in front of his house. Josh and his brother are twins, and until Zack broke his nose in football their senior year, it was almost impossible to tell them apart. They're both big guys, tall and broad shouldered. Zack always had a more intense look in his face, while Josh is more laid-back, quick to smile or tease—especially me, it seemed. In high school I was invisible to most people, having been a little too round, a lot too plain, but Josh noticed me.

He used to pull on my horrible curls as he'd walk past me at school, and of course because he was two years ahead of me, and a football star, I was crazy about him. My hair naturally falls in tight ringlets, but I've since straightened it, thank God.

I haven't seen much of Josh over the years. Each of us went away to college, and since we've both returned, I may catch a glimpse of him at the grocery store or in a restaurant, but never long enough to talk to him. I wonder if the rumors of his woman- izing are true.

They were in high school.

I just hope he hasn't turned into one of those cowboys who wear tight Wrangler jeans and straw cowboy hats.

My lips twitch at the thought as I pull myself out of my compact Toyota. The front door swings open, and there he is, all six foot three of him. Only with great effort does my jaw not drop.

Jesus, we breed hot men in Montana.

Josh's hair is dark, dark brown and he has chocolate-colored eyes to match. His olive skin has acquired a deep tan, and when he smiles, he has a dimple in his left cheek that can melt panties at twenty paces.

Dark stubble is on his chin this morning, and he flashes that cocky smile as he steps onto the porch. His jeans—Levi's, not Wranglers—ride low on his hips, and a plain white T-shirt hugs his muscular chest and arms. I can't help but wonder what he smells like.

Down, girl.

Following directly behind Josh is a tall, blond woman I don't recognize, laughing at something he must have said just before he sauntered through the door. They stop on the covered front porch long enough for him to smile sweetly down at her. He pulls his large hand down her arm and murmurs, "Have a good day, and good luck."

"Thanks, Josh," she responds, and bounces down the steps of the front porch, nods at me, and hops into her Jeep.

"Carolina Donovan," Josh murmurs, and stuffs his hands in his pockets.

"You know I hate it when you call me Carolina." I roll my eyes. "My parents should have been brought up on child-abuse charges for that name."

Josh laughs and shakes his head. "It's a beautiful name." He frowns and rocks back on his heels. "You look great, Cara."

"Uh, you've seen me around town over the years, Josh," I remind him with a half smile. "I hope I didn't interrupt anything?" I grimace inside, regretting the question immediately. *Mom always said, never ask a question you don't want the answer to.*

He shrugs one shoulder and offers me that cocky grin. God, he's such a charmer. "Nah, we were finished."

I frown at him. *What does that mean?*

"So, where is Seth?" I ask, changing the subject.

Josh frowns in turn and looks toward the big house. "He should be on his way in a few minutes. I have to warn you, Cara, working with Seth may not be a day at the beach. He's a good kid, but he's having a rough time of it." Josh rubs his hand over his face and sighs.

"Why is he here and not with his mom?"

"Because the bitch dropped him off here so she can be footloose and fancy-free. She's filed for divorce. Good riddance. I wish she'd brought him to us years ago."

"Oh." I don't know what else to say. I never liked Kensie King. She was a bitch in high school, but she was pretty and popular, and I'm quite sure Zack never planned on knocking her up.

But none of that is Seth's fault.

"What areas does he need help in?" I ask, and pull my tote bag out of the passenger seat. When I turn around, Josh's eyes are on my ass and he's chewing on his lower lip. I frown and stand up straight, self-conscious of my round behind.

"Josh?"

"I'm sorry, what?" He shakes his head and narrows his eyes on my face.

"What areas does Seth need the most help in?"

"All of them. He failed every class this spring."

"*Every* class?" I ask incredulously.

"Yeah. He's a smart kid, I don't know what his problem is."

"I don't need a tutor!" a young male voice calls out. I turn to see Seth riding a BMX bike from the big house down the driveway.

"Seth, don't start." Josh's eyes narrow and he folds his arms over his chest. "Ms. Donovan is here to help. You will be nice."

Seth rolls his eyes and hops off the bike, laying it on its side, and mirrors his uncle's stance, arms crossed over his chest.

God, he looks just like his dad and his uncle. He

could be their younger brother. He's going to inherit their height and has the same dark hair, but his eyes are hazel.

He's going to be a knockout someday.

And right now he's scowling at me.

"Hi, Seth. I'm Cara."

"What is it, Cara or Ms. Donovan?" he asks defiantly.

"Seth!" Josh begins, but I interrupt him. Seth isn't the first difficult child I've come across.

"Since it's summer, and I'm in your home, it's Cara. But if you see me at school, it's Ms. Donovan. Sound fair?"

Seth shrugs his slim shoulders and twists his lips as if he wants to say something smart but doesn't dare in his uncle's company.

Smart kid.

"Where do you want us?" I ask Josh, who is still glaring at Seth. They're clearly frustrated with each other.

"You can sit at the kitchen table. The house is empty during the day since I'm out working, so you shouldn't be interrupted." Josh motions for us to go in ahead of him, and as I walk past, he reaches out to pull my hair. "What happened to your curls?"

"I voted them off the island," I reply dryly, then almost trip as he laughs, sending shivers down my spine.

He leans in and whispers, "I liked them."

I shrug and follow Seth to the kitchen. "I didn't."

Josh's home is spacious; the floor plan is open

from the living area right inside the front door through to the eat-in kitchen with its maple cabinets the color of honey and smooth, light granite countertops. The windows are wide and I can see all over the property from inside the main room.

I immediately feel at home here, despite the obvious bachelor-pad feel to it. Large, brown leather couches face a floor-to-ceiling river-rock fireplace with a flat-screen TV mounted above it. Fishing, hunting, and men's-health magazines are scattered on the coffee table, along with an empty coffee mug. Not a throw pillow or knickknack to be found anywhere.

Typical guy.

Seth pulls a chair away from the table and plops down in it, resting his head on his folded arms.

"Seth, sit up." Josh is exasperated and Seth just sinks deeper into his slouch.

"I think we're good to go." I grin at Josh but he scowls.

"Are you sure?"

"Yep, we're good. You get to work and leave us be so we can too."

I turn my back on him, dismissing him, and begin pulling worksheets, pens, and a book out of my bag.

"I'll be working nearby today, so just call my cell if you need me."

"Fine." I wave him off, not looking over at him. I sense him still standing behind me. Finally I turn and raise an eyebrow. "You're still here."

He's watching me carefully, leaning against the

countertop, his rough hands tucked in his pockets. My eyes are drawn to his biceps, straining against the sleeves of his tee. "You got really pushy."

"I'm a teacher. It's either be pushy or die a long, slow death. Now go. We have work to do today."

"You'll have lunch with us before you go." Josh pushes himself away from the counter and saunters to the front door, grabs an old, faded-green baseball cap, and settles it backward on his head. "I'm pushy too."

He grins and that dimple winks at me before he leaves the house, shutting the door behind him.

Good God, I will not be able to focus if he doesn't leave us be while I'm here.

"You ready to get to work?" I ask Seth, thumbing through my writing worksheets until I find the one I want.

"This is a waste of time," he grumbles.

"Why do you say that?"

He shrugs again and buries his face in his arms.

"Well, I don't consider it a waste of time. What's your favorite subject?"

No answer.

"Least favorite?"

No answer.

"I personally like math, but I always sucked at it."

Seth shifts his head slightly and one eye peeks at me.

"Are you good at math?" I ask him.

"It's easy."

"Not for me." I sigh.

"But you're a teacher." Seth finally sits up and frowns at me.

"That doesn't mean I'm good at everything. Teachers aren't superhuman or anything."

"I can do math."

"Okay, let's start there."

Seth eyes me for a minute and then shrugs. It seems shrugging is his favorite form of communication.

"Are you really going to stay and have lunch?"

"Does that make you uncomfortable?" I pass him the math worksheet.

"No, I don't care." He picks up a pencil and starts marking the sheet, digging right in, and I grin.

"Does the food suck?"

"No, Gram packs us a lunch every day."

"Well then, I'll stay."

His lips twitch, but he doesn't smile—yet somehow I think I just won a big battle.

"So, looks like fried chicken and potato salad, homemade rolls, and fruit." Josh pulls the last of the food out of the ice chest and passes Seth a Coke.

"Your mom goes all out."

"She's been making lunch for ranch hands for almost forty years. It's habit."

We're sitting on Josh's back patio. It's partially covered, with a hanging swing on one side and a picnic table on the other and looks out over a large meadow where cattle are grazing.

"Do you get a lot of deer back here?" I ask.

He nods and swallows. "Usually in the evening and very early mornings. A moose walked through last week."

"That was cool," Seth murmurs, and Josh looks up in surprise.

Does Seth never talk to him?

"Yeah, it was," Josh agrees softly.

"Do you fish?" Seth asks me as he takes a big bite out of a chicken breast, sending golden pieces of fried batter down the front of his shirt. His dark hair is a bit too long and falls over one eye. I grin at him. He's adorable.

"No. I hate fishing."

"How can you hate to fish?!" Seth exclaims, as if I'd just admitted to hating ice cream.

"It's dirty." I wrinkle my nose and Josh bursts out laughing.

"Everything here is dirty, sweetheart." Josh shakes his head and nudges me lightly with his elbow.

He's such a flirt!

"But you live in Montana!" Seth exclaims, examining me as if I were a science project, his chicken momentarily forgotten.

"I live in town, Seth. Always have. My dad loves to fish. I just never really got into it." I shrug and take a bite of delicious homemade potato salad.

"But you like horses, right?" He shovels a heaping forkful of potato salad into his mouth.

"I've never ridden one." I chuckle and shake my head as I watch him eat. "Are they starving you here, Seth? The way you're eating, you'd think you haven't seen food in days."

Seth just blinks at me. He slowly smiles, but I cut him off before he can voice the idea I can see forming in that sharp brain of his.

"I'm not getting on a horse."

"Why not?" Josh asks with a broad smile.

"Well . . ." I look back and forth between the two guys and then sigh when I can't come up with a good reason not to. "I'm not dressed for riding."

Josh's gaze falls to my red sundress before his brown eyes find mine again. "Wear jeans tomorrow."

"I'm not here to learn how to ride a horse, I'm here to teach Seth."

"No reason that you can't do both," Josh replies with a grin, and winks at me, his dimple creasing his cheek, waking those butterflies in my stomach.

"Am I keeping you from work?" I change the subject and pop a piece of watermelon in my mouth, doing my best not to squirm in my chair.

"I have to go paint the fence," Seth mutters, and swigs down the last of his Coke, making me laugh.

"What?" he asks.

"When I drove up to the house and saw the white

fence, I thought to myself, 'I don't envy the person who has to paint this every couple of years.'"

"It was either paint the fence or shovel the horse shit," Seth replies matter-of-factly.

"Mouth!" Josh scowls, pinning Seth with a look, and Seth rolls his eyes.

"Horse crap."

"I think I'd take the fence too," I agree, but Seth just shrugs his thin shoulders and frowns. "You look so much like your dad." I shake my head and reach for another piece of watermelon before I realize that both Seth and Josh have gone still.

"I do not," Seth whispers.

"Well, you look just like your uncle Josh, and Josh and Zack are twins, so . . ." I tilt my head to one side and watch Seth's face tighten.

"I'm nothing like my dad," he insists.

"Okay, I'm sorry."

Seth pins me with a scowl, then grabs his trash and lets himself into the house to dump it, stalks through the house, and slams the front door behind him.

"I'm sorry," I whisper again.

"It's okay. He's pissed at my brother. Won't talk about it, just won't have anything at all to do with him." Josh purses his lips and sighs, still watching the path Seth took through the house. My eyes are glued to his lips and I'm mortified to realize that I want him to kiss me.

And not just a sweet thank-you-for-teaching-my-nephew kiss, but a long, slow kiss that lasts forever and makes me forget how to breathe. I want to sink my fingers into his thick, dark hair and feel his large, callused hands glide down my back as he pulls me against him.

I want him to touch me.

Josh begins to pack up the remains of our lunch and I take a deep breath and join him.

"When he smiled at you earlier? That's the first time I've seen him smile since he's been here."

"Josh, I'm so sorry. He's a great kid, and he's really smart. I think we'll have him back on track with his grades without a problem."

"Thank you." Josh replaces the lid on the fruit and throws it in the cooler. "You know, Kyle didn't tell me who he was sending out here. I was surprised when I saw it was you."

"Why?"

"I don't know, but I'm glad you're here. I wasn't kidding before—you look fantastic."

I blush and concentrate on rewrapping the chicken and placing it in the cooler.

"I'm not a hermit, Josh. Like I said before, you've seen me around."

"In passing. Not like this. I like it."

I stand up and cross my arms over my chest, then frown when he stands too and is more than a foot taller than me.

I've always been so damn short.

"Are you flirting with me?" I ask.

"Maybe." He pushes the lid down on the ice chest,

then moves around the table to stand right next to me, and I have to tilt my head way back to see his eyes. "You always were a little thing."

"Little?! Oh my God." I giggle and throw a hand over my mouth. "I'm just short. Hell, in high school I was f—"

"If you say *fat*, I will take you over my knee, Carolina. You were not fat then, you're not fat now, and next to me, you *are* tiny." He sets his mouth in a disapproving line and pulls on a lock of my hair. "Your pretty blond hair is soft."

"Don't f-flirt with me," I stutter halfheartedly. Instead of moving away, I sway toward him, my heart racing.

"Why not?" He grins and continues to gently pull my hair between his thumb and forefinger, watching the strands as they fall out of his grasp.

"Because I'm your employee for the summer, and I like my job. It's not like there are dozens of middle schools here in town that I can work at if I get fired." I step away, pulling myself together, doing my best to remind myself of the blonde I saw leaving his house this morning and how I do *not* want to be another notch in Josh King's bedpost. I open his sliding screen door and gather my tote bag and purse and turn to find him standing right behind me again. "I have to go."

He sighs, props his hands on his hips, and looks as if he wants to say more, so I turn on my heel and walk briskly to the door.

"I'll walk you out," he mutters, and walks quickly to keep up with me. He holds his front door open for me, and I feel his hand on my lower back as he guides me to my little blue car.

He opens the door for me and settles my bags into the passenger seat.

"You're very chivalrous," I inform him dryly.

As I move to sit in the driver's seat, he runs his hand down my bare arm, very much as he did with Blondie this morning, and smiles.

"Thanks for doing this, Cara. Don't forget to wear jeans tomorrow." With that he winks and shuts my door, stepping back to watch me drive away.

Looks like I'll be wearing shorts tomorrow.

CHAPTER

Two

"Where are your jeans?" Josh asks as he meets me at my car the following morning.

"These are jeans." I pull my tote bag out of the car and walk toward the front door of his house. "Is Seth here yet?"

"No, he'll be a few minutes. I have him feeding the dogs at the big house."

"Okay."

"Those are not jeans." Josh is scowling down at my denim shorts as if they were the devil incarnate.

"They're denim."

He narrows his chocolate eyes at me, but I see the humor there, and my stomach clenches.

I love riling this guy up.

"Fine, they'll have to do. Go ahead and get settled, Seth will be here in a minute. I have to ride out with a few of the guys to repair a fence, so I'll see you at lunchtime." He pulls on some gloves and settles his green baseball cap on his head.

"You don't wear cowboy hats?" I ask without thinking.

"Not usually. I have one, if you'd rather I wear it." He smirks.

"No, just curious," I mumble, and head toward the house.

"Don't leave before I get back. I have plans for you."

He grins wide, winks, and saunters off toward the massive barn that sits between his house and the big house.

Well, isn't that view nice? His Levi's hug his ass perfectly and sit low on his hips, and as he walks, I can see his buttocks and thighs flex.

Dear God, I'm lusting after a rancher.

Pulling myself together, I go inside and begin pulling out materials for today's lesson.

Do I even *want* to get on a horse?

Not really.

But I have a feeling these two guys are going to talk me into it.

The front door bursts open and Seth strolls in. "I'd rather be helping the guys with the fences today."

"I'd rather be lying on a beach in Hawaii today, but neither of us is going to get our wish." I sigh and gesture for him to sit, pulling the book he'll be reading this summer out of my tote bag. "This is going to be your homework."

"I'm going to have homework?" he asks, shocked. "But it's summer!"

"I'll make sure you finish all of the worksheets while I'm here each day, but I also want you to read this book, and we'll talk about it every day so I know you're reading it."

"I hate the books the school makes us read," he grumbles. I smirk and mentally agree. Some of the mandatory reading material is dry, and I understand why the kids don't go crazy about it.

"This isn't a book the school would make you read. It's a book for fun, and I'm going to read it with you."

"Really?" This piques his interest and he takes the book from me. It's *Exiled* by M. R. Merrick.

"Really. This book is science fiction, and it's about a boy who has to deal with demons and hunters and all kinds of stuff. I think it's going to be fun."

"It'll probably suck," he states defiantly, but he flips the book over and immediately begins reading the blurb on the back.

Adolescent boys are fun.

"You're right, it probably will suck, but we can talk about all of its suckiness together." I smile sweetly and push a math worksheet under his nose, hand him a pencil, and we get started with today's lesson.

Halfway through fractions, my phone chirps with an incoming text. Seth is hard at work and not paying any attention to me, so I quickly check it and smile when I see Jilly's name.

What are you doing?

Typical Jill, just get right to the point.

Good morning. I'm working. What are you doing?

I set the phone aside and check Seth's work. All of the answers are correct, and he's worked through them quickly.

"Impressive," I murmur with a grin. "You were right, you *are* good at math, Seth."

His lips twitch, as though he wants to smile, but he keeps his eyes on the paper, working diligently, and mutters, "Thanks."

I give him another worksheet with more of the same type of problems just as my phone chirps.

Just closed on a house & on my way to show another. Miss u. Talk soon?

I smile and respond. **Miss u too. Call me.**

Glancing up while tucking my phone back in my pocket, I see Josh riding to the back fence of his house with two other guys. The horses are beautiful, two black and one white with red patches. The guys are dripping in sweat, dirt clinging to their clothes and skin. They stop to talk, pointing to various parts of the ranch and even laughing once in a while.

While still in the saddle, Josh pulls his cap off, pushes his hand through his sweaty hair, then pulls his T-shirt over his head to wipe his face with it.

Holy Mary, mother of God.

Wow.

He's more than built. His muscles are toned and

defined, thanks to all the work he does on the ranch. He has an amazing abdomen, and I can see the top of a sexy V rising out of the waist of his jeans, but it's his arms and shoulders that have me mesmerized and my panties suddenly soaked.

His biceps have to be the size of my thighs, and not in a gross he's-gotta-be-on-steroids way. I wonder what it would be like to have those arms wrapped around me, to feel the muscles flex beneath my hands.

His shoulders are broad and tanned, and he has just a light sprinkle of dark hair over his chest.

I could eat him with a spoon.

Josh pulls a bottle of water out of a saddlebag, takes a drink, and then laughs at one of the other guys. He swings his leg over the horse, dismounting easily, ties the rein to the fence, and waves as his companions ride off toward the barn.

"Why are you looking at him like that?" Seth's voice is hard and angry.

"What?" Oh, crap, he caught me. I'm so embarrassed. "I'm not looking at anything. Just daydreaming, I guess." My face is bright red when I look down at Seth, but he scowls and pushes his worksheet toward me.

"Girls are dumb. You shouldn't look at him like that. He's a jerk."

Josh saunters in through the sliding glass door off the kitchen, his shirt still off, and I bite my lip as my eyes wander down his torso. When I glance back up, he's grinning, that sexy dimple is winking at me, and I flush.

Maybe I should start working with Seth over at the big house.

"Are you guys almost done?"

"Almost." I nod.

"I'm going to catch a quick shower and then put you up on a horse, my friend."

"Cool!" Seth exclaims, surprising us both.

"Um, I wore shorts."

"I noticed. You have gorgeous legs. We'll make it work. I'll be out in a minute." With that, he saunters down the hall and I hear a door close.

"Why do you think he's a jerk?" I ask, still stuck on the *gorgeous legs* remark. Does Josh mistreat him?

"Because he's my dad's brother. They're twins."

"And you think your dad's a jerk?"

"He *is* a jerk," Seth insists emphatically.

"I don't remember your dad being a jerk, Seth." I check over Seth's work.

Something is wrong. Well, not something, *everything*. Every single answer on this sheet is wrong. But as I read through the work, it's correct. He's purposefully worked out every problem the right way and marked the wrong answer.

"What the heck, Seth?"

"What?"

"All the answers are wrong." I frown at him and wait for his answer.

"So?"

"So, the work is right, and you wrote down the wrong answers on purpose." I sit back in the chair and cross my arms over my chest. Seth squirms in his chair, his mouth set in a tight line as he frowns.

"Doesn't matter if it's wrong."

"Well, yeah, it does because you're being graded on these, Seth." I tilt my head and watch him squirm some more. "You are so smart. Why are you doing this?"

His startled gaze meets mine, making my heart ache for this boy. He seems so lonely and sad. I just want to pull him to me and hug the defiance right out of him.

"I'm not doing anything," he whispers, and looks down at his sheet.

"Okay, let's do this," Josh says, returning. His dark hair is wet from the shower and he's changed into clean jeans and a white tee.

"Why did you put on clean clothes?" Seth asks with a frown. "They're just gonna get messed up again."

"Because I'm sure Cara doesn't want to stand next to me when I smell funky, kid. That's gross."

"You smell funky no matter what," Seth taunts.

Josh's eyes light up with humor. "Back at you. I'm glad you're staying over at the other house because I hate to think of what your bedroom must smell like."

I watch the banter with a huge grin plastered on my face. I don't think they joke with each other like this often.

"It smells like stupid air freshener because Gram keeps sticking smelly stuff in my drawers and stuff." Seth wrinkles his nose.

"Take it from me, kid, air freshener in a young man's room is mandatory." Josh shakes his head and laughs. "Shall we?"

"Really, I—"

"Yep, we shall!" Seth jumps up and runs out the back door.

"I guess we shall," I mutter, and stand to follow him.

When we step outside, Seth has already reached a tall, black horse and is petting its nose, talking to it softly.

"What if the horse doesn't like me?" I whisper to Josh. He smiles down at me gently and tugs on my hair. I want to lean into his touch, so I step away.

"She'll love you. She's a gentle horse, Cara. I wouldn't put you on one of the mean stallions. Magic is a sweet mare and she's patient with the newbies."

"Uh-huh."

"Besides, she's *my* horse. I know her better than any other animal on this ranch. You'll love her."

"I could love her from afar," I mutter.

He laughs at me, and as we approach the horse, I hang back and watch Josh and Seth pet Magic, both crooning softly to her. She does seem sweet. She nudges their hands and nods her head as if she knows what they're saying.

And her big, brown eyes shine with intelligence.

"I'm gonna go get her an apple!" Seth runs back to the house with excitement.

"Come here, Cara," Josh murmurs gently, and holds his hand out for mine. I take it and immediately love the way his large, callused hand feels wrapped around mine. He tugs me to his side and places my hand on the mare's nose. "Just pet her."

"Hi, pretty girl." I pet her nose, then run my hand down her long, soft neck. "Are you going to be gentle with me?"

Magic snorts softly. I smile at her and continue to pet her gently. Just when I'm beginning to relax, she steps to the left a bit, her heavy foot startling me, and I jump back in surprise.

"Easy, girl." Josh steps up behind me, his chest pressed to my back, again covers my hand with his, and I don't know if he's talking to me or the horse, and frankly I don't care. "Easy." He guides my hand down her neck and then leads me to the side of the horse.

"She's really tall."

"This is one of the smaller horses," Seth informs me as he rejoins us with an apple in his hand. He holds it out for Magic and she eagerly, and gently, takes it from him, munching happily.

"Okay, you're going to put your left foot in the stirrup, and I'm going to boost you up into the saddle."

"No." I try to take a step back but crash into Josh's hard chest.

"Why are you scared, honey?" Josh asks gently.

I swallow as I look up at the saddle. "It's really high up and I don't like heights."

"Once you're up there, you'll see it's not that far." He's running his hand up and down my back in a soothing, calming pattern and leans down to whisper in my ear, "I'm right here. I won't let you get hurt."

"What if she takes off running and I hit a tree branch?"

Josh laughs and shakes his head. "You watch too many movies. Trust me, Magic is a sweet girl. You'll be fine."

"Okay." I take a deep breath as Josh places my foot in the stirrup.

"Just bounce up and I'll boost you."

"Um, okay."

"Cara, you're gonna love it!" Seth tells me from Magic's head, where he's snuck her another apple. I'm floored at the difference in him from just a few moments ago. This ranch might be the best place for him.

I bounce twice and suddenly Josh grips me at my waist and boosts me into the saddle.

"Here, take the reins." Josh hands me the soft leather straps and Seth helps me find the other stirrup with my right foot.

"I'm on a horse," I breathe.

"You are." Josh grins up at me, then looks at my legs with a frown. "The saddle might pinch your thighs a bit. From now on, when I tell you to wear jeans, wear the damn jeans."

"And you call *me* pushy?" I smirk down at him and then take a deep breath, starting to feel comfortable up here on this horse.

Although the saddle isn't terribly comfortable.

"My ass is going to hurt tomorrow," I grumble.

"Probably," Josh agrees. "Okay, we're going to walk you around the field."

"I'm fine just sitting here. No need to get fancy."

"Don't be such a wimp." Josh laughs and guides Magic slowly along the fence line.

"Oh, God." I bite my lip and white-knuckle the reins. I *am* being a monumental wimp.

Finally, my body falls into the rhythm of Magic's gait and it almost starts to feel good.

"How are you doing, honey?" Josh tosses a smile at me, admiring me as he leads Magic through the pasture. "You look great up on my horse."

"I'm good." I smile down at him, my stomach clenching. *He thinks I look great!* "This isn't so hard."

"It's only the company that sucks." Seth is walking behind us, picking up rocks and throwing them, his scowl back on his face. *And we're back to the attitude.*

"What's wrong, Seth?" I ask, attempting to look back at him without falling off this horse.

"Nothing." He tosses another rock into the pasture as he rolls his eyes. I have no idea if this sudden change in attitude is because he's preadolescent or if he's truly angry about something.

Before long we're back where we started from. Josh helps me dismount, his hands again on my hips, lifting me. I plant my hands on his shoulders, and when my feet hit the ground, he doesn't immediately let me go. His brown eyes are soft and smiling, and I just want to stay right here, all day.

So I pull gently away and turn my attention to the horse, rub my hand down her neck.

"Seth, you have chores to do." Josh pats Magic's neck as he moves to tie the reins to the fence.

"I don't want to do them today," Seth mutters.

"We do chores every day," Josh reminds him.

Seth squares his shoulders, and I know Josh is in for a fight.

"I want to play video games."

"After your chores are done."

"I'm not doing it." Seth turns and stomps off toward the house.

"Seth King, you will do what you're told!"

I watch in awe, and in utter shock, as Seth turns around, flips his uncle off, and runs for his bike.

"Oh my God."

"I'm gonna kill him." Every muscle in Josh's body is tight, the muscle in his jaw is flexing, and I can feel the frustration coming off him in waves.

"There are moments when he's so happy and sweet, and I can tell he's a good kid. What is going on, Josh?" I lean my hips on the top rail of the fence and cross my arms over my chest.

"I don't know what to do with him, Cara." He pushes his hands through his hair as he paces in front of me. "He talks like this to my mom, my dad,

even the ranch hands. Punishing him doesn't help."
Josh throws his hands in the air and keeps talking.
"We've taken away all of his privileges: his video
games, his music, he doesn't get to ride the horses,
he has to paint the fences. It doesn't matter."

Josh takes a deep breath and props his hands on
his hips, shaking his head in frustration. "I know he's
had a rough time of it the last few years, and God
only knows what that woman said to him and what
he saw when he was still with her." Josh swallows
hard and swears under his breath. "Obviously, the
way he talks about Zack, it isn't good. But he won't
talk about it, and I don't know what to do with his
disrespectful attitude."

"I have an idea."

Josh snaps his head over to look at me and takes
a deep breath, calming himself. "I'll take all the ideas
I can get right now."

"I want to take him on a field trip tomorrow."

"Absolutely not. We don't reward that behavior
with field trips." Josh shakes his head, fisting his
hands at his side.

"No, a different kind of field trip. Trust me."

"I do trust you, but . . ."

"Have you ever seen that TV show *Scared
Straight*?"

Understanding brightens his brown eyes and a
slow smile spreads across his lips. "I'm going with
you."

"Can you get away for a whole day?"

"I'm the boss, sweetheart, I can do whatever I want." He pushes his hand through his hair and sighs.

"If you're coming with me, you need to understand that I'm in charge. You keep quiet and you let me do all the talking."

Josh narrows his eyes at me and steps closer, until he's close enough to touch me. "Okay, but enjoy it while you can, honey, because I'm not a man that gives up control easily." He tucks a piece of my hair behind my ear before pulling his thumb down my cheek to my chin. I can't move. My eyes are caught in his dark gaze.

"Your eyes are amazing, Cara."

"They're kind of weird," I whisper.

"No, they're not weird." He shakes his head slowly. "I've just never seen eyes that go from amber to hazel to green. I wonder what color they are when you're turned on?"

Whatever color they are right now!

This is not the kind boy I knew as a girl. This man is still kind, and gentle, but is self-assured and sexy and calls to me in ways I thought existed only in the romance novels I read.

Think about Seth! Think about your job!

I take a deep breath and step back, close my eyes for a moment, and then square my shoulders. "I'll pick you guys up at seven tomorrow morning."

"That's early." Josh's eyebrows shoot up as he shoves his hands in his pockets.

"I'm sure you'll have been up for a few hours by then." I smirk. "It's going to be a long day. You might want to make sure Seth gets a good night's sleep."

"You mean business, don't you?" Josh asks with a chuckle, then he sobers when he sees how serious I am.

"If this doesn't mellow Seth's attitude out, I don't know what will."

"We'll see you then."

CHAPTER

Three

JOSH

I wonder what she has up her sexy little sleeve.

Seth, yawning, is in the backseat of Cara's car, and I'm sitting shotgun. I can't help but look over at her and grin. Her sunglasses are perched on her cute nose, her shoulder-length blond hair is pulled back into a ponytail, and she's wearing jeans—imagine that—that hug her full ass perfectly. Between those jeans and the red, V-neck T-shirt that shows just a hint of cleavage, my cock has been at half-mast since she picked us up.

It's going to be a long day.

I've tried to respect her space, and her position as Seth's teacher, but I'll be damned if I can stay away from her. I love the way she feels, and I need to find out what it feels like to have her beneath me, to be inside her.

Jesus, I'd be happy to just hold her while we watch TV, and I haven't had that urge in a long, long time.

Cara was always a sweet kid, if not a little, well, plain. Not ugly, just not someone who would have made a teenage boy pay attention.

Until Monday, it hadn't occurred to me to pay much attention. Thank God Kyle sent her to my place.

Cara glances over at me and offers me a soft smile. "What?"

"Where are we going?"

"Breakfast."

"You wanted to take us out for breakfast?" I ask, surprised. My gut clenches when she laughs. Has her smile always been that amazing?

"We need to eat something, it's going to be a long day."

"I already had breakfast," Seth grumbles. "Where are we going, anyway?"

"That's fine, you can watch me eat the best waffle in town." She smirks and turns in to Ed's Diner, and despite my having had breakfast a couple hours ago, my stomach growls.

"Ed makes the best waffles," I agree, and hop out of the car.

"Who's Ed?" Seth asks as he shuffles along behind us.

"My uncle." Cara smiles at him, and I wish she'd turn that smile on me. I adore her smile. "He owns this place."

"Gee, imagine that, with it being called Ed's Diner and all."

"Watch your smart mouth," I warn him with a glare, and he glares back at me.

"You agreed," Cara whispers, reminding me that she is in charge today, and I fidget. I don't like giving up control, and I definitely need to be able to protect her from any harsh words Seth might decide to fling at her. "I've got this."

She leads us into the diner and to a booth. We order three waffles with bacon and orange juice on the side.

Seth makes quick work of his own waffle and polishes off half of Cara's. He definitely hasn't lost his appetite.

As we are finishing up, Ed himself comes out of the kitchen, smiling when he sees Cara sitting in the booth. Cara stands to give him a big hug. "Hey, darlin', it's always good to see you."

"Hi, Uncle Ed. You look great." She grins up at the aging man lovingly. Ed is short for a man, but still much taller than Cara. He's stick thin and gray, with kind eyes.

"So, I see you've brought me a new worker." Ed narrows his eyes as he gazes at Seth.

Seth's eyes go wide with surprise. "Worker?" Seth squeaks.

"I have. Seth is going to help you out this morning. Ed's short a dishwasher today, so you'll be filling in, Seth."

"I am not!" Seth's gaze turns to me. "What the hell, Uncle Josh?"

"You will be respectful and do as you're told," I tell him softly, barely keeping my temper leashed.

"Aren't there laws against kids working?" Seth grumbles, making my lips twitch. This kid is really too smart for his own good.

"Not for just a few hours. Come on." Ed walks briskly through a swinging door and into the kitchen. Seth follows, with Cara and me bringing up the rear. On one side of the kitchen is a large tub sink with a nozzle that pulls down from the ceiling and is used to power-wash dishes. Quite a stack is already waiting for Seth.

"This is gross!"

"Breakfast dishes usually are, son." Ed winks at him and flips an egg. "Gravy and syrup are the worst."

"You have an electric dishwasher! Why are you making me wash these?" Seth crosses his arms and scowls at all of us.

"Because," Cara begins softly, "you said yourself yesterday that it doesn't matter if you work hard. It doesn't matter if you pass school, or if you fail. Today, I'm going to show you just a few of the reasons why it does matter."

"I'll pay you seven dollars an hour to wash those." Ed gestures with his spatula. "That's minimum wage."

"I can wash some stupid dishes. It's not hard." Seth scowls and sets his jaw.

Ed's lips twitch. "Okay, get started then." Ed shows

him how to work the nozzle and how to wash them properly, then leaves him to it. Cara and I stand to the side and watch. I can feel her body heat next to me. I glance down and tuck her hair behind her ear, smiling when she looks up at me in surprise.

"This one has a spot on it. Rewash it." Ed hands a plate back to Seth, who scowls at him.

"It does not! It's clean!"

"I say it's not. Rewash it."

I feel my hands clench. I want to argue with Ed—it looks clean to me—but I remind myself that they're trying to teach my nephew a lesson.

Fuck, I hope he learns it.

Cara sighs beside me, flinching when she shifts her feet. I have a feeling it's because her ass and inner thighs are sore from riding yesterday.

Without thinking, I reach down and cup her ass in my hand. "Are you sore?"

She gapes at me, looks over at Ed in a panic to make sure he's not looking, which he's not, and then gapes at me some more.

"Yes," she hisses, and moves out of my grasp. "Stop that."

Her face flushes as she clears her throat, crosses her arms under her round breasts, and unknowingly presses the fabric against them, showing me that her nipples are puckered.

Damn, I want to take her right here.

"I'm done," Seth announces, his voice tight with anger.

"Here's some more." A waitress drops off a tub full of more dirty breakfast dishes, and Seth growls before pulling them out and washing them.

So it goes for the next hour, Seth washing and grumbling and Ed barking orders at him. Finally, at around nine thirty, Cara kisses Ed's cheek and turns to Seth.

"Okay, I think we're done here. Dry your hands."

Seth quickly dries his hands and starts to walk out of the kitchen without a word to anyone, but Ed stops him.

"This is where you can thank me, son."

"Thank you for what? You should thank me for washing those gross dishes."

Before I can step in and remind Seth of his manners, Ed shakes his head and says sternly, "No, you can thank me for the seven bucks an hour."

Seth just shrugs and nods and walks sullenly out to the car to sit in the backseat. "Are we going home now?"

"How was that?" Cara asks rather than answer his question as she pulls out of the parking lot.

"It sucked."

"Okay." She nods thoughtfully. "Was it as easy as you thought it would be?"

Seth shrugs and looks down at his feet.

"Answer my question, please." Her voice is strong, leaving no room for disagreement.

He exhales as he drops his head back against the seat. "No, it wasn't easy."

"Was it something you can see yourself doing for the rest of your life?"

Seth's eyebrows rise in surprise. "Not for the rest of my life!"

"Well then, an education might be a good thing to have, Seth." She winks at him in the rearview mirror.

I glance back to find Seth with his jaw dropped, staring at Cara in shock.

Cara pulls the car to a stop at the curb in the heart of downtown, right in front of a law office. My longtime friend Ty Sullivan is a partner here.

"Are we going in to see Ty?" I ask Cara.

She smiles and nods.

"Why do I need a lawyer?" Seth asks, his voice suddenly scared.

"You don't, but you might work for him for a little while." Cara leads us into the air-conditioned building as Ty walks out of his office to greet us.

"Hey, man, good to see you." Ty moves toward us, extending his hand out for mine.

"You too. We need to go shoot pool one night soon, catch up." I grin and shake his hand.

"I'm up for that." Ty smiles softly at Cara and kisses her cheek, and my defenses immediately go up, even though I know being jealous of my best friend is irrational and ridiculous. Still, I can't help but wonder, are Ty and Cara an item? If they are, I haven't heard about it. "Hey, Carolina."

"Hey, Ty, thanks for this."

He just shakes his head, and when he looks down

at Seth, Ty's eyes grow cold and his face gets tight.
This is exactly how he looks in a courtroom.

"Seth?"

"Yeah." Seth's voice is soft but still defiant. His eyes
are large and he takes a step toward my side, which
surprises the hell out of me.

"I've heard that you're looking for a little work."

"What can I do here? I'm just a kid!"

My thoughts exactly.

"Cara tells me you're pretty smart. You know the
alphabet, right?"

"Duh."

Ty narrows his eyes at him and waits for a different reply.

"Yes."

"Good, then you can do some filing. It's important that you file them perfectly. If papers get lost,
bad things happen and important people get really
pissed off."

"I can file."

Ty nods and leads us into his office, where he has
a stack of papers about two inches thick that need
to be filed away.

I pull Cara back out to the hallway. "There could
be sensitive files in there, Cara. Is this appropriate?"

"He assured me over the phone that there was no
confidential information in the paperwork, and it's
a big enough pile to keep Seth busy for a while." She
smiles as she rests her hand on my arm. "Trust me."

"How much do I get paid?" Seth asks.

"Seven bucks an hour, kid."

"But this is a lawyer's office!"

"You're just filing, not saving someone from the death penalty," Ty responds dryly. Seth settles in to work and Cara and I sit across from Ty at his desk.

"Can I listen to my iPod while I do this?" Seth asks hopefully.

Cara looks to me and I nod.

"Sure," she responds.

Seth eagerly plugs in his earbuds and turns the volume up.

"How's Jillian?" I ask Ty.

"Cara would be the one to ask, she talks to Jill more than I do." Ty looks at Cara expectantly.

"She's good. Working hard." Cara smiles at us and shrugs. "We have a phone date tonight."

"A phone date?" I ask.

"Yeah, we try to carve out a few hours every month to catch up. Tonight's our date night."

"Why did she decide to stay in California after the divorce?"

Ty frowns and rubs his forehead. "Good question." He glances at Cara, his face sober. "Has she ever confided in you about what happened with the asshole?"

Cara shakes her head and sighs. "No. Even when we've had too much to drink, she won't tell me."

"She's so damn frustrating," Ty mutters as he pulls his hands down his face and back up through his hair in agitation. "I wish she'd talk to me about it so I'd know how to fix it."

"You're always fixing things for the women in your life," I mention quietly, and cross my ankle over my knee, memories of not so long ago echoing through my mind. "Maybe she wants to take care of this on her own."

Ty just stares back at me and cocks an eyebrow. "Would you leave it alone if it were your sister?"

"Fuck no." I sigh.

"I wish she'd come home," Cara murmurs. "For good. Not just to visit."

"Yeah, I need someone to harass," Ty agrees with a sad smile.

"You guys always did torture us endlessly. What was up with that?" Cara turns to me, looking all exasperated and adorable.

"You were girls, we were teenagers, and it was our God-given right as older brothers—and friends of older brothers—to torment you." She bites her lip to keep from laughing, her eyes sparkling with memories.

"But no one else would dare give us a hard time for fear of your wrath," she says, laughing, and she's absolutely right.

If anyone else had fucked with them, we would have killed them.

"Where is Zack these days? Is he still deployed? I haven't talked to him for a while." Ty grabs a paper clip off his desk and slowly begins to straighten it.

"He's been in Afghanistan. He should be back in Texas this week, and then he'll be on his way here once he processes out of the army." I sigh and glance over at Seth to make sure he's still listening to his music.

"What the fuck was Kensie thinking?" Ty breathes.

"Who cares? Seth is safe, and Zack will be home soon, and hopefully things will calm down for everyone."

"What will Zack do here? The army is all he's known for more than ten years." Cara frowns and crosses her short legs. I wish she'd worn shorts again today. Her legs are toned and soft. I wonder what they'll feel like wrapped around my waist.

Or propped on my shoulders.

"I'm not sure what his plans are." I shake my head, attempting to focus on the topic at hand. "I think he's just anxious to get here and make sure Seth is okay. We'll take it from there." I'm ready for my brother to be home full-time. As Cara said, he's been gone for more than ten years, and it's time for him to come home. He's a good man, and given the chance, he'd be a good dad, no matter what lies his bitch ex-wife put into Seth's head.

"I'm done." Seth stands and pulls his buds out of his ears.

Ty joins him and checks over his work. "That was faster than I expected. Good job."

Seth grins proudly and waits while Ty checks Seth's work.

Ty pulls a few files back out of the drawer. "These three were out of order," he accuses, his tone hard.

"Someone could have gone to jail or lost a lot of money because you filed these incorrectly."

"I tried my best." Seth sets his jaw and frowns.

"I told you, it has to be perfect."

"I don't care about your stupid papers."

"Seth," Cara warns just as I'm about to shove to my feet. "Ty is your employer. He deserves your respect."

"Sorry," Seth mumbles.

"Overall, you did good, Seth. Thank you."

Seth turns to me. "Can I go to the car?"

"Sure."

He rushes out of the building and Ty sighs. "That sucked. I don't want to play the scared-straight game again."

Cara laughs and rubs his arm soothingly, and I suddenly want to punch my best friend in the face. "Thanks for helping."

Ty's eyes are on mine, and he smiles slowly, the bastard. "My pleasure, little one." He bends down and kisses her cheek, runs a finger down her face, and Cara gapes up at him.

So, they're not a couple, and Ty thinks he can have some fun with me. Bastard.

"Let's go." Cara turns toward the door. "We have one more stop to make."

"You're an ass," I mutter to Ty after Cara leaves through the door.

"I know." He grins and then sobers. "You like her."

"Yeah, I like her."

"She's grown up nicely." Ty nods.

I narrow my eyes on him again. "Why am I just now noticing?"

"I don't know, man." He slaps my shoulder and holds the door open for me. "Good luck."

I follow Cara to the car and climb in. "Where to now?"

"Just one more stop." She checks the mirrors as she pulls into traffic. "How was that?"

"Ty's an ass," Seth says.

"Watch your damn mouth!" I yell before I can stop myself. "Ty is my best friend, and an adult, and you will respect that."

Seth crosses his arms defiantly and I sigh. "I'm sorry I yelled, but, Seth, you've got to stop with this disrespectful attitude."

"We're here." Cara pulls the car to the stop and I gape at her.

"The jail?"

She turns her amber eyes to me and nods solemnly, and I think I'm going to throw up. There is no way in hell I want my nephew in the *jail*. He's only twelve years old!

"Come on." Cara climbs out of the car and we follow behind her.

"Hey, Cara, Josh." Brad Hull, one of the police detectives, meets us and greets us warmly.

"Hey, Brad."

"You must be Seth," Brad greets Seth, and shakes his hand. "I've heard a bit about you."

"Yeah, I suck."

I gasp and stare at Seth in shock. He does *not* suck. Sure, he's a pain in the ass, but what kid isn't?

"Actually, that's not what I was told." Brad frowns down at Seth. "I've heard that you're a really good kid."

"You did?" Seth asks skeptically. "Then why am I here?"

"Because even good people screw up." Brad sighs and leans against the wall, crosses his arms and ankles as he looks down at Seth. Seth's eyes are glued to Brad's gun. "You interested in firearms?"

"Having a gun and a badge doesn't make you cool," Seth sputters, then frowns as if he's not sure why he said that.

"You're right." Brad nods thoughtfully. "They don't make me cool. They help me to keep people like Cara safe from people like you." The last part of the sentence is said quietly, but Seth's face pales and tears fill his eyes, and I want to hug him tight and tell him that he's going to be okay.

But I wait to see where Brad's going with this.

"I would never hurt Cara!" Seth exclaims, and turns his sad gaze to the woman next to me. "Cara's great."

"Do you think your words don't hurt her? Or your grandparents? Or even Josh?" Brad changes his stance and tucks his hands in his pockets. "What if you get really, really mad at them?"

"I don't start fights," Seth argues. "I've never hit anybody. I just keep to myself."

"But, Seth, not everybody goes to jail just because of their fists. You don't treat anyone with respect and you are thoughtless with your words. Who's to say that one day you won't decide you can hurt someone physically too? Or take something that doesn't belong to you?"

Seth is shaking his head, processing what Brad is saying. "I wouldn't do that."

"I'm going to show you something, Seth." Brad doesn't touch Seth, he just motions for him to follow and leads him through a heavy metal door and down a long line of jail cells. He walks into one, but Seth stops at the door. "Come inside."

Seth does as he's told and stands in front of Brad.

"I believe Cara when she said that you're a good kid, Seth. I don't ever want to see you in here after today. Do you hear me?"

"Yes, sir." Seth's voice is nothing but a whisper. It's tearing me apart.

"Okay." Brad shakes his hand and leaves us alone, waiting for us by the main door. Cara steps inside the cell with Seth, and it takes everything in me to not follow her in and hold her close, to yank both of them out of this godforsaken place and make sure they're safe for the rest of their lives.

They shouldn't be here.

"Seth." Cara takes his shoulders in her hands and looks him dead in the eye. "Everything you do *matters*. Your classwork, your chores, your family. It all matters. How you talk to others and treat them matters too. If you don't change your attitude, bad things are in store for you, and I know that you don't want that. You are such a bright kid, and you, my friend, are going to be an amazing adult. But you have to change your attitude."

Seth's lips quiver as he watches Cara's face while she talks to him.

"I'm sorry," he whispers.

"I know. Come on, let's go home." She hugs him close for a minute.

He actually hugs her back before walking over to me and looking up at me. "Can we go home now?"

"Yep. Let's go home."

The drive home is quiet. Seth doesn't say a word from the time he gets in the car until Cara pulls into my driveway.

After we've all climbed out, Seth stands awkwardly and shuffles his feet. "Do I have any chores to do this afternoon, Uncle Josh?"

"No, I think you've done enough work for the day. You can go do whatever you like." I look down into Seth's face, so similar to my own and Zack's. For the first time since that bitch dropped him off to us a little over three months ago, I feel hope.

Seth nods. "Okay, thanks. Bye, Cara. See you tomorrow." He grabs his bike and rides it down the driveway, then cuts right to the barn.

"He'll go talk to the horses," I murmur, and reach down for Cara's hand. It's so small, like the rest of her, and yet she's one of the strongest people I know.

I couldn't admire her more than I do right now.

"I'm sorry it was so hard for him today," she whispers with tears in her eyes.

"Rough day for you too, honey."

She looks up at me and nods and bites her lip, and I just can't stand it anymore. I need to taste her.

I cup her face in my hands and lean in, keeping eye contact with her as I do, and I brush my lips over hers, so lightly that I can barely feel her. I nuzzle her nose with my own and nibble the corner of her mouth. Her eyes flutter closed on a sigh.

"I'm not interested in cowboys," she whispers.

"Why?" I breathe.

"Because I don't think tight Wranglers and cowboy hats are hot."

I chuckle against her ear and gently tug the lobe with my teeth. "Then it's a good thing I wear Levi's."

God, she smells like heaven. Her hair smells like strawberries and her skin is soft. I want to lose myself in her.

"What about Blondie?"

What the fuck? "Who?"

"The blond chick I saw leaving your house the first morning I was here."

"That was Erica. She's with Fish and Wildlife. I think I have a wolf issue."

"Oh, I thought she might be your girlfriend or . . . something," Cara mutters as color rises to her cheeks.

"I don't have a girlfriend or . . . something." I grin.

"Cara, you live in the same small town I do." I look her in the eyes and hold her face in my hands. "Rumors are just that: rumors. I haven't been with a woman in over a year."

Her gorgeous eyes go round and she blinks up at me, processing this information.

"I didn't think I was your type," she murmurs, making me chuckle.

My hands glide down to her perfectly round ass as I pull her against me so she can feel my hard cock against her stomach. "I think it's pretty obvious that you're my type, whatever the hell that means."

But taking her now would be too fast, and she's had a rough day.

I pull back and tug her hair gently before stepping away. She's panting, her cheeks are flushed, and her eyes are bright green.

So that's what color they are when she's turned on.

CHAPTER

Four

CARA

He freaking kissed me!

And damn if I don't want him to do it again.

I pace across my colorful living room, cell phone gripped firmly in my right hand, waiting anxiously for Jill to call. I'm all keyed up, still emotional from the outing with Seth and more than a little hot and bothered by Josh's kiss.

Josh King is just as sexy and sweet as he ever was, and I'm losing the tenuous grip I had on my professionalism.

Today sucked, that's all there is to it. I hated making Seth feel small, but I think our little field trip today might have done the trick where his attitude is concerned. Time will tell.

And Josh had done exactly what I'd asked of him;

he'd let me run the show today and I know how hard that must have been for him.

I stomp past the dining room table, where my uneaten dinner has been resting for the better part of an hour, and into the kitchen to pour myself a glass of wine. It's seven fifteen.

Jill's late.

Just as I turn to stomp back to the living room, wine in one hand and phone in the other, my cell rings.

"You're late." I narrow my eyes and take a sip of the cold, sweet wine.

"I'm sorry. I was showing a house and the damn couple kept wanting to hem and haw over the master bathroom."

I hear road noise in the background. "Are you in the car?"

"Yeah, I'm driving home so you're on speaker. Can you hear me?"

"I hear you." I plop my ass into an overstuffed red chair and lean my head back with a sigh.

"So, how's your day, dear?" Jill asks happily.

"I had the shittiest day of my life."

"Worse than that time during junior year when we were dissecting frogs and you threw up?" Jill laughs, bringing a smile to my face.

"Worse," I confirm.

"Worse than when you decided to get your bangs cut and they looked like someone tried to murder you in your sleep with scissors?"

I laugh and take a sip of wine. "A little worse, yes."

"It definitely can't be worse than prom." Her voice is incredulous, and I can't help but laugh as I remember back to our prom night and my date spilling beer all down my beautiful, perfect dress at the pre-party.

"Okay, it's a close second," I concede.

"What's up?" she asks in her carefree, Jillian way. I miss her.

"I'm working for Josh King." I take a sip of wine and then set the glass on the end table so I can rub my eyes.

"Josh needs a tutor?" Jill asks dryly. "Last time I checked, he graduated two years ahead of us."

"No, smart-ass, Josh doesn't need a tutor. Kensie dropped Zack's boy off unexpectedly and ran off with some guy."

"Damn, I'm missing all the good stuff." I hear her shut off her car. "I'm home."

"Good, pour yourself a glass of wine and join me."

"Sounds perfect. You were saying?"

"So, Seth flunked out of school and has just had a hard time of it, and Josh hired me to tutor him over the summer." I take another sip and am beginning to feel my lips tingle. I haven't had anything to eat since breakfast, not to mention I've always been a lightweight.

I'd better slow down.

"Okay, so why did your day suck?" I hear the pop of a cork and the *glug-glug* of Jill pouring her wine. "Josh is a nice guy."

"He's nice. I had to do the tough-love thing with Seth today." I set my wine back down and trace the seam on the arm of the chair with my fingertip.

"*Tough love?*" Jill chuckles. "What does that mean?"

"I took him to Uncle Ed so he could wash dishes, took him to the jail. All the fun stuff." I swallow another sip of wine and lean my head back. "I'm glad I don't have to do it often. I hate it."

"Right. Just like I hate it when people hem and haw over master bathrooms. Jesus, it's just a bathroom, people!"

I grin and nod. "Exactly. You know, I roped Ty into helping me today. I would not want to go against your brother in a courtroom. His stern face is a little scary."

"Don't let him fool you, he's not that scary. So does Seth come to you every day or are you going out to the ranch?"

"I go to the ranch."

"How is Josh doing?" Jill sighs. I picture her sitting in her living room, her shoes kicked off, still in her power suit.

"He's good." I try to make my voice light as though I were speaking about anyone else in town.

Jillian's not stupid. "Good, huh? I saw him when I was home at Christmas. Those King boys are as hot as ever. I wouldn't kick Josh out of bed for eating crackers, unless he wanted to do it on the floor." She giggles hysterically, so amused with herself, and instead of laughing with her as I normally would, I chew on my lower lip and continue to trace the pattern on the chair.

"Cara?"

"I'm here."

"Spill."

"He kissed me."

"Reeeeeeeally. And?"

"And what?"

"Don't be a bitch, you know I need details."

"It was nice."

"Well, if it was just 'nice,' what's the problem? Move on. Ain't nobody got time to settle for 'nice.'"

"It was—" Suddenly the doorbell rings. "Hold on, someone's at the door."

I walk to the door, the phone pressed to my shoulder, and open it to find Josh standing there, his face hard and serious, hands propped on his lean hips. His eyes search my face, and suddenly he moves inside, grabs the phone from my hand, pushes the END button, and tosses it on the key table next to the door.

"What are you—"

Before I can complete the question, he grips my face in his hands and lowers his lips to mine. This is no gentle kiss like this afternoon's. This is a hard, deep, powerful kiss that rocks me back on my heels. I grip his forearms and hold on as bold lust settles in my belly.

He pushes me back against the wall and pins me

with his hips as he buries one hand in my hair, holding my head still for his lips. His other hand grips my waist.

Dear God, I just want to climb him.

I wrap my arms around his neck and kiss him back, just as firmly and passionately as he's delivering. He growls low in his throat and cups my round ass in his hands, boosting me up against the wall so my legs wrap around his hips and I'm eye level with him.

His chocolate-brown eyes stare into mine and he again pins me, his pelvis cradled against mine. He lifts one hand to brush the hair away from my face.

"What are you doing here?" I whisper, my breath coming in pants. I don't know if I'm light-headed from the wine or Josh's kisses.

He shakes his head, nuzzles my nose, and I can feel his erection pressed to my center.

I grip his face in my hands and stare him in the eye. "What are you doing here?"

"I don't know." He closes his eyes and sighs, leaning his forehead against mine. "One taste of you wasn't enough. I can't get you out of my head."

He lowers his lips to mine again, gently this time, and he slowly brushes them back and forth, nibbling at the sides of my mouth, licking my lower lip with just the tip of his tongue. I'm vaguely aware of my cell ringing, but I don't care.

I roll my hips, just a tiny bit, and grin when he groans against my lips. He pushes more firmly against me, shooting sparks through my clit and up my spine.

I want him. Now.

Both of his hands glide up my hips, my sides, and cup my full breasts. He worries the nipples with his thumbs as he sweeps his amazing lips down my jawline to my neck.

"You're so sweet," he whispers. "You've been drinking wine."

I grin and nod. He chuckles softly against my skin, making me tingle even more.

"Can I pour you a glass?" I ask, my voice trembling.

"No, I'm drunk enough on you, sweetheart." He settles his lips over mine again and boosts me higher against the wall, even tighter against him.

I plunge my hands in his thick, dark brown hair and hang on for dear life as his mouth plunders mine, his tongue dancing and rubbing with my own. Finally he pulls back, panting raggedly. He kisses my cheek softly and brushes his thumb over my lower lip.

"I'd better go before I rip the clothes off your delectable little body and take you against this wall."

"Go ahead." I enjoy the way his eyes widen as he swallows thickly. *Holy shit, did I really just say that?*

"Not yet." He shakes his head and slowly lowers me to the floor. "It's too soon, and as much as I want you right now, I don't want to rush this."

"Why not?" I whisper, his words a balm to my

ego. I want him. I shouldn't, and this is nuts, but I so, so want him.

"Because this isn't a one-night stand for me, Cara. I don't know where this will go, but it's not a quick fuck against the wall by your front door."

"I have a bedroom," I offer with a smile.

He grins down at me, his eyes happy and warm. "Soon," he promises, and cups my cheek in his hand once more, gently kisses me, and then sighs. "I'll see you in the morning."

He opens the front door and looks back at me, almost hesitating as if he wants to say something more, but he turns and shuts the door behind him, and I'm left leaning against my wall, a panty-soaked, gasping-for-breath mess.

So much for maintaining my professionalism.

Taking a deep breath, I reach for my phone and call Jillian back to reassure her that I wasn't just attacked by a serial killer.

I'm a complete wimp.

I called in sick this morning for the first time in four years.

I shake my head in disgust and pour more beige paint into the pan, run my roller through it, and smooth it over the wall. I couldn't face Josh today. I need to get a handle on my emotions, and I can't do that when I'm around him.

He's too . . . *Josh.*

How can he just come into my home, kiss the hell

out of me, and then leave as if nothing happened? Okay, so he didn't leave as if *nothing* happened, but still. Who the hell does that?

And why do I so desperately want him to do it again?

Because he's hotter than sin and you want in his pants.

"Cara?"

I frown and turn at the sound of Seth's voice coming from my front door.

"Seth, you're supposed to knock, for God's sake!"

And there's Josh, right behind him.

"I'm back here!" I yell out with a resigned sigh, set the roller in the pan, and wipe my hands on the rag resting on my shoulder.

I turn to find Seth and Josh staring at me from the door. Seth wrinkles his nose and sighs. "I do not want to paint. Tell me you're not going to make me paint."

Josh leans casually against the doorframe and smirks at me. "Sick, huh?"

I shrug and turn around, cleaning up my mess.

"Are you feeling better?" Seth asks.

"I'm fine," I mumble.

"Seth, why don't you go wait for Cara at the kitchen table." Josh hasn't taken his eyes off me, and I squirm as Seth leaves the room. "What's wrong?"

"I'm fine," I repeat as I place the lid on the can of paint.

"You called in sick this morning."

I shrug again, not wanting to admit that he's the reason I didn't come to work, and pissed that my lust for him is interfering with my job.

"Look at me." His voice is firm. I close my eyes and cross my arms over my chest.

"Maybe you should find Seth a different tutor. I can make some calls."

Josh moves into the room, grips my chin between his thumb and finger, and tilts my head back to look him in the face. "No."

"Josh . . ."

"No." He shakes his head. "Seth actually smiled at me this morning, Cara. He was respectful to my parents when they told him to feed the dogs and collect the eggs this morning. That's because of *you*. I'm not hiring someone else."

"I'm so glad, really, but I think—"

"Stop thinking so hard." He offers me a half smile, that sexy dimple winking at me, and I feel myself soften. "I'm not going to ravage your body in front of him. I can control myself." Josh frowns and narrows his eyes. "But when he's not around, I plan to touch you as much as possible."

I can't stop my gasp or the way my eyes go round in surprise. "This is crazy," I whisper.

"Call in sick again and I'll come find you, if nothing more than to make sure you're okay." He smirks arrogantly and backs away. I immediately miss the warmth of his body so close to mine.

"I'm not helpless."

"If you don't want me to pursue you, say the word and I'll stop. I'm not in the habit of harassing women." He crosses his arms over his chest, his biceps flex under his white T-shirt, and I am once again a quivering, wet mess.

I should tell him I'm not interested. But I can't form the damn words.

"Okay." He nods and smiles. "I'll pick Seth up at two."

"You didn't have to bring him here," I mutter.

"Yeah, I did. I'll see you later, sweetheart."

I follow Josh out of the room and into the living space. He leaves without another word.

Seth is watching me as if I might die of the plague any moment. "Are you really sick?"

"I'm feeling better." I shrug and offer him a small smile, and he returns it, a bright, sweet young-boy smile. "Let's get started on fractions."

"I hate fractions."

"I'm with you, kid."

"So, he didn't call you at all over the weekend?" Jill asks over the phone. I press it between my ear and shoulder as I pull the bag of popcorn apart to empty it into a bowl. The screen on my back door is suddenly slammed, hard, and I hurry over to secure it.

"Storm's coming in." I love summer storms. They move in fast and hard, blowing wind and spitting rain, and then they move out just as fast. "The wind is nuts right now." I eye the tree in the backyard and remind myself for the hundredth time to call Mr. Eckles to come over and trim it.

"Is there thunder?" Jill asks, making me laugh. She's so in-your-face most of the time, but a total wimp when it comes to storms.

"Yes, and lightning."

"Ugh, I'm glad I'm not there. Now, focus. You didn't hear from Josh over the weekend?"

"Nope. It's been a week since he showed up here the day I called in sick. He didn't lie before. He hasn't touched me in front of Seth, but when Seth isn't around, he definitely does."

"Touches you how?" She's chewing on something crunchy.

"You know, brushes against me when he walks past, tucks my hair behind my ear, that kind of stuff. Like yesterday—" I stop short.

"If you stop now, I swear to God, I'll shoot you the next time I see you."

"You don't know how to fire a gun."

"I'll learn. Keep talking."

"Well, yesterday, I was leaning over Seth's shoulder to read the worksheet he was working on, and Josh moved up behind me and rubbed his hand up and down my back, and when I looked up at him, he winked at me."

"But no more kissing?"

"No."

"Boring." Jill sighs.

I laugh. "I'm so sorry that I'm not more enter-taining."

"Hey, you're getting more action than I am these days." She takes another bite of the crunchy. "So maybe *you* should just kiss *him*."

"Maybe he came to his senses and realized that a sexual relationship is a bad idea."

"Maybe pigs will fly out of my ass." I can practi-cally hear her roll her eyes.

"I've always hated that expression." I frown and stuff a handful of popcorn in my mouth.

"I think he's being a nice guy. Getting to know you. Letting you get used to him, and all that boring shit."

"Probably. Did you watch *Dancing with the Stars* last night?" I ask, changing the subject.

"Of course. I'm so glad they brought Max back this season. That man melts my panties off."

Suddenly call waiting is beeping in my ear. When I pull the phone away, it's Josh's name on the caller ID.

"Jill, I'll call you later. Josh is on the other line."

"I want all the details!"

"Good-bye, Jilly." I chuckle as I switch over. "Hello?"

"Hey." His low voice sends shivers through me and I immediately set my popcorn aside while wiping my hands on my jeans.

"Hey, what's up?" My voice sounds a bit too high even to my own ears and I wince.

"What are you doing?"

"I was chatting with Jill."

"Do you want me to let you go?" I hear him shifting in the background and I wonder if he's lying down.

"No, I hung up with her. Are you okay?"

"I'm fine, I was just thinking about you." I pull the phone away from my ear and frown down at it. This is the first time he's called me just to chat.

"What were you thinking?" I ask, genuinely curious.

"That I wish you were here with me. Is it weird that I miss you and I just saw you four hours ago?"

No, it's not weird because I feel exactly the same way! "I always knew you were weird," I respond playfully, and am rewarded with his deep chuckle. My panties dampen as I picture that sexy dimple in his cheek, but then I grow quiet.

"Okay, you're quiet. What are *you* thinking?"

"Well, it's weird. You miss me, but I haven't heard from you much the last few days."

He sighs deeply. "I had a few foals born over the weekend. One didn't make it. A portion of the fence line on the far side of the ranch went down, I have no idea how, and a few head of cattle got out. Had to round them up. It was a shitty weekend."

"I'm sorry about the foal," I murmur, and close my eyes.

"It happens. Seth took it hard."

"He didn't mention anything about it today." I pop a kernel of popcorn in my mouth and munch thoughtfully. "What are you up to? Before you called me, that is."

"I was reading, gonna call it a night. Wanted to hear your voice." The last sentence is whispered and I've never been more tempted to jump in my car and race over to a man's place.

"It's kind of early to go to bed." I glance at the clock and am surprised to see it's only eight thirty.

"I have to get up at five to feed the horses and meet with my guys before the day gets started."

I settle in deeper against the cushions of my couch, enjoying the deep timbre of his voice. "That's right, you're a morning person."

"It's habit now," he agrees with a chuckle. "Are you a night person?"

"Depends on my mood, I guess." The back screen door slams against the house again and I walk through the house to secure it. "It's windy tonight."

"Are you okay?" I hear the concern in his voice and I grin.

"Yeah, the screen door keeps coming unlatched from the wind."

"Do you need me to come in to town to help you out?"

I'm so, so tempted to say yes, just so I can see him, but it's only a silly storm.

"I'm fine, Josh, but thanks for the offer. I'll probably head to bed soon too."

Silence.

"Josh?"

"I'm here." His voice is soft and the line is still.

"What's wrong?" I whisper.

"The thought of you in a bed conjures all kinds of images, and you're a good fifteen minutes away from me right now."

I laugh and shake my head, but my nipples have puckered at his words and my toes curl. "I'll see you tomorrow."

"I want to see you this weekend, just you and me."

"Like on a date?" I lean my head back against the couch, biting my lower lip.

"Yes, on a date. I want to take you to dinner, in public. Take a walk. Go to the movies. You know, a date. What do you say?"

"Is this a good idea?" I ask softly, and close my eyes, wishing with all my might that it *were* a good idea.

"It's just dinner, Carolina. Stop overthinking it."

"We both know it's not going to end at dinner."

"Fuck, I hope not," he agrees with a smile in his voice.

"It's a date."

I'm jolted awake by what sounds like warfare. The house is trembling as though I'm under fire, pounding and groaning, splintering wood. It's pitch-dark, and snow is falling inside my room, but it hurts when it hits my skin. My heart is beating so hard I swear it's going to come out of my chest, and I can hardly breathe.

I sit straight up and, to my horror, see my ceiling

falling apart above me. Water is spilling inside, along with what looks like snow, but I quickly realize it is insulation from the roof.

Holy fuck!

My lungs are screaming in pain from inhaling the sharp shards of fiberglass, and then I don't feel anything at all as adrenaline kicks in.

I have to get out of here!

I leap from the bed and yank the yoga pants I tossed at the end of my bed up over my hips, step into flip-flops, and run outside to the sound of sirens and wind. My neighbors have come out of their homes, and someone wraps me in his arms and holds on tight.

"Thank God you're okay."

Ty! Ty lives just four houses down from me.

"My God, Ty!"

I pull from his arms and turn toward the house. The tree from the backyard has toppled over, its old, rotten trunk splintered in half. It's lying across the entire left side of my house. The roof is completely collapsed, and the wall to the master bathroom has crumbled.

I could have been killed.

A fire truck pulls up, and then another, their sirens blaring. An ambulance approaches behind them, and my street is suddenly in a flurry of activity. More neighbors are filtering out of their homes, gasping and crying, and all I can do is stand in shock, not caring that I'm getting wet and dirty, and not even feeling Ty's strong arms looped around me, holding me up.

I'm thankful for Ty, but suddenly all I can think about is being in Josh's arms. I need him.

And I don't even have a phone.

"My phone is under the tree," I mutter.

"Who do you need to call?" Ty asks.

"Jill. My parents." I swallow hard. "Josh," I whisper.

"I called Josh," Ty responds with a warm smile. "He's on his way."

I nod and turn back to the house, unable to tear my eyes away from the destruction.

"Cara, we have to check you over and make sure you're not hurt."

One of the paramedics, Sam Waters, takes me by the arm, pulls me over to the ambulance, and sits me down inside. Ty stands vigil at the ambulance door and speaks into his phone.

"She's getting checked out now."

Who's he talking to?

I can't bring myself to care. I don't feel anything.

Sam and his partner are running their hands over my arms and legs, checking for breaks and scrapes.

"Wow, there's hardly a mark on you. You'll have some little cuts and scratches from the insulation, though." Sam's face is worried as he looks into my eyes. "Her eyes are dilated."

"She's in shock."

Someone wraps a thin hospital blanket around my shoulders, making me frown. Should I be cold?

"Cara."

I don't respond.

"Cara." Sam shakes me, forcing me to look up into his face. "Maybe we should take you to the hospital anyway."

"No." I shake my head and grip the blanket around me. "I'm fine. I'm not hurt."

"Cara," he begins again, but I clamber out of the ambulance and down to Ty, who wraps his arms around me again and kisses my temple. The rain has stopped, but the wind is still vicious.

"Where is she?" someone is shouting in a panic, and my heart fills with joy at the sound of Josh's voice. I turn to see him pushing his way through the crowd, his eyes wild with fear. "Where the fuck is she?"

"Josh!" He wraps his arms around me and I burrow into his chest. For the first time since waking up, I feel safe at last.

CHAPTER
Five

JOSH

"'Lo?" My voice is groggy as I answer my phone and check the time: 2:09 in the middle of the damn night. "What's wrong?"

"It's Ty. I need you in town now, man." I can hear rain and voices around him. I immediately jump from bed, pull on my jeans and a shirt, and pull my shit together. "We're gonna need your generator and lights too."

"What's wrong?" I ask again, my voice hard and awake.

"I heard a loud boom about two minutes ago and came running outside to find a tree lying across Cara's roof." My heart stops as I pause in tying my boots. "The power's out and it's black out here, man."

"Have you called 911?"

"Of course, and they're on their way, but—"

"Is Cara still in there?" I close my eyes and pray that he says no, that she's right there next to him. Please, God, let her be okay.

"Yeah, she's not out here yet. Jesus, man." I hear the fear and the shock in his voice and it spurs me into action. I grab my jacket and keys and run out to my truck.

"I'll be there in fifteen." I end the call and immediately dial Louie, our head ranch hand, and instruct him to call the other guys, grab the lights and generator, and come to town.

There's no way in fucking hell I'm wasting time gathering that shit when I need to get to Cara. Now.

Jesus, what if she's hurt?

I punch the accelerator on the way down the long driveway, swerving around fallen tree limbs and other debris thrown around by the windstorm. Once on the highway I punch it hard, driving much faster than is safe, especially in this weather, but I don't care. I have only one thought in my head: get to Carolina.

Ten minutes later my phone rings again.

"Ty!" I bark.

"She's out and she's okay. Shaken up, but not hurt."

I close my eyes with relief. The knot I didn't even know was there loosens in my chest, allowing me to take a deep breath.

"Have the paramedics looked at her?"

"She's getting checked out now. How far out are you?"

"I'm almost there. Louie and the other guys are bringing the equipment."

"Thanks, man."

I hang up and toss the phone on the seat beside me, relieved to see the edges of town in my headlights. People and official vehicles and barricades at both ends of the block stop me as I approach Cara's street, so I jump out of the truck and run. The crowd in the street is surprisingly thick and full of movement and flashing lights and confusion, and the more I have to search for her, the more panicked I become.

"Where is she?" I yell, and push neighbors aside, frantically searching the crowd. "Where the fuck is she?"

"Josh!"

I see her now, not far from the ambulance with Ty; his arms are around her as though he's holding her up. Her beautiful hair is covered in white, and she's wearing nothing more than a black tank top and yoga pants. She flings a thin hospital blanket off her shoulders and pulls out of Ty's arms to run to me. I wrap my arms around her shoulders, pulling her close.

"She's covered in insulation, man. Be careful."

I watch Ty's serious face over Cara's head and nod gravely. I want to bury my face in her hair and breathe her in, but I won't do her any good if I'm in the hospital from inhaling fiberglass, so I just run my hands up and down her back, soothing her.

"A tree fell on my house," she mutters, her voice thin and flat.

"I see, honey." My calm voice masks the fear coursing through me. Holy fuck, the tree practically sliced her house in two.

I could have lost her, and I just found her.

"It fell on my house," she repeats, and I look down to find her cheek pressed to my chest and her eyes glued to her house. I turn her away and tilt her head back with my fingers, needing to look her in the eye. Her eyes are wide and glassy with shock.

"You're fine, baby." Her eyes fill with tears, but she swallows and blinks them away. "It's okay. The house can be fixed."

"Where am I gonna go?"

"You can stay with me, Cara," Ty begins, but I scowl at him and wrap my arms around her again, pulling her into me. I'll be damned if I'll let her out of my sight.

"She'll stay with me."

She frowns up at me and I can see the wheels turning in her gorgeous head. "I have a spare bed-room, Cara."

She looks back at Ty, who just smiles and shrugs, and then she turns those amazing amber eyes back at me. "Are you sure?"

"Yes." I cup her face in my hands and brush the white flecks on her cheeks with my thumbs, feeling tiny pricks on my skin. "In fact, we need to get you out of here and cleaned up. You're going to get cut up from this insulation."

She frowns as if she's just now realizing that she's covered in it. "It stings."

I growl and bend her over, shaking it out of her hair the best I can, ignoring the pokes on my own skin. She sways on her feet when she rights herself, and I lift her easily in my arms.

"I'm taking her home."

Ty nods and waves at my men as they pull up with the equipment. "Thanks for this, Josh."

"This is what we do. Call if you need anything." With that, I carry Cara, her head resting on my shoulder, to my truck and set her carefully in the passenger seat. I buckle her in and frown when she doesn't relax against the seat. She's begun to shake, her eyes still pinned to her house.

I need to get her the hell out of here.

I wrap my jacket around her, jog around the truck to climb in the driver's side, and head off toward home.

By the time we reach the ranch Cara is trembling violently, tears streaming unchecked down her cheeks. I need to get her into a hot shower quick. Jesus, I have to do *something*.

"Come on, baby." I smile down at her as I lift her out of the truck, carrying her through the house to the master suite.

"I thought I would have my own room," she murmurs, her voice thin and trembling.

"You will, but we need to get you cleaned up."

"You're not showering with me." She clenches her eyes closed and shakes her head.

"Hey, Cara, stop this." I set her carefully on the closed toilet and kneel before her, gripping her shoulders in my hands. "You're in shock, baby. I can't let you take a shower by yourself. It's okay."

"I'm so embarrassed," she whispers.

I sigh. "No need. You're gorgeous, but I'll be good. Let's get this fiberglass off you." I turn and quickly turn the hot water on in the shower, giving it time to heat up. I turn back to her and my heart clenches. She looks so small and defeated. I grip the hem of her tank in my hands and pull it over her head. Her breasts are as beautiful as I knew they would be, but I keep my face calm and focus on the task at hand.

She stands and strips out of her yoga pants, and I gather the ruined clothes and shove them in the garbage.

I'm thankful that when I built this bathroom, I installed a separate walk-in shower and bathtub. The shower is large enough for two. When the bathroom is steamy, I shuck out of my own clothes, leaving my boxers on, and guide her into the shower and under the hot water.

"You have shorts on," she states matter-of-factly.

"Yep." I grin down at her.

"Why?"

"To make sure you behave yourself." I raise an eyebrow as I guide her under the hot water and wince when she flinches.

"Too hot?"

"No, my skin is just really sensitive." She won't look me in the eye, and I know she's embarrassed.

This is not how either of us envisioned seeing each other naked for the first time.

She leans her head back into the stream of hot water, and when I'm satisfied that she's no longer in danger of being cut, I wash and rinse her hair and soap up a washcloth, running it over her curves and soft skin. Despite the hot water, she's begun shaking violently again and her skin is covered in goose bumps.

As I wash her hair for the third time, she looks up at me with wide amber eyes and bites her lip, watching my face as I rinse the suds from her thick locks.

God, she's so fucking beautiful.

"You're good at this," she whispers.

I smile down at her gently and cup her cheeks in my hands. "Are you still cold?"

She shakes her head but continues to shiver. Her eyes fill with tears. "Thank you for being so nice to me," she stutters.

"Come here." I pull her into my arms and we stand here, under the scalding water, pressed against each other. I've never before felt so close to another person, not even when I was making love to one.

Not even when I was *inside* one.

She breaks down into sobs, her forehead against my sternum, and lets go.

"It's okay, baby, let it out. You're safe." I continue

crooning to her, gently rubbing her back and her arms, kissing her wet hair, until the shivering slows and she takes a big, deep breath.

"I'm sorry."

"What do you have to be sorry for?" I tilt her head back to look me in the face, and her eyes fill with fresh tears.

God, she's killing me.

"For everything. Making you bring me here, falling apart. We're naked, for God's sake!"

"You didn't make me do anything, Cara. I want you here. I've wanted you here for a while. You needed to fall apart, and having you naked is a fantasy come true, although I was planning on it being under very different circumstances." Her shoulders relax and I lean down to plant a chaste kiss on her pouty lips. "Let's get you dressed."

I lead her out of the shower and begin drying her with soft towels. "How does your skin feel?"

"A little raw and it's really itchy." Her arms, face, and chest are irritated from the insulation, but her face is still far too pale, and I'm suddenly filled with more rage than I've felt in months.

She could have been killed.

"I don't even have any underwear." A single tear falls down her cheek and she just looks so defeated.

"You can borrow some of my things for the rest of the night, baby."

I take her hand in mine and lead her to the bed, then step away from her to shuffle through my dresser drawers, pulling out a T-shirt and a pair of boxers and handing them to her.

She quickly pulls my T-shirt over her head and steps into the boxers, all way too big for her.

Even scared and upset she's fucking adorable.

I lift her in my arms again and climb into my bed with her, pull the covers up over us, and turn her away from me, tucking her against me.

"You don't need to keep me in your bed," she whispers, but nuzzles more securely against me.

I'll be damned if she'll sleep one night in that damn spare room.

"I don't want to be alone tonight, Cara."

She looks over her shoulder at me, surprise written all over her face as she turns fully and wraps her arms around my waist. "Are you okay?"

"Don't worry—"

"Are you okay?" she demands again, small tremors wracking her body.

"I'm better now that I know you're safe," I respond truthfully. "You scared the shit out of me." I pull her against me and run my hands down her back. She rubs her sweet, small hands up and down my back at the same time, her amber eyes watching me. How she can try to soothe me after all she's been through in the past hour is beyond me.

"Go to sleep," I whisper, and kiss her forehead.

"You too," she murmurs.

I smile against her forehead, suddenly exhausted. It feels amazing to have her here, safe and whole in my bed. "Sleep, sweetheart. We'll figure everything out tomorrow."

The ranch is a damn disaster.

After just a couple hours of sleep, wrapped around Cara, I pulled myself out of bed to tend to the ranch. None of the guys got any sleep last night, and we have a hell of a mess on our hands today. I've sent half the guys out on ATVs to check the fences, opting to stay close to home, and Cara, today. Seth is gathering scattered branches and other debris and throwing it all in a pile that we'll roast marshmallows over later.

All of the animals are safe and accounted for, thankfully.

I left Cara sleeping in my bed this morning, and I hope she's still knocked out. She needs the rest. I scowl at my watch when I discover that I've been gone longer than I thought.

When I push inside the house, I see Cara sitting on the couch, still in my T-shirt and shorts, staring wide-eyed at the TV.

Fuck, she's watching the news.

". . . can see, the tree fell across the entire left side of the house. The fire chief tells us that if it had fallen just two feet to the left, the homeowner would have been killed."

"Cara, don't watch this shit." I hastily turn off the TV and lift her into my lap, settling back on the couch.

"I'm too heavy," she whispers, and plays with the buttons on my shirt.

"No, you're not. How are you this morning?"

She shrugs and sighs. "I need to go into town and look at my house."

"It's being taken care of."

"Josh, it's my house. I need to go look at it."

I don't like it. I want to protect her, and I definitely don't want her going anywhere near that house.

"It's not safe."

"What are you doing here?" Seth asks from the doorway, his face full of surprise.

Cara tries to pull herself out of my lap, and because Seth is here, I let her go.

For now.

"The storm did some damage to Cara's house last night, so she came here. She's going to be staying with me for a while."

Seth's solemn gaze turns to Cara and he walks over to her, watching her carefully. "Did you get hurt?"

"Just scared more than anything."

"What happened?" he asks, sounding much older than his twelve years.

"A tree fell on my roof."

Seth blanches and his face goes pale. He suddenly throws his arms around Cara and hugs her tight.

She blinks back tears as she pushes her fingers through his dark hair soothingly. "I'm okay, sweetie. The house will be fixed."

"I don't give a shit about your house! You could have gotten really hurt."

I love this kid.

Cara gives Seth a quick squeeze and brushes a tear from her cheek. "Can I borrow some sweats, Josh? I need to get some clothes from my place today."

"You're not going back there alone," Seth insists, scowling. "I'll go with you."

"You can come," she agrees, and looks up at me expectantly. "Sweats?"

"Seth, go help Louie for a few minutes. I'll come get you when we're ready to go to town."

Seth nods and runs out to help in the pasture.

"I have sweats you can wear." I pull her back into my arms, tilt her head back, and gaze into her eyes. "Are you sure you're okay?"

"I will be," she whispers. "You help."

"Good." I nod and lead her to the bedroom to find her some sweats.

"Should I move into the spare room?"

"Fuck no. You're with me, sweetheart." I stare over at her, daring her to argue, but she smiles slowly and pulls my sweats over her hips, over the shorts. They're at least five sizes too big, and I want nothing more than to strip her out of them.

"We'd better go."

CHAPTER

CARA

The house looks no better in the light of day, but the storm has cleared, leaving warm sunshine and a cool, light breeze.

Aside from the house being crushed by a hundred-year-old maple tree, and debris thrown all over the neighborhood, you'd never know the storm ever happened.

And with the sunshine, and a breath of fresh air, I've found my resolve.

"I need to go in and get some clothes." I look up at Josh, standing next to me, his hands propped on his hips, and he stares down at me as if I've lost my mind.

"You're not going in there."

"No way," Seth agrees, his hazel eyes glued to the house.

I'm surrounded by overprotective men.

"Hey, Charlie!" I call out to the tall, handsome member of the crew helping with cleanup, smiling at him as he approaches. "When did the tree come off the house?"

"Early this morning." He takes off his hat and wipes his sweat-covered brow. "Now we have to clean up."

"I need to go in and get some clothes and stuff."

"I said—" Josh begins, but Charlie interrupts.

"Not a chance." Charlie shakes his head. "It's not sound in there, Cara. Plus, the insulation is all over your clothes and things."

"So I'll wash them." I shrug.

"They have to be sent out to a special cleaner to make them safe for you. I'm sorry, but I can't let you in there."

I just stare at him, processing. "So, I won't have clean clothes for *days*?"

"At least we don't have to throw them out." Charlie shrugs and walks back to the house. "I'll call you when I know more."

"I don't have a phone!" I call after him in frustration.

Josh is watching me with a half grin on his face, his arms crossed over his chest. Seth giggles.

"What is so damn funny?" I demand.

"You are." Josh grins and that dimple softens me, just a bit, but I keep the scowl on my face. "I guess we'll go shopping next."

"I hate shopping," I grumble, making Seth laugh even harder.

"Hey, guys!" Ty calls, and jogs across the street to us. He's in faded blue jeans and a Metallica T-shirt, showing off the tattoo sleeve on his right arm. It's easy to forget when he's got on his lawyer suit that he's very much the bad boy underneath.

"Hey, Ty," I say.

He wraps his arms around me and squeezes me tight. "How are you, bird?"

"I'm better. What a mess."

"That it is." He nods, shakes Josh's hand, and ruffles Seth's hair. "Have you called your folks?"

"Shit, no!" I glance down at Seth and grimace. "Sorry, Seth."

"I don't care." He shrugs.

"I don't have a phone," I remind everyone. "It's in the house. I have to call Jilly too."

"I called her this morning. I had to talk her out of jumping on the first plane out of LAX."

I rub my forehead with the tips of my fingers and sigh. "My parents are going to freak out."

Josh has moved up behind me, rubbing my shoulders with his big, strong hands, and I lean back into him, absorbing his strength and warmth.

"I can call them for you," he offers, but I shake my head and cover one of his hands with my own.

"I'll do it. I guess I'd better get a new phone when we go shopping."

"You're going shopping?" Ty asks incredulously,

then chuckles. "That might get Jill on the plane after all."

"Screw you." I glare at him, then laugh. "I needed some new things anyway. I've been putting it off."

"Why do you hate to shop so much?" Seth asks. "Don't girls live for that crap?"

"Not this girl." I shudder and push my hands through my hair, enjoying the feel of Josh's hands still kneading my shoulders. "I usually wait until Jill's home or I go visit her and then I can't avoid it any longer. She drags me."

Seth's eyes are now glued to Josh's hands on my shoulders. "Why are you touching her like that?"

I go still just as Josh's hands stop moving. Ty smothers a grin.

"Seth . . ." I begin as his hands form fists and he scowls at his uncle. Josh moves me easily aside and stands directly in front of Seth.

"What's wrong?" Josh asks his nephew calmly.

Seth shrugs and looks at his feet, his hands crammed in his pockets, a scowl on his handsome little face.

"Talk to me," Josh tries again.

Seth's head comes up and he pins Josh with a harsh glare. "You shouldn't touch her like that. She's not like my mom." He's got tears in his eyes, but he fights valiantly to keep them at bay as his cheeks flush with anger.

I gasp. Ty swears under his breath, and Josh's hands fist at his sides and his jaw clenches.

"Do you think I'm taking advantage of Cara?" he asks in a low voice.

"You better not." Seth pushes his chin out defiantly and I want to hug him to me, so moved that he wants to protect me.

"Seth, Josh isn't trying to take advantage of me," I say. Seth watches us both carefully. "He's being supportive and a good friend." *Dear God, what did he see when he lived with his mom?*

"Seth, I care about Cara. Very much." Josh relaxes his body and smiles down at the boy as he links his fingers with mine. "I like that you care about her too and want to protect her."

Seth shrugs again and frowns.

I think I just fell in love with both of them.

"Just don't do gross stuff in front of me," he grumbles, and stomps off to the truck.

"Well, there's more of his dad in him than he thinks," Ty observes, and grins at Josh.

Josh looks over at me, his eyes roam over my face, and I'm not sure what he's looking for, but I squeeze his hand with my own and offer him a small smile.

"Here are three words I never thought I'd say willingly: let's go shopping."

If he touches me one more time, I swear I'll combust.

He's had his hands on me all day: resting a hand on the small of my back to lead me into a store, holding my hand, brushing my hair behind my ear. And he keeps smiling at me, winking.

Flirting.

Dear God, I want him.

I finally have a few moments to myself, in the spare bedroom. I'm hanging the few new pieces of clothing I bought today in the closet, stuffing underwear, bras, and socks in a drawer and pulling tags off my new flip-flops and sneakers.

"What are you doing?"

Josh is leaning casually against the doorframe, his hands in his pockets. I take a moment to soak him in.

His long, jean-clad legs are crossed at the ankle; torso and shoulders are molded in a black T-shirt. His dark hair is messy and his lips are quirked in a smirk, his brown eyes happy and trained on me.

"I'm putting my things away," I mutter, and turn back to the task at hand.

"You're in the wrong room." I hear him approach behind me, his bare feet quiet on the plush carpet.

"It's better if I stay in here."

He grips my shoulders in his hands and turns me to face him. "Why?"

"I'm much better, Josh. You don't have to keep an eye on me."

He jerks me up against him, pressing his pelvis—his erection—into my belly, and his hands grip me tighter.

"Me wanting you in my bed has nothing to do with your damn tree."

I frown up at him and then look down, shaking my head.

"Why is it so hard for you to believe that I want you, sweetheart?" His voice is soft as he leans in and whispers in my ear. "Answer me."

"It's not that I don't believe it." My eyes flutter closed at the feel of his breath against my ear. "Hell, I can feel it. But we've known each other for ages, and now . . ."

"Now what?" His lips glide down my neck and back up to my ear.

"Now we have more to think about than whether or not we're attracted to each other. There's Seth to consider," I whisper.

"Do you trust me?" He pulls back just a few inches so he can look me in the eye, and I swallow.

"Yes."

His eyes flare and he smiles softly, cups my neck in his hands, and lowers his mouth to mine.

I love the way he kisses!

His full lips cover mine and he stills, not moving them, just breathing me in. I glide my hands up his shoulders and into his hair and press myself against him, my nipples puckering, and he growls as he sinks into me, licking the seam of my lips, asking for entrance.

I kiss him back, sucking and pulling on his lower lip with my teeth. His eyes narrow as he bends down and lifts me easily in his arms, carrying me out of the spare room and into his bedroom, never taking his lips from mine.

It's as if he can't get enough of me, and I feel the exact same way.

I need him.

I need *this*.

"Are you sure?" he asks, his deep voice heavy with lust.

"Yes." He sets me on my feet and I immediately pull my shirt up over my head. "I want you."

"Damn, baby." His eyes are on my round breasts, and I'm shy for a moment. I move to cover myself with my hands but he pulls them away and kisses my palms. "Don't."

"You need to get naked."

"I will." He grins.

"Now."

"Be patient."

"No, I need you. Hard and fast, Josh." I'm panting now and pulling at his jeans, but he stops me, his eyes narrowed and on my face.

"What's the hurry?"

"I need to feel alive," I whisper, and clench my eyes shut. He cups my face in his palms. I open my eyes to see him looking down at me so tenderly it makes me hurt. "I don't need soft and slow, I need to remember that I'm alive and I need you to fuck me."

He sucks in a breath and crushes his lips to mine, strips me out of the rest of my clothes, cups my ass in his hands, and lifts me the way he did the other night at my house. I don't have time to be shy in my nakedness. He's devouring me.

Claiming me.

And I fucking love it.

He braces me against the wall as I'm pulling at his T-shirt. He finally pulls his mouth away from mine long enough to yank it over his head and throws it to the floor.

"You're so fucking beautiful," he growls, and buries his face in my neck, kissing and suckling me. His hands cup my breasts and he lifts them to his lips.

"Oh my God." I reach between us and unfasten his jeans, pushing them with my feet down his hips, unleashing his impressive cock. "This is beautiful," I mutter.

He grins wolfishly and hoists me up higher against the wall. "I'm clean, I promise."

"On the pill," I mutter, and bite his neck. "Now, Josh."

And with that he pushes inside me, all the way, in one long, slow thrust. His cock is long and thick and fills me perfectly.

As if he were made just for me.

"Damn, baby," he growls. "Look at me."

I open my eyes and bite my lip.

"Your eyes are so green." He kisses me softly and groans. "You're so snug, babe."

"Move," I beg, and roll my hips.

"Cara, don't do that . . ."

"Fuck me," I beg, and roll my hips again as he begins to pound in and out of me, hard. He reaches between us and thumbs my clit, and I suddenly see stars. I'm going to come, hard and fast.

"That's right, sweetheart." He's panting hard now,

moving faster and harder. "God, your pussy is so damn good."

"Josh," I mutter.

"Let go, Cara." He pushes on my clit, just a bit harder, and my world explodes around me, scattering in thousands of pieces and then gathering again at the center of me. I cry out and grip his hair in my fingers, bucking my hips against him.

He stops, buried to the root, and leans his forehead against mine, breathing hard.

"How was that?"

"Holy shit," I whisper, and open my eyes.

"I'm not done."

He carries me to the bed, still inside me, and lays me flat on my back, my lower legs hanging off the edge. He kisses me, then pulls out of me, making me groan.

"Josh . . ."

"Shhh." He circles a nipple with his tongue and then nuzzles the underside of my breast. "Just relax and enjoy."

"What are you doing?"

"What I've wanted to do since you got out of your car two weeks ago. I'm tasting you."

He drags his lips down my belly, over my navel, and to the small patch of curls that cover my pussy.

He kneels between my knees and lifts my legs over his shoulders, tilts my pelvis up with one hand on my ass, and pulls one finger down my slit from my clitoris all the way down to my ass.

"You're so swollen and wet for me." His voice is a deep whisper. He leans in and gently kisses that sensitive nub, licks it, then kisses it again.

"Josh," I whisper, closing my eyes.

"Yes, baby." Now I feel the flat of his tongue against me and he pushes it down into my folds and inside me.

"Shit!" I cry out as he sucks my lips into his mouth, and I feel him grin against me before he does it again, making me writhe and move against him, circling my hips against his face.

If he stops, I might kill him.

"Oh, God, I can't." My head is thrashing side to side, and the tension is coiling tighter than it ever has. This orgasm is going to kill me.

"You can," he mutters, and pushes two fingers inside me as he continues to lap at my clit and lips. "I want you to come again, honey."

I link my ankles over his shoulders and push my pelvis against his face and feel the world fall away from me as I come so hard I can't breathe.

Through my orgasmic haze, I feel him kiss the inside of my thighs, my pubis, and up my torso. He sucks each nipple gently, and I frown at the change in him.

Minutes ago he was a man possessed, obsessed with taking me hard, and now he's gentle.

Loving.

He pushes me farther up on the bed and covers me with his body, cradled in the apex of my thighs, braced on his elbows on either side of my head.

He buries his fingers in my hair, nuzzles my nose with his own, while gently rocking his hard cock against my folds.

"Do you have any idea how fucking gorgeous you are?" he whispers.

Rather than answer, I drag my fingertips down his cheek and lift my head to brush his lips with my own. I can taste myself there, and it only makes me want him more.

"You needed me to fuck you, baby, but I need to make love to you. It feels like I've been waiting forever for this." He frowns down at me and nibbles the side of my mouth. "Say something."

"I need you inside me."

His lips quirk against mine as he moves his hips back until the head of his cock is nestled against my opening. "Now?"

"Now."

And slowly, so slowly it brings tears to my eyes, he fills me, all the while watching me with a look of complete and utter contentment on his amazing face.

"You feel so good," I whisper.

"It's all you, baby."

He begins to move, long, slow strokes, pushing me higher and higher, but then he stops and waits for me to come back down.

"That was mean."

He chuckles and licks a trail from my collarbone to my ear. "We're gonna make this last, Carolina."

"I hate that name," I remind him, and gasp as he begins to move again.

"I love your name," he whispers, and wraps his lips around my nipple, suckling softly, and I feel it down to my clit. I squirm beneath him, silently begging him to speed up again, but he stops.

"Every time you try to control this, we start over again."

My eyes burst open at his soft declaration. "What?"

"You heard me. You had it your way." He lifts one of my legs up onto his shoulder, opening me wider, and pushes in deeper, making me gasp. "Now I get to take you places you've never known before, baby."

"I can't do this," I mutter, and shake my head, but he stills me with a soft kiss on my lips and his hand gently smoothes up and down my side.

"You can. Just enjoy, honey."

He starts to move his hips again, slowly but steadily, and I'm amazed at how deep he is. No one has ever before been so deep.

No one has ever made me feel like this.

My muscles contract around him and he clenches his jaw and eyes shut, lowers his forehead to mine, and circles his hips, moving his cock in and out, brushing my G-spot with every damn stroke.

I grip his ass in my hands and urge him to move faster, but he maintains his rhythm.

"Love your hands on me," he mutters, and reaches behind him to grip my hand in his, linking our fingers, and pins my hand to the bed above my head.

Finally he speeds up, his lust carrying him now, and he pushes against my clit with every thrust. I tighten my thighs against his hips and arch my head back as he buries his face against my neck.

"Come, Carolina." He bites the top of my shoulder and I unravel beneath him, crying out, squeezing his hand and his ass, and he growls as he finds his own release.

I've never felt anything else like it in my life.

He releases my leg and my hand and cups my face gently, kisses me thoroughly, sweeping those lips over mine, tangling our tongues and nibbling as if he were a starved man at a buffet.

"Did I hurt you?" he asks quietly as we regain our breath.

"No." I smile softly at him and kiss his cheek. "You definitely didn't hurt me."

"Stay here."

He kisses me one last time and pulls out of me, walks naked into the bathroom, and I hear running water. He quickly returns with a wet, warm washcloth and cleans me up, then tucks us both into bed.

Between the tree falling on my house last night, and the amazing bout of sex with Josh this evening, I've never been so tired in my life.

He tucks me against him the way he did last night, but I turn in his arms, preferring to face him, and nuzzle against his chest. He kisses my head and rubs his hands up and down my back.

"So tired," I mutter, and yawn deeply.

"So beautiful."

"You say that a lot." I lean back and look up into his dark face. I can see his smile in the moonlight.

"I think it a lot."

I smirk and kiss his sternum.

"How did you get your hair this straight?" He pushes his fingers into my hair, brushing it with his fingers.

"I used to use a flatiron every day, but then I discovered the Brazilian Blowout."

"Sounds kinky." He wriggles his eyebrows at me playfully.

I laugh and smack him on the shoulder. "Pervert."

"You bring it out in me, babe."

"The BB is a hair treatment to make my hair straight and frizz-free. I'm religious about it."

"I liked your curls," he whispers, and kisses my forehead.

"So you've said," I sigh. "I didn't. I like it better straight."

"Hmm."

He continues to caress my back, his lips resting against my forehead, and before long my eyes are heavy and I fall into a deep, hard sleep.

"Wake up, sweetheart."

Warm lips are moving across my face, over my forehead, kissing me tenderly. I reach out for him and frown when my hands grip cotton.

"Why are you dressed?" I ask, still not opening my eyes.

"I've been up for a little while. Wake up."

I hear the smile in his voice, but I turn onto my stomach and bury my face into the pillow. "No."

"Come on, I need you to get up." He's chuckling now.

Why did I have to go and be attracted to a morning person? "Time is it?" I ask against the pillow.

"Five thirty."

"Are you here for sex?"

"Unfortunately, no."

"If you leave now, I'll let you live." I turn over onto my other side, facing away from him, and pull the covers over my head.

He laughs loudly and pulls the covers off my face. "You're adorable in the morning."

"I'll show you just how adorable I can be at this hour with no coffee."

"Open your gorgeous eyes, baby."

He leans over me and kisses my cheek and I sigh. "Why am I awake?"

"I need to show you something."

"I've seen it. You said you weren't here for sex." I open one eye and scowl at him. "Don't play with my emotions."

"Get dressed, there's something you need to see."

I sigh and scrub my hands roughly over my face and sit up, letting the covers fall into my lap, exposing my breasts.

Josh sucks in a breath and swears under his breath. "Get dressed fast before I join you and meet me in the kitchen."

With that he stalks out of the room and I grin, remembering last night.

I climb from the bed, stretching and flinching as muscles I haven't used in too long moan in protest. I'd love a hot shower, but I don't think Josh is patient enough to wait that long, so I pull on a new blue T-shirt and jeans, slide my feet into my new sneakers, and meet him in the kitchen.

"I'm dressed."

"Come on, we have to hurry. I don't want you to miss it." He grips my hand and pulls me out of the house to a waiting ATV parked at the bottom of the porch. "Hop on."

As soon as I climb on behind him, he takes off at full speed, and I have to loop my arms around his middle to keep from falling off the back. We race down the driveway toward the big house, then veer over to the barn. He parks, cuts the engine, and helps me off the four-wheeler.

"That was fun," I mutter dryly.

"Come on, smart-ass." He takes my hand and pulls me into the barn, down a row of stalls. I see Seth sitting up on one of the stall walls, grinning down inside and talking to Louie, the longtime ranch hand of the Lazy K.

"She's so small! And she has knobby knees," Seth giggles.

"She'll get bigger fast enough," I hear Louie respond, and my gaze immediately finds Josh's.

"A baby?" I ask quietly.

"Yeah, Starfire had her foal just a little while ago. I don't think she's stood up and walked yet, and I want you to see that part. It's pretty amazing." Josh is grinning down at me, his eyes shining and happy.

He loves this ranch.

He opens the door to the stall, an extra-large one at the end of the row that I assume is used for expectant mothers. The smell of hay is strong, but the barn is clean and tidy. The animals are well cared for here.

He motions for me to follow him inside and shuts the door behind us. Starfire is munching happily on breakfast while her baby lies comfortably on a pile of straw, sleeping soundly.

"Oh, how sweet."

"Starfire had her baby!" Seth informs me, a wide grin on his face.

"I see that." I smile back at him, then watch as Starfire turns to her baby and licks and nuzzles her gently.

"She needs to eat," Josh tells me, and wraps his arms around me, pulling me back against his chest. "So, Starfire will help her get on her feet so she can nurse."

Sure enough, over the next ten minutes, Starfire coaxes her baby onto her feet, and the foal wobbles, unsure of her footing. Finally, she takes a few steps and roots around under her mother's belly until she finds a teat and begins to nurse.

"Gross." Seth scrunches up his nose.

"How else will the baby eat?" I ask him, and smile.

He shrugs, watching the mama and the baby closely, and the teacher in me can't help but appreciate what a learning tool this is for the boy.

We spend a few hours there, watching the new foal get used to life on the "outside," as Seth puts it with fits of giggles.

"I think it's time for us to get to work, Seth." I laugh when he scowls at me.

"But I should get today off, to help with the baby."

"She'll be here when you're done," I reply sternly, and run my hand down Josh's arm before walking out of the stall. "I'll give you a break in a couple hours so you can come check on her."

"Okay." Seth looks longingly at the foal and then jumps down off the stall wall and walks out of the barn ahead of me.

"Come check on me while you're at it," Josh murmurs as he moves up behind me and kisses my neck, just below my ear. I pull out of his grasp, pointing at Seth walking ahead.

"Will you need checking?" I ask with a grin.

"I've got something you can check, sweetheart." He swats my ass as I walk away, laughing and shaking my head.

I'm so coming out to the barn in a few hours.

CHAPTER

Seven

"We could have gone somewhere more casual," I murmur, and take a sip of wine, enjoying the sight of Josh sitting across from me at the table in his white button-down shirt, with the sleeves rolled up on his forearms, and black slacks. His dark brown hair has been tamed, and I can't wait to run my fingers through it and mess it up.

His brown gaze finds mine over the leather menu in his hands and he smiles softly. "This is our first official date."

"I'm aware," I respond with a raised eyebrow.

"So we should be somewhere nice on our first date. Besides," he adds with a smirk, "you love it here."

"How do you know?" I ask, surprised. This Italian restaurant is new to town and has quickly become my favorite. "We've never talked about this place before."

"You should have seen your eyes light up when I mentioned it." He glances back down at his menu, his lips pursed.

He's observant, which is one of the things that I've come to appreciate about him. He pays attention to my moods, my body language, both in and out of the bedroom.

It's nice to be away from the ranch for the evening. I enjoy the ranch, and in the past few days that I've been staying there, in Josh's bed every night, I've come to have a greater appreciation for how much work it is, and how dedicated Josh is to his family legacy.

I smooth my hands down my thighs, over the cotton fabric of my orange sundress, thankful that my clothes came back from the hazmat cleaner in time for this date.

Shorts and a tank top would not have been appropriate for tonight.

Folding his menu, he sets it on top of mine at the edge of the table and takes my hand in his, weaves our fingers together. I catch a few curious glances from other patrons at nearby tables.

If news of my staying at the Lazy K hasn't already begun circulating around town, our being out together tonight will be fodder for conversation by tomorrow morning.

The young, bubbly waitress appears and takes our food orders, then leaves us alone.

"What are you thinking?" Josh asks, his eyes searching mine.

"We are going to make the grapevine news before morning," I murmur with a smile, and play with the stem of my wineglass.

"Good." He shrugs. "Does it bother you?"

"No." I shake my head, then frown as I think about it further. "It's really no one's business, although I am blurring the line where my job is concerned."

"They can't fire you for what you do on your own time, Cara. You're allowed to have a personal life." He grips my fingers more tightly. "You haven't done anything wrong."

I nod, but bite my lip.

"What?"

"I just hope you're right."

Our salads are served, along with the most delicious chicken I've ever tasted. At the first bite, I close my eyes and moan, letting the flavors explode on my tongue.

"Oh, dear God, that's good."

"Don't do that," Josh murmurs, his voice hard, and I open my eyes to find him staring at me intently.

"Do what?" I ask innocently.

"You know what. I already want you, Carolina. I'd be happy to skip dinner and take you out to my truck and make you come until your brain is numb." He hasn't touched the food in front of him.

I swallow hard and twirl my fork in the noodles and garlicky chicken. I take another bite, licking my lips and moaning in happiness, enjoying the way his eyes flare and his throat moves as he swallows.

"You should eat your food before it gets cold," I tell him sweetly.

"You're so getting spanked later." He laughs and finally picks up his fork, twirling it in his fettuccine.

"We can play in the truck." I shrug and grin at him, stuffing my face with more of the delicious food. "I'm hungry."

"So am I," he whispers, and watches my mouth.

"Eat!" I laugh and take a sip of wine. "What are we doing after this?"

"It's a surprise."

"Truck fun?" I ask with a giggle.

"I love the way you laugh." He smiles and sips his own wine, and just like that the butterflies are back in my stomach. "And, yes, there may be truck fun later, but I have something else planned first."

"Okay then," I murmur, and continue working my way through the meal. "I'm looking forward to it."

"Movies!" I exclaim, and smile over at Josh as he pulls the truck into the parking lot across from Cunningham Park. The park is just over twenty acres in the heart of town, with a large playground for parents to bring their kids to play, walking paths, benches and picnic tables, and a large grassy area where in the summer the town sets up a portable movie screen every Friday night. The townspeople bring blankets or lawn chairs and spread out on the grass to enjoy a double feature.

"I thought you might like it." He grins and reaches over to tuck my hair behind my ear.

"I love going to the movies."

He leans in and kisses me softly before reaching into the backseat to retrieve a small picnic basket and a soft blanket. He leads me out onto the manicured grass.

"What's playing tonight?" I ask, and help him spread the blanket on the ground toward the left edge before the screen, against a tree.

"I'm not sure. Probably a chick flick." He wrinkles his nose at the thought and makes me laugh.

"Not into chick flicks?"

"I'm a guy."

"Yes, you are." I kick my shoes off, sink onto the blanket, and glance around at all of the people. "Sit with me."

"Happily." He sits, his back to the tree, and pulls me against his chest, between his legs, knees bent. The previews begin and I sigh, completely content. The sun is almost down, leaving us in the glow of the screen and the moonlight behind us.

A few people I recognize, colleagues and parents of students, wave or call out greetings. Some look curiously between Josh and me, and I'm surprised to realize that it doesn't bother me.

He's a great guy and I'm happy to be out with him.

Josh wraps his arms around my chest and hugs me to him, kisses the top of my head, and we settle in to watch the movie. The first show is usually family friendly, and the second for more mature audiences, when parents leave to tuck their little ones into bed.

True to form, we are watching *Tangled*.

"I love this movie," I murmur, and snuggle against him.

"You do?" He rubs my arms with his palms.

I nod happily and rest my hands on Josh's thighs. I immediately feel a reaction to my touch: his thigh muscles clench and his cock comes to life against the small of my back. I can't help but grin.

"Behave yourself," I mutter, keeping my eyes trained on the movie screen. "There are kids here."

"Your sexiness is distracting me," he growls into my ear, and kisses the sensitive skin behind it, sending shivers through me. "Are you cold?"

"No."

He chuckles and hugs me tight before releasing me to pull the picnic basket to our side. "I brought dessert."

"What did you bring? Please say chocolate. Raisinets would be good."

He raises an eyebrow quizzically.

"We're at the movies. Candy? Popcorn?"

He smirks. "First date," he reminds me with a smile, his dimple winking down at me.

"What did you bring?"

"Strawberries," he replies with a straight face. "Covered in chocolate."

"God bless you," I say as he holds one up to my lips. I bite through the hard milk chocolate and sweet, juicy berry, and Josh's eyes greedily watch my mouth. Suddenly I forget about the movie and the dozens of people sitting around us as I take another bite of the delicious treat.

"More?"

"My turn," I whisper, and reach into the basket for another strawberry and offer it to his mouth. His eyes shine with mischief as he takes a bite and then bends down to kiss me, the chocolate and the juice from the berry on his lips. I lick them clean and he kisses me firmly.

"I'm about to make a scene," he whispers, making me chuckle.

I pull away from him and munch on chocolate strawberries as he pours me a glass of sweet white wine.

"Red Solo cups are so romantic," I giggle softly.

"I can't pour it into wineglasses." He shakes his head, a wide grin on his face. "Alcohol is prohibited in this park." He places his finger over his lips, warning me to keep our secret between us, and then takes a sip of my wine before handing it to me.

"You're not having any?" I take a drink.

"I'm driving us home."

"Not for a while."

"That remains to be seen." He runs the backs of his knuckles down my cheek. "I'm having a very hard time keeping my hands off you."

Just like that, it's as if the wind were knocked out of me. He says the sweetest things.

The first movie ends and the crowd stirs, people standing and stretching, gathering blankets and bags of snacks. Kids whine about having to go home to bed. Some parents let their little ones simply sleep on the blankets on the ground while they stay for the second show.

"I'm gonna go use the restroom." I stand and raise my hands over my head, stretching up on my toes. "I'll be back."

"Okay, babe."

A line wraps around the small brown-brick restroom building, but it seems to be moving fairly quickly. I move to the back of the line and notice a group of women about five people ahead of me.

If there had been "mean girls" in my high school, it would have been two of those three girls. Sunny Lawson and Lauren Cunningham were classmates of Jillian's and mine, and they were *horrible*. Both from wealthy families, they were pretty and popular and incredibly snobby. I frown, remembering. Actually, that's not true. Lauren was always just quiet. She was never cruel, she just hung out with girls who were.

I wonder why?

The third woman, Misty Maddox, is newer to town. I believe she's only been here for a couple of years, but, boy, does she ever fit in well with that group. I've never met a cattier woman.

". . . Cara Donovan."

My ears immediately perk up at the sound of my name.

"He's not interested in Cara." Misty smirks.

"Didn't you see them sitting together?" Sunny asks. "He looked interested to me."

Oh, trust me, he's interested.

"Why would he be interested in that fat bitch? Trust me, he just feels sorry for her because the tree fell on her house. You know how he is, always saving someone from something." Misty shakes her head condescendingly.

"Stop that," Lauren interrupts. "Cara's a nice person."

"I didn't say she wasn't," Misty agrees. "But she's so not his type. He's a ten and she's a three on a good day."

"At least she's straightened her hair." Sunny giggles. "Remember her hair, Lo? Oh, God, what a mess!"

"Tell me about her hair!" Misty is smiling giddily and I just want to throw up. I'm mortified. I want to run away, but I can't make my feet move. They still haven't seen me, and the people in front of me haven't noticed me standing here either.

"She had this horrible, curly frizzy hair." Sunny gasps for breath from laughing so hard. "It was all over the place."

"I think it looks nice now." Lauren is scowling at both women. "You two are ridiculous. This isn't high school."

"Oh, loosen up, Lo." Misty waves Lauren off dismissively. "It's all in fun. And trust me, girls—Cara Donovan is no threat."

"You're right," I call out, to the surprise of everyone around me.

The three women turn, eyes wide and mouths open. Lauren and Sunny both blush, but Misty quickly recovers and narrows her eyes viciously at me.

I can't stay quiet one moment longer. "There's no threat because Josh has *chosen* to be with me. I guess he's just not into catty bitches." I prop my hands on my hips and tilt my head to the side. My heart is racing with adrenaline. "It's good to see Lauren has grown up. When are you two going to join her?"

Before either Misty or Sunny can respond, Lauren grabs both their arms and yanks them into the restroom.

"Those girls always were trouble."

I spin around to see Mrs. Baker, my eighth-grade math teacher, standing behind me, her eyes narrowed and hands planted on her ample hips. She always was a force to be reckoned with, and retirement hasn't changed that.

"It doesn't matter," I murmur.

"It does too matter. I don't like that new girl one bit. If she were in my classroom, I'd make her life a living hell."

I smirk and silently agree. Maybe Misty needs a scared-straight field trip.

The line moves, and before long all three girls leave, walking quickly, not glancing my way.

By the time I walk back toward Josh, I can't help

but feel just a little twinge of doubt because, at the end of the day, what if Misty was right? What if Josh just feels the need to swoop in and save me?

The part that pisses me off the most is that she's made me doubt *why* he's attracted to me, despite the fact that Josh himself has never given me a reason to doubt him.

God, Jillian would smack the shit out of me right now. After she smacked the shit out of Misty and Sunny.

I almost trip on my own feet when I see Misty sitting on our blanket next to Josh, smiling up at him adoringly, her hand planted on his shoulder. Her raven hair is pulled over one shoulder, exposing her other naked shoulder and showcasing her cleavage.

She's thin, with big gray eyes and plump lips.

And her hands are on the man I'm currently sleeping with. The woman has balls of steel.

I'm going to rip her hair out by the roots.

I force my feet to move, propelling me forward as I glance at Josh for the first time. He has a small smile on his lips, but it's forced. His eyes are combing the crowd, and when he finds me, his smile widens and he immediately stands, ignoring whatever it was that Misty was saying.

She glares at me, but I ignore her and focus on the magnificent man striding toward me.

"There you are." He takes my hand in his and pulls it up to his lips.

"There was a line," I mutter, and offer him a small smile. He narrows his eyes at me, sensing the change in my attitude, I'm sure.

I've been stupid to just jump into whatever this man is offering without being cautious.

"As I was saying," Misty begins. "My parents own a house . . ." Her voice fades as Josh drapes an arm over my shoulders and turns us to look over at her. She's standing next to the blanket now, twisting her fingers at her stomach.

"Hey, Misty, let's go get our spot back for the next movie," Lauren calls from a few feet away and gives me a sympathetic smile as if to say, *Sorry.*

"I'll call you, Josh." Misty smiles sweetly and joins her friends.

"What's wrong?" Josh asks me when she's gone. "What happened?"

I just relived my junior year, that's what. "Nothing. I think I'm ready to go now if you don't mind."

"I'll take you wherever you want to go. What I mind is whatever has upset you."

Before he can stop me, I begin gathering the blanket and the picnic basket. He takes the basket from me and I immediately walk toward the truck.

I'm embarrassed. That's what it is. I'm just so damn embarrassed.

He's silent as he stows the blanket and basket in the backseat and helps me into the truck, turns the ignition, and pulls away from the park.

"Where would you like to go?"

I really want to go home.

But that's not an option.

"Your place is fine."

His eyes narrow on my face, watching me. "Talk to me."

I swallow and look out the passenger window and ignore the expletives he mutters under his breath. The lights from the city dwindle as we head out of town toward the ranch, and with each passing mile I get more and more angry.

I'm pissed at those bitchy, stuck-up women. They need to grow the fuck up already. And I'm pissed at myself for letting those toxic women get into my head.

"Are you fucking me because you feel sorry for me?" I blurt out, and immediately wish I could grab the words out of the air between us and stuff them in my pockets.

Josh's head whips around, his eyes wide in shock and anger. He clenches his mouth shut, tightens his grip on the steering wheel, and ignores the question altogether.

"Well?" I demand as he angrily flips on the blinker to turn down his driveway.

"Shut up, Carolina."

"What did you say?"

"You heard me."

"No, I must be mistaken, because if you just told me to shut up, I'm going to kick your ass."

He pulls in front of his house, kills the engine, and

turns in his seat to glare at me. "Why in the name of all that's holy would you ask me that?"

"Just answer the question."

"Cara, I'm going to warn you right now, I'm fucking pissed that you would even think for a second that I would *fuck you*, as you put it, because I feel sorry for you. Why is that thought even in your head?"

God, I'm stupid. I sigh and rub my forehead with my fingertips.

"Is this about Misty?" he asks, and my head whips back up to glare at him. "Shit."

"What's going on with you and Misty?" I ask, despising the accusatory tone in my voice.

"Nothing's gone on with her for over a year."

"You slept with her?" I ask incredulously.

"No, I dated her exactly twice, and then I found out what kind of person she is and stopped seeing her." He shakes his head and brushes a finger down my cheek, but I flinch away from him. "What did she say to you?"

"She didn't say anything to me."

"Carolina," he growls in warning.

"I overheard them," I whisper, and look out the window, loathing the tears I feel trying to form at the corners of my eyes.

He doesn't say anything, he just waits, and I love him and hate him for understanding.

"Misty clearly has a thing for you." I clear my throat as though it's not a big deal. "She made it clear that a fat, ugly chick like me is no threat when it comes to a ten like you. You clearly just feel sorry for me and are trying to save me."

"And you fucking believe that bullshit?"

"No, I don't believe her!"

"Then why are we fighting about this?"

"I don't necessarily believe Misty's bullshit, but a tiny part of me can't help but wonder why you're attracted to me." The last few words are whispered shamefully.

Josh stomps angrily out of the truck, slams the door shut, and moves in angry strides around the vehicle, yanks my door open, and, before I can do anything, pulls me easily over his shoulder, lifting me from my seat.

"Hey!"

"I've heard enough." He slaps my ass—hard— and carries me into the house, slamming the door behind us with his foot.

"Ow!"

"I warned you." He sets me on the kitchen island, slams his palms on the granite on either side of my hips, and pushes his face into mine. "I warned you the first day you were here that I'd spank your ass if you called yourself fat. It pisses me off."

"So I'm gathering," I whisper.

"Misty and her friends are bitches and most likely have been since the day they were born. I don't give a fuck what they think about you or me or you and me together." I hesitantly touch my fingertips to his cheeks and pull them down his face. "The only two people in this room are you and me, Carolina, and we're the only ones who matter."

He cups my face in his hands, his brown eyes on fire, and kisses me hard, his mouth claiming mine, marking me.

He grabs my hand in his, leading it to his erection, still covered by his slacks. "Trust me, sweetheart, this doesn't happen around women I feel sorry for. Feel what you do to me."

My cheeks flush and I just want to slink away and be mortified while he's not watching, but he makes me meet his eyes with my own.

"Pull that dress over your head." He takes a small step back, giving me room to do as I'm told.

I bite my lip, embarrassed all over again because I'd been brave earlier and gone without panties. Now I wish I'd worn them.

"Carolina," he whispers, and drops to his knees, spreading my thighs wide. "You're so beautiful."

I whimper as he traces my labia with a fingertip and presses a light kiss over my clitoris. "Soft. If I'd known you weren't wearing panties all night . . ." He swears under his breath and then gently kisses my clitoris again.

I white-knuckle the edge of the countertop as electricity shoots through me at the touch of his mouth. "Josh."

"That's right, baby." He pushes two fingers inside me and nuzzles the most sensitive nub with his nose. "I fucking love your pussy."

I push my fingers into his thick, soft, dark brown hair and hold on as he laps at my core, sucking and nibbling and making me crazy. I'm panting and whimpering, begging him to stop, but then begging him to never, ever stop.

He pulls away and lifts me off the counter. Stripping his clothes off quickly, he turns me around and bends me over. Before he slams his hard cock inside me, he slaps my ass again, the loud *thwack* echoing throughout the great room. He growls as he buries himself balls-deep inside my slick pussy.

"Get it through that gorgeous head of yours, baby, this is not pity, charity, or just because I'm fucking horny. I want you, Cara. *You.*" He grips my hair in his fist and pulls me back so he can whisper in my ear, "You."

"Josh," I whisper, and hold on for dear life as he smacks my ass again and then loses himself in the fast, hard rhythm of taking me from behind. There is just the slapping of skin and our harsh, ragged breaths filling the room until I can't stand it anymore and I convulse as my orgasm rips through me, clenching around his cock.

Josh growls and finds his own release, holding himself buried to the hilt as his own shudders rack through his body. He kisses my back gently and slides out of me, turns me to him, and wraps me in his strong arms.

"Do you want to hear my list?" he murmurs as he brushes his lips across my temple.

"What list?"

"I have a whole list of reasons that I'm attracted to you, sweetheart. It goes without saying, although I've repeated it many times, that you're beautiful. But more than that, you're funny. You are dedicated to your job and you're proud of what you do."

His hands glide up and down my back in long, sweeping motions, soothing me.

"You're kind and generous. You're so fucking smart, baby. I plan to spend a lot of time making you see you how I see you because the view is un-believable."

I bite my lip and will the tears that have gathered in my eyes at bay.

"What I feel for you is so big, Cara. No more doubts." He tips my chin up to look me in the eye. "You're with me because there's nowhere else I want you to be. Got it?"

I offer him a small smile and nod. "Got it."

"Good." He lifts me and carries me toward the bedroom. "But just in case, I think I'll work on re-minding you some more."

CHAPTER

JOSH

The house is quiet as I let myself in the back door. I've been at work for a few hours, having left Cara in my bed before the sun was up this morning.

She is not a morning person.

I rinse out my coffee mug and grab a clean one from the cupboard above the sink, and as I turn to the coffeepot to pour both Cara and myself a cup, I hear her shuffle up behind me. She wraps her arms around my waist and presses her sweet little body against my back, nuzzling her face between my shoulder blades.

And just like that, I'm hard.

"Good morning," she murmurs sleepily into my back. I grin and grip her hands in my own, turn in her arms, and loop my arms around her shoulders as she snuggles into my chest.

God, she's so fucking adorable.

"Good morning, sweetheart." I press my lips and nose to the crown of her head and take in a long, deep breath. She smells like strawberries and Cara, her own soft, sweet scent mingling with the berries. It's intoxicating. "I'm pouring you some coffee."

"Mmm." She rubs her nose against my chest.

I lean back against the counter, holding her to me, content to stand with her as she wakes up. "Did you sleep okay?" I glide my hands up and down her slender back, enjoying the feel of the soft cotton of my faded, old college T-shirt over her skin.

"Slept fine." She tilts her head back to smile up at me.

Dear God, I'd give anything to wake up to this smile for the rest of my life, and that thought is more than a little unnerving.

"Good." I kiss her nose and then her lips softly before offering her the mug of steaming-hot coffee.

"Thank you," she murmurs, and, holding the mug between both her hands, takes a long sip. "How did you know how I like my coffee?"

"I pay attention." I shrug and take a sip of my own coffee, watching her over the brim. She's all mussed up, her blond hair a bit tangled and messy, and her face is clean of makeup, glowing and flawless. My old University of Montana T-shirt hangs on her petite frame covering her yoga shorts and leaving her smooth legs bare. "You have great legs."

Cara takes another sip of her coffee and blushes.

Since the other night after the movie, she hasn't said one negative word about her body. Instead, she simply blushes and smiles when I compliment her.

Remembering Friday night both pisses me off and turns me on. That anyone could look at Cara and call her fat or ugly is pure insanity and fills me with such rage that I can't see straight. But the aftereffects when I fucked her against this kitchen counter and then showed her over and over all night long how beautiful I think she is made it one of the best nights of my life.

As her eyes widen and begin to shine, I can see that she's remembering too.

"We don't have time for this," I mutter regretfully, and take another sip of coffee.

"Time for what?"

"For me to haul you back to my bedroom and bury myself inside you for the rest of the morning."

She swallows hard, making me grin.

"Rain check?" she asks with a half smile.

"Absolutely."

"What are you doing in here, anyway?" She refills her mug. "I don't usually see you until lunchtime."

"I have a surprise for Seth."

"You do?" She grins widely and leans a hip against the countertop. "What is it?"

"You'll see; you're coming with us."

"Well then, I guess I'd better get dressed."

"I guess you'd better." I slap her ass as she saunters past me and back to my bedroom to change.

I'm thinking about following her to cash in on the rain check now rather than later when a sleepy Seth wanders through the front door, munching on a breakfast burrito.

"Mornin'."

"Good morning. How are you?"

"Sleepy." He plops down at the kitchen table. "I don't want to do any schoolwork today."

"Didn't sleep well?" I pour him a glass of orange juice, which he gulps down quickly.

"I stayed up too late reading the book Cara gave me." He shrugs and takes a bite of his burrito.

"Pretty good, huh?"

He shrugs again, then nods reluctantly. "Yeah, it's good. I finished it already."

"What did you finish?" Cara asks as she joins us. She's changed into jeans and a green V-neck T-shirt that shows off those amazing tits of hers perfectly and makes her eyes glow.

I should have come back to the house earlier to make love to her before Seth got here.

"The book you gave me," Seth replies as if it were no big deal.

Her eyes widen in surprise and then she laughs. "I haven't even finished it yet."

"Slowpoke," Seth taunts her, and she shoots him a mock glare.

"You were only supposed to read a chapter a day."

"Too slow," he mutters. "Do I have to build that

model of the solar system this morning?" He stuffs the rest of the burrito in his mouth.

"No," I answer before Cara can, earning a surprised look from both of them. "At least not this morning. Cara, do you mind if you have class this afternoon instead?"

"I don't have a problem with that."

"Why?" Seth asks skeptically.

"I want to take you somewhere. Come on, let's hop in the truck."

"I don't want to wash dishes again. I've been good." Seth turns his wide, hazel eyes to Cara. "Don't make me."

"This isn't that kind of field trip," I inform him dryly. "You'll like it."

"Okay!" He jumps up and runs out the front door and to the truck, hopping in the backseat.

"You're coming with us." I take Cara by the hand and lead her out to the truck as well, helping her climb in the front seat.

"Cara, where are we going?" Seth asks, bouncing in the backseat.

"I don't know, Josh didn't tell me either."

"I really hope I don't have to wash any dishes." Seth buckles himself in and watches out the window as I pull away from the house and down the long driveway to the highway.

The poor kid is going to need therapy because of that field trip.

Among other things, such as a bat-shit-crazy mother.

We don't have to drive far. I pull into Louie's driveway and come to a stop at the side of his small, ranch-style home. He saunters outside and waves, smiling at Seth as he jumps out of the truck.

"Hey, Louie!"

"Good morning." Louie fist-bumps Seth, then motions for us to follow him to his small barn behind the house.

"You have a barn too, Louie?" Seth asks.

"A small one. But I don't keep livestock."

Cara and I walk behind Louie and Seth. I grip her hand in my own, lacing our fingers together, happy to hang back and let Louie reveal Seth's surprise.

"Why are we here?" she asks with a smile.

"Wait for it."

My eyes are glued to the barn door as Louie slides it open and Seth walks through.

"Puppies!"

Cara's eyes find mine, laughing. "Puppies?"

"Puppies." I lead her into the barn. Louie has a large corner fenced off with blankets, dog beds, bowls for food and water, and six Lab puppies, four black and two yellow.

The mama dog sniffs Seth's hand and offers him a friendly lick before backing away so her pups can beg for attention.

"I didn't know you had puppies!" Seth lets himself in the pen and sits on the floor, right in the middle of the pups, laughing as they climb over him, licking his face and pulling on his clothes.

"Lola had her pups almost three months ago and they're ready to go home," Louie tells him, grinning as he watches Seth with the pups.

"Do they have homes?" Cara asks, also grinning at the boy. "They're adorable."

Louie nods. "Five of them do."

"Only five?" Seth frowns.

"One of them still needs a home." Louie points to one of the black puppies. "One of the black males isn't spoken for yet."

"Well, Seth," I say, wrapping my arm around Cara's shoulders, "I thought that maybe you might like to take him."

"Me?" Seth asks, his eyes wide. "Really?"

"A boy needs a dog." I shrug.

"Which one is mine?"

"I guess that's a yes," Cara murmurs with a laugh.

"That little black fella you're holding right now," Louie informs Seth, and props a booted foot on a bucket.

The little guy just curls up for a nap in Seth's lap.

"I think he likes me." The boy's face is all smiles, his eyes are shining in excitement.

"Looks like," Louie agrees, and helps Seth out of the pen with his new friend. Louie clasps a simple leash to the dog's collar and hands it to the boy.

"I can take him home?" he asks me hopefully.

"You can. But he's your responsibility, Seth."

"I get it." He shakes his head and buries his nose in the fur on top of the pup's head. "I'll take care of him."

"He's so adorable." Cara takes the puppy out of Seth's arms and snuggles him. "Oh, I love that puppy smell."

"We'll all think he's great until he's chewing our shoes and anything else he can get his paws on," I remind her as I lead them out to the truck. Seth jumps in the back and Cara hands him the pup before shutting the door and climbing into the passenger seat.

"I'll train him," Seth announces. "I'll look at videos online and learn how."

He giggles as the puppy licks his face and then burrows in Seth's neck to take a nap.

Cara clasps my hand in hers and squeezes tightly. "This is good for him," she whispers.

I nod and drive us back to the ranch.

"What are you going to name him?" Cara asks as I pull up to the house and we all climb out.

"Optimus Prime," Seth announces proudly, making me laugh.

"That's a long name," Cara reminds him with a chuckle.

"He's not a Spider-Man." Seth furrows his brow, deep in thought.

"No, he's not," Cara agrees dryly.

Seth leads the dog around the yard, waiting for him to relieve himself before going into the house.

"I know! Thor!"

"Thor?" I ask. The kid obviously loves comic-book movies.

"Thor." Seth nods his head decisively.

"I like it." Cara's smile is sweet and happy.

"Thor it is."

"Come on, Thor, we have to do our science project."

"We don't have any supplies for him." Cara frowns up at me as Seth guides Thor into the house.

"We have other dogs on the ranch, honey. I brought a dog bed in. He can eat with the other dogs in the morning, and we'll get him some toys the next time we go to town."

"Okay." She pulls me to her and stands on tip-toe so she can brush her lips over mine. I immediately grip her hips and pull her against me, sinking into her.

Each time I kiss her it's like the first time.

"What was that for?" I ask as I pull back to give us both a chance to breathe.

"I just like you." She shrugs as if it were no big deal.

"Gee, that's convenient." I swat her ass, then soothe it with my palm. "You're not so bad yourself."

"Convenient," she agrees, and plants a sweet kiss on my chin, then pushes her hands into my hair and pulls me down for another all-consuming kiss, practically climbing me. It's all I can do to not pull her into the backseat of my truck and take her hard and fast.

"Thor peed!" Seth announces as he comes barreling out of the house with a happy Thor.

"You go back to work." Cara laughs and pulls away reluctantly. "I have to teach science and potty-train a puppy."

"I didn't mean to add more work for you." I grimace as I realize that's exactly what's just happened.

"It's fine." She shrugs. "You owe me."

"I'll make it up to you, sweetheart." I feel the smile grow across my face as I picture exactly how I'll make it up to her.

She answers with a grin of her own. "I know."

"So did you find the Mustang?" I ask my brother, my phone pressed to my ear, as I stride toward my house. The sun is shining brightly again today, making my head sweat under my green hat. I need a shower.

"Yeah, the bastard sold it back to me." Zack sighs on the other end of the phone. "I have a feeling I paid more than what he bought it for."

"Kensie didn't tell you what she sold it for?" I ask with a frown.

"I haven't spoken to her since before she left Seth with you." He sighs again. "Is Seth nearby?"

"He's in the house with Cara, working on math or something."

"He still won't take my calls." I hate hearing the defeat in my brother's voice.

"I wonder what that woman told him," I murmur.

"I'm sure she told him many, many things that aren't fucking true and are pretty fucked-up."

"I'm sure you're right." I walk through the back door of my house, a smile spreading across my face at the sight of Cara sitting at my table, looking all fresh and sexy in her jeans and green T-shirt. Her honey-blond hair is tucked behind her ears and I want to push my fingers through it.

I can't get enough of her.

She looks up and grins back at me, those hazel eyes shining in happiness.

"Hello?"

"Sorry, Bro, got sidetracked."

Seth's head snaps up and he eyes me warily, but Thor hops up from his napping place at Seth's feet and greets me energetically, dancing around my legs, his pink tongue hanging out of his mouth.

"So when will you be here?" I ask as Seth leads Thor back to his feet at the table. I pull a bottle of water from the fridge, twist off the cap, and guzzle it down in one long gulp. Cara's eyes are glued to my neck, her mouth slightly open and her eyes wide, and when the tip of her little, pink tongue peeks out to touch her upper lip, I almost grab her and take her to my bedroom to keep her under me for hours.

She recovers and blushes, looking down at her papers. Fuck, she's adorable.

"I'll be there by this weekend."

"Awesome, I can use the help."

"I miss you too," he mutters dryly. "Be nice to my kid."

"Seth's being taken care of," I assure him, wave at Cara and Seth, and head for the shower.

"Is he as bad as Mom says?"

"He's doing better. Cara's been great for him. He's enjoying the ranch and we put him to work every day with chores, but I think he secretly loves it, he just doesn't want us to know it." I start the shower and start stripping out of my sweat-soaked, smelly clothes. "Louie's Lab had pups a few months ago. He gave one to Seth."

"Sounds like us at that age." Zack chuckles. "A boy needs a dog. I'm nervous about seeing him, man. Kensie has him hating me."

"So prove the bitch wrong, Z. Seriously, Seth will come around with time. You deal with eighteen-year-old kids fresh out of boot camp every day. You can handle one kid who secretly hero-worships you."

"I don't need him to hero-worship me. I'd settle for speaking to me over the phone."

"He'll come around." I watch the mirror go cloudy with steam. "Do you need me to pick you up from the airport?"

"No, I'm driving up. I'll leave tomorrow morning."

"Drive safe. Call if you need me."

"I will. Thanks, man. Later."

"Later." I hang up and step into the shower, washing up quickly so I can join Cara and Seth. I yank on a clean pair of worn blue jeans, pull an old red T-shirt over my head, and join Seth and Cara in the kitchen.

"...don't care!" Seth yells.

"Seth," Cara's voice is hard and her hands are fisted on the table.

"What's going on?" I ask, and narrow my eyes at Seth, who just glares at me as he jumps out of his chair, his feet planted, shoulders square, as if ready for a fight.

"Why didn't you tell me my dad was back in Texas?" he demands.

"Seth, you refuse to listen to anyone when your dad's name comes up."

"If he's in the States, why hasn't he come here?" His lip quivers slightly but he tightens his mouth to hide it, and a ball of lead takes up residence in my gut.

"He had to finish up some things in Texas before he could come home," I explain calmly.

"No one told me," Seth repeats stubbornly.

"Seth, your dad tries to talk to you every time he calls and you refuse to take his calls. I know you don't want to see him, but—"

"You don't know anything about it!" Seth yells as tears fall from his eyes.

"Okay, explain it to me." I lean against the counter and tuck my hands in my pockets, as if my body weren't tense and longing to pull him to me to reassure him.

I need him to talk to me.

"No one cares." He shakes his head and looks down at his feet, his dark hair falling into his eyes.

"That's not true, Seth," Cara begins.

"Yes, it is," he interrupts, and glares at her. "What do you know, anyway? You're banging him." He points at me. "You're no better than the rest of them."

Cara gasps, and before I realize what I'm doing, I've gripped Seth's lean shoulders in my hands and pulled his face within an inch of my own.

"I'm going to tell you this one time." My voice is low and hard. Measured. "If you *ever* disrespect Cara like that again, I will make you regret it." I loosen my grip but keep his eyes on mine. "I love you, kid. *I love you.* I care. I want to know what's going on in your head, but I won't force you to tell me."

He continues to cry silently and it's killing me.

"I'll answer any questions you have. I'll talk to your dad for you or call him back right now and put you on the line with him. He wants to talk to you, Seth."

He shakes his head in denial, and I just sigh deeply and cup his face in my hand.

"Seth, your dad loves you," Cara adds. "He's trying to get here as fast as he can. Maybe talking on the phone with him will make you feel better."

"I don't want to talk to him," Seth whispers, and turns tear-filled eyes to Cara. "I'm sorry about what I said. I didn't mean it."

"I know." Cara offers him a smile. "You're angry. But talking to us, or your dad, will help, sweetie."

He shakes his head again and I pull him in for a hug.

"It's going to be okay, buddy."

"Can I take Thor to the barn?" he whispers.

"Yeah, go ahead."

He pats his leg and Thor happily follows him out the front door.

"My brother really needs to get here and work some things out with that boy," I mutter softly.

"He's so angry," Cara agrees softly. "I wish I could kick Kensie's ass."

"Get in line, sweetheart."

She gathers Seth's papers and tidies the table swiftly. I pull the papers out of her hand and set them on the table and pull her into my arms, tucked under my chin. I love the way she fits against me.

I tighten my arms around her shoulders, gliding my hands up and down her back, and just hug her.

"It's amazing how you calm me," I murmur.

"Same here," she whispers without moving her cheek from my chest. "Zack's on his way home?"

"He should be here this weekend."

"Good. Seth needs him, whether he believes it or not."

"I know what I need," I murmur, and kiss her head.

"What?" She pulls back to look into my eyes. Her hazel eyes get me every time.

"You," I whisper, and kiss her forehead. "You,

curled up with me on the couch, pretending to watch a movie while I seduce you."

She raises her eyebrows and smiles softly. "Do I get to pick the movie?"

"Since neither of us will actually be watching it, yes."

CHAPTER

Nine

CARA

I stretch lazily, enjoying the way the soft white sheets shift over my naked body, still sensitive from a night of incredible lovemaking. Without opening my eyes, I reach to my right, searching for Josh, but his side of the bed has gone cold.

I love that he lets me sleep in, but I'd love to wake up with him once in a while.

I'll have to request that sometime soon.

I roll to my back and take a deep breath, registering the smell of coffee. Has he come back to the house to make me coffee again?

A girl could get used to this.

Excited to see him, I jump from the bed and pull on a pair of yoga shorts and a skimpy tank top and shuffle out to the kitchen quietly while I rub the sleep from my eyes. I turn the corner from the hallway to the great room, and there he is, with his back to me, facing the coffeepot, waiting for the last of the coffee to brew.

Something about him seems to be different this morning, something in the tenseness of his shoulders, and I wonder if everything is okay. Did something happen with one of the animals?

I move up behind him and wrap my arms around his waist, bury my face in the center of his back, just as on the other day when we took Seth to get his puppy.

"Good morning," I murmur, just as I realize that he smells . . . *wrong*.

"Well, that's one way to welcome Zack home," a familiar voice mutters behind me.

I jump back, my heart hammering and my face flushing as the man that I just had my breasts pressed against turns and grins down at me. His face is exactly like Josh's, aside from that small bump on his nose where he broke it his senior year in high school. "Good morning, Carolina." He laughs at my stunned expression.

"Zack!" I wrap my arms around him and hug him close, happy to see him after all this time. "I'm sorry."

"You'll never hear me complain about a gorgeous woman pressing herself against me first thing in the morning."

"Watch yourself, Brother," Josh warns him, and pulls me out of Zack's arms.

"So that's how it is?" Zack asks with a raised brow.

"That's how it is," Josh confirms, and earns another big grin from his brother.

"How what is?" I ask, narrowing my eyes on the sexy identical twins.

"It's a guy thing." Josh kisses my forehead and then frowns down at my outfit. "What are you wearing?"

"Seduce-Josh-in-the-kitchen clothes." I shrug and laugh when his eyes glass over. "I guess I got the wrong brother."

"Go away," Josh orders his brother, and buries his face in my neck and wraps his arms around my waist, pulling me into him, making us both laugh. I pull away and pour myself a cup of coffee.

"You made good time, Zack. When did you get in?" I ask as Josh leaves the room and quickly returns with one of his oversize sweatshirts and pulls it over my head, his eyes hot with lust.

"I don't share this beautiful body with anyone, sweetheart, even my brother," Josh whispers in my ear, then pours himself a cup of coffee, leaving me slightly breathless and a whole lot turned on.

"Weather was good." Zack shrugs, sits at the kitchen table as we join him. "Got in around three a.m. Crashed in J's spare bedroom for a few hours."

"Have you seen Seth?" Josh asks quietly.

"No." Zack shakes his head and takes a sip of coffee. "I just got up not long ago. Thought I'd wait for him here."

"It's Saturday," I remind him. "He might not be

down here for quite a while, especially now that he has a puppy to get into trouble with."

"Lost track of my days." Zack gulps down the rest of his coffee. "I'll go find him. Thanks for teaching him, Cara. Josh tells me you've been great with him, even when he's had a piss-poor attitude."

"He's a good kid, Zack." I grip his forearm in my hand soothingly, earning a glare from Josh.

What a caveman.

"Thank you," Zack repeats with a deep sigh. "I've missed him."

"If you missed me, why were you gone for so long?" Seth is standing just inside the front door, his eyes wide and angry, his hands in fists at his side and his pup whining at his feet.

"Seth." Zack stands and walks to Seth, who steps back angrily.

"Don't touch me!"

"Seth, I was in Afghanistan. You know that." Zack's body is tight with anger, but his voice is completely calm.

"Mom said you didn't have to go, but you wanted to be away from us. You don't care about me."

"That's not true." Zack's brown eyes are blazing with anger now. "The army didn't give me a choice."

Seth frowns and looks at Josh and then at his dad. "You never wanted to talk to me."

"*You* refused to take *my* calls, not the other way around." Zack is still standing back from Seth, but his face is lined in anguish. Clearly, he desperately wants to pull the boy to him and reassure him.

But Seth would not accept that right now.

Seth shakes his head, ready to argue some more.

"Why don't you guys go spend the day together?" I suggest softly. "Go fishing, or ride the horses or something."

"I hate horses and fishing," Seth insists, crossing his arms over his chest.

Josh is a tense ball of fury, sitting silently next to me, letting his brother handle the young boy, and I have a newfound respect for the man who constantly needs to be in control.

"You love those things, Seth," Zack reminds him calmly.

"Not with you," he spits out, and runs out of the house, Thor following close behind.

We sit in silence for a few long minutes, not sure what to say.

"Well, that went well," Zack finally says, and roughly rubs his forehead.

"He'll come around," I murmur. "He just needs to punish you for a little while before he's ready to hear you out."

"It's working."

"Can I make you guys breakfast?" I offer.

"No." Zack shakes his head. He grabs his keys and wallet from the kitchen counter. "I'm going to go take care of some business in town, give Seth some space." He waves and slams out the front door, fires up his Mustang, and speeds off toward the highway, the rear tires kicking up gravel as he drives away.

"It's just us," I mutter to Josh.

"I want to take you somewhere today." His face is perfectly serious, and I'm instantly curious. "Let those two circle around each other. I finally get you all to myself."

"Where are we going?"

"I want to show you my ranch on the ATV today because I don't think you're ready for a full day on horseback."

"It's going to take us all day?" I ask incredulously.

"A good portion of it." He nods. "I've packed a lunch and some supplies. I want to share my home with you."

"You have been." I walk to him and sit in his lap, wrapping my arms around his shoulders. I press my lips to his softly. "You have been sharing your home with me."

"There's so much more than what you've seen." He leans his forehead against my own and sighs. "Let me show you."

"Okay, let's go." I lean back and grin down at him. "Do I get my own ATV?"

"Hell no, you get to sit behind me and wrap those sexy arms around my waist."

"We'll see." I bounce up to go get dressed. "Maybe you'll sit behind me and hold on to *my* waist."

"You're feisty this morning." Josh laughs and

pivots in his chair, watching me with humor-filled brown eyes.

"You haven't seen feisty yet!"

He wasn't kidding when he said it would take all day. I had no idea Josh and his family owned so much land.

"This place is huge." He's parked the four-wheeler beside a row of cabins and cut the engine, giving us a chance to sit and look around. "I didn't know you offered hunting cabins in the winter."

"You're not much of a hunter, are you?" He tucks my hair behind my ear and kisses my forehead.

"Uh, no. Not unless it's a spider that needs to be killed." I glance back at the well-kept, simple cabins. The sun is shining brightly, making me thankful for my tank, but I long for my shorts rather than the long blue jeans that Josh insisted I wear today. My hair feels heavy on my neck and my brow sweaty.

"Like I said earlier, the ranch is more than beef cattle. We offer these cabins for tourists who want to hunt, along with a guide. I'm hoping Zack will want to guide this winter." Josh throws me a grin that says that he'll talk his brother into it.

"Do you get a lot of customers?"

Josh nods. "We're booked solid through next hunting season."

"Wow, good for you." I rub my hand up and down his back, ridiculously proud of Josh and his family. "Maybe Seth would like to join Zack and the hunters this winter? He's old enough to take hunter's education this fall."

"You're right. I'll mention it to Z. Seth would love that."

Josh starts the ignition again and I happily link my arms around his middle and snuggle up against him.

"I have a special place I want to show you."

He rests one hand on my thigh and drives us through the brush with one hand, leading us behind the cabins and into the woods again. The canopy of evergreen trees gives us a reprieve from the hot summer sun, and I sigh in relief.

"Getting too warm?" he asks.

"A little."

"Good thing we put sunscreen on you."

I blush furiously and bury my face in Josh's back as I remember his slathering the coconut-scented lotion on my arms, shoulders, neck, and face right before we left the house.

Only Josh can turn basic skin care into an erotic event. I've been turned on all morning, damn him.

I can feel the vibrations from his laughter against my cheek as he pulls the ATV to a stop and kills the engine, whose sound is replaced by the sounds of water and a light breeze blowing through the trees overhead. Birds sing as Josh and I stay where we are, sitting on the four-wheeler, me leaning against him, breathing in the fresh air.

Finally, I kiss his back and lean away from him, swing my leg over, and hop off, and he follows suit.

"This is a great place," I murmur, and turn in a complete circle, taking everything in. The forest is thick here, but with a clearing by a wide pool of water, which is being fed by a creek that empties into it via a beautiful waterfall about twenty yards away. Slabs of rock frame the pond, making a natural ledge to sit on and enjoy nature.

"This is where I've always come whenever I'm happy or mad or just need to think." Josh wraps his arms around me from behind and kisses the top of my head.

"You brought me to your happy place?" I ask, half kidding, and turn my head to kiss his biceps. I can't seem to keep my lips off this man.

And he doesn't seem to mind.

"It seems that anywhere you are is my happy place these days, Carolina."

I gasp and look up into his soft brown eyes.

"So, I brought the person who makes me happy to my happy place," he clarifies.

Well . . . wow.

Before I can respond, he kisses my lips quickly and then pulls away to grab a blanket out of a saddlebag. He takes me by the hand and leads me up onto the rocks by the water. He spreads the blanket out and pulls me down next to him.

"Are you hungry?" he asks, and pushes my hair back over my shoulder.

"Not quite yet."

He nods and his eyes heat as they rake down my

face, my neck, and over my tank top, which I know shows off the girls nicely.

If he is going to keep me perpetually turned on today, I am happy to return the favor.

"You are so beautiful," he whispers, and leans in to claim my mouth. His lips are gentle and soft, sweeping across my own rhythmically yet slowly, sending shivers down my arms and making my stomach clench.

He has only touched me with his lips and my panties are wet. I'm panting, ready for him to take me right here, in the middle of nature.

He cups my cheek in the palm of his hand and pulls me closer, sinking into the kiss, but then he abruptly pulls back, his brows pulled into a frown.

"You really are warm," he mutters, and feels my neck and forehead.

I laugh at him as I rub my hand up and down his firm chest. "It's hot outside, Josh."

"Let's cool off." He smiles down at me wickedly and begins to peel me out of my clothes.

"We might give the wildlife quite a show," I warn him mildly, excitement coursing through me.

"That's the plan." He winks at me and quickly strips out of his own clothes. He pulls me up onto my feet and peels my jeans and panties down my legs.

"Now what?" I ask with a wide smile.

"Now we cool off."

Before I can think, he lifts me into his arms and tosses me into the pond. I immediately swim to the surface and sputter, gasping for breath at the shock of the cold water.

"It's so cold!"

"It's mountain runoff, of course it's cold." He's treading water beside me. "We're cooling off, remember?"

"You just wanted to skinny-dip," I accuse him, and playfully narrow my eyes at him.

"I wanted to get you naked," he corrects me. "It worked."

He pulls me to him and kisses me hard and then dunks me under the water. He's laughing when I surface and I swim after him. My body has adjusted to the temperature of the water, and it feels cool and refreshing on my skin. I latch onto Josh's back, wrapping my arms around his neck and my legs around his waist, and he swims around the pond, carrying me around piggyback.

After playing in the water like kids for a while, Josh leads me to the edge of the pond and shows me where to step to safely climb out. Despite the canopy of trees, the air is warm. A light breeze blows across my wet body, sending more shivers through me and raising gooseflesh.

"Are you cold?" he asks as he guides me back to our blanket.

"No, I'm naked, wet, and there's a breeze."

We are standing in the center of the blanket, on the highest rock above the water, for all of God's creation to see. He's holding my hands in his, but has stepped back so he can look his fill, his heated eyes traveling up and down my nakedness, and I'm thrilled by the lust and the want I see on his handsome face. When his gaze meets mine again, I offer him a shy smile, and his breath catches as he swallows hard.

"Carolina," he whispers, and steps to me, keeping his hands linked with mine, but now I can feel his body heat and I yearn to feel him against me. "I love your body. I love every curve on you, how soft you are, how smooth your skin is."

He's seducing me with his soft words, and if we weren't standing so close, the mountain breeze would have blown the sound away.

"But the sexiest curve on your body is your sweet smile."

My breath catches and I feel my eyes go wide as he smiles softly down at me, and in this moment I know without a shadow of a doubt, I've fallen in love with Joshua King.

He lightly pulls the backs of his knuckles down my face and cups my jawline in his palm. With my hands now freed, I link them around his waist at the small of his back. I can't look away from his eyes. Droplets fall from his wet hair and run down his cheeks. I want him to kiss me silly. I want him to touch me everywhere.

I want him inside me.

"Josh."

"Yes, love." He kisses my forehead tenderly.

"I'm gonna need you inside me now."

"I was just thinking the same thing." He guides me down onto the blanket-covered rock and onto my back, but rather than cover me with his large, hard body, he kneels between my thighs and kisses the insides of them. He cups my right calf in one hand and runs his other hand up and down the length of my leg.

"Have I told you how great your legs are?"

"You've mentioned it," I reply dryly, enjoying the sight of him looming above me, the sunshine poking through the trees overhead. "But I have short legs. I'm a short girl."

"They don't have to be long to be amazing." He kisses my calf and then pays equal attention to my other leg, kissing and kneading the flesh. He's sitting back on his heels as he skims his lips over my ankle and then starts the journey up the other leg, and my gaze lands on the impressive erection jutting from his body, bobbing with his movements. I reach down between my legs, wrap my hand around him, and pump up and down the length twice.

His heated gaze finds mine as he pulls out of my grasp, grinning as I moan in protest, and nibbles on the inside of my left thigh, working his way up to my center.

Instead of burying his face in my folds, he runs his forefinger from my anus, through my labia, and over my clit, then holds it up for me to see. It's dripping with my juices.

"You're always so wet for me, baby." He sticks his finger in his mouth and licks it clean. "I love that."

With that, he leans down and follows the path his finger just took with his tongue. He repeats the motion three times before he circles the tip of his tongue around my clit, lifting the hood with his thumb so he can lick it more deeply. I push my hands into his hair and grip him hard, rocking my hips up against his face.

"Oh, God."

I feel him grin against me before he pulls the lips of my labia into his mouth and hollows his cheeks to suck on them, softly at first, then more firmly, making me squirm and moan.

He finally pushes two fingers inside me, sweeping his fingertips over that tiny rough spot that makes me lose my ever-loving mind.

"Josh!"

"That's right, baby," he whispers, and moves his fingers faster, presses his lips against my clit, then licks it hard with the flat of his tongue, making me see stars.

"I'm gonna—" I can't complete the sentence. I don't even know if I spoke it out loud. I can't hear the rush of the water anymore, or the birds, or anything except the roaring of blood in my head and my desperate groans.

Josh growls against me, the vibrations shooting me out into orbit, and I come hard, my pussy spasming and clenching around his thick fingers, my hips rocking against his face, shamelessly asking for more.

When my body calms, he pulls his fingers out and licks me again, along the length of my sex, then licks and kisses his way up my torso. He kisses and pulls on my already firm nipples, making me moan again.

"God, I love the sounds you make," he murmurs, and glides his lips up my collarbone, up my neck and to my jawline, where he nibbles as he settles against me, his elbows planted at either side of my head and his hard cock resting against my center. I raise my knees and cradle him against me, rocking just a bit so he slides against my wetness.

"Jesus, Cara," he whispers against my ear. "You feel so fucking good."

"Mmm," I agree, and rock again. He pulls up so he can look down into my eyes as he rears back, the blunt head of his cock resting against my opening.

"There is nothing in the world like sinking into you," he murmurs, and slowly pushes his length into me, inch by inch, so damn slowly. I close my eyes at the amazing sensations, but he grips my hair in his fists and growls, "Watch me."

I quickly open my eyes as he bottoms out, pressed inside me balls-deep. He brushes a stray strand of wet hair off my cheek and lowers his mouth to mine as he slowly begins to move, pumping his hips in a long, steady rhythm.

He licks my bottom lip and then pushes his

tongue into my mouth, mirroring his cock moving in and out of me. It's too much. It's not enough.

In this moment, it's *everything*.

I wrap my arms around him, digging my nails into his back and hitching my legs up around his hips. He begins to move a little faster, and with every drag of the head of his cock, the nerves in my pussy shoot sparks of electricity up my spine. I can feel the orgasm gathering low in my belly, and as my pussy begins to contract around him, he pushes in hard and stops.

"Josh!"

"Yes, baby, let go."

This orgasm is like nothing I've felt before, full of emotion and intensity and a newly discovered love for this man above me.

As I begin to recover, he begins to move in earnest, chasing his own release. He thrusts hard, and fast, and buries his face in my neck as he growls while coming inside me, panting and gasping for breath.

"You'll be the death of me," he whispers against my neck, but I feel him smile.

"Damn, you're good at this."

"*We're* good at this, Cara. It's never been like this for me before." He lifts his head and gazes down at me, his eyes happy and bright.

"Me neither," I agree softly.

He pulls out of me slowly and winces as he shifts off his knees.

"Maybe we're too old to be fucking on rocks," I smirk at him, but sober at the anger in his eyes as he turns his face to me.

"I don't fuck you, Cara. Ever."

"I'm sorry . . ."

"You should know by now that you mean much more to me than a fuck buddy."

"I'm sorry." I run my hand up and down his muscular arm. "It was just an expression. I've used it before."

"I know." He shakes his head, but when he looks at me again, his eyes have softened. "And there are times when it's sexy coming out of your mouth, but not right after we've . . ."

"I get it." I kiss his cheek and smile at him. "I get it."

"Okay." He nods and then helps me dress, just smiling serenely when I remind him that I'm capable of dressing myself.

Control freak.

"Are you hungry yet?" he asks me mildly.

"Starving."

"Good. I brought lunch." He quickly pulls on his white T-shirt and faded blue jeans and walks to the ATV to pull a collapsible cooler from another saddlebag and brings it back to the blanket, along with our phones.

"You get a signal out here?" I ask, surprised.

"Sometimes. It gets spotty." He shrugs and pulls hoagies, pasta salad, and fruit out of the cooler and offers me a bottle of water, which I gratefully take as I look down at my phone.

"My mom called."

"How are your folks?" He takes a bite of his sandwich.

"They're good. They enjoy Florida. They were going to come home this summer, but with the tree falling and everything, they decided to just stay down there this year."

My parents moved down to Florida five years ago to escape the harsh Montana winters. I bought my childhood home from them.

"You should call her back so she doesn't worry."

"You're a nice guy, you know that, right?"

He winces and shrugs. "Well, I'd worry if you didn't answer or call me back."

"Good point." I highlight Mom's name on my phone and press the green call button.

She picks up on the second ring. "There you are!"

"Hi, Mom, sorry I missed your call." I take a bite of pasta salad and grin when I hear my dad yell in the background for my mom to tell me hi. "Tell Dad I said hi back."

"She said hi back!"

"Not in my ear, Mom," I remind her dryly when she doesn't pull the phone from her mouth.

"Sorry, honey. How are you?"

"I'm good."

"What are you doing?"

"I'm having lunch." I smile over at Josh, who is drinking his water and watching me. "Is everything okay with you guys?"

"We're fine. I just wanted to check in. How is the house coming along? Are you sure you don't want us to come up and help you?"

"The house is coming along well. The roof will be repaired after the Fourth of July. And, no, I don't need you to come up and help." I take a bite of my sandwich and sigh in appreciation. It's damn good.

"Well, let us know if you change your mind."

"I will." I lower my sandwich and clear my throat. "I love you, Mama."

"I love you too, darling girl. I'll call soon."

"I know." I smile. "Talk soon."

I hang up and realize that I also have a text from Jill.

"Sorry, I'm just gonna check this text from Jill."

"I'm fine, babe. Do your thing."

I grin at him and open Jill's message: **Can you pick me up from the airport tonight?**

I feel my eyes go round and I drop my sandwich into its wrapper.

"What's wrong?" Josh asks.

"Nothing. Jill's coming home. She's asking me to pick her up tonight."

I immediately respond, **Of course.**

"That's unexpected," I murmur.

"Maybe she's coming home for the holiday?" He pops a strawberry in his mouth.

I'm immediately caught up in watching his lips as he chews.

"Cara?"

"Sorry?"

He laughs and shakes his head. "I can't make love to you again right now because I'll make you sore and I have plans for tonight."

I blush and look down at my phone when it beeps at me.

Jill: **Thx. I'll get in at 10pm. See you soon!**

"Hey." He grips my chin and makes me meet his gaze. "Don't be embarrassed, baby. I want you just as badly."

"I'm not embarrassed." I shrug and grin at him. "I've just never had a man call me out on my lustful looks before."

"I don't like thinking about you giving other men looks, lustful or otherwise." He scowls, making me laugh.

"I give Paul Walker lustful looks every time you make me watch *Fast Five*."

Josh laughs and shakes his head at me. "You make me laugh."

"How are *your* parents? I'm surprised we don't see more of them, given that you live on the same property."

"They're doing well. Staying busy." He shrugs and reaches for another strawberry.

"Did you always know that you wanted to take over the ranch?"

"Pretty much, yeah, although I thought Zack and I would run it together." Josh takes a deep breath and gazes at the trees around us. "This is our home. I love it here."

"It's beautiful out here."

He pulls me to my feet and swats my ass firmly. "Come on, feisty girl, let's head back to the house."

"I want to drive!" I bounce on the balls of my feet and clap my hands, making Josh laugh.

"No." He shakes his head and props his hands on his hips, grinning happily.

"Please?" I move over to him and run my hands down his torso. I grip his ass in one hand and cup his growing cock in the other. "I'll show you how amazing my mouth can be later tonight."

"Are you offering me sexual favors in exchange for driving my four-wheeler?" he asks with a fake glare.

"Absolutely."

"Deal."

CHAPTER

The three-gate airport is pretty much empty, aside from a few other people standing about waiting for the plane to land.

It's an hour late.

Jill texted when she boarded the plane at LAX. I'm excited to see her. It's only been a few months since we last spent time together, but it feels like forever. Jill is the closest thing I have to a sister, and I miss her like crazy.

I should plan a trip to LA soon. We usually alternate our visits, and it's been too long since I made the trip down to spend time with her.

This airport is tiny. Only two airlines fly in and out, making flights expensive and hard to find, especially in the summer and winter months when the tourism kicks up to full speed. Sculptures and local artwork are displayed, and the décor is rustic, fitting in with the Western theme.

My phone pings in my pocket and I check the incoming text.

Josh: **Did she land okay?**

I smile and immediately respond, **Not yet. Plane is late. Not sure when I'll be back.**

I lean my shoulder against the wall directly across from the security doors that separate the common area from the boarding area and sigh contentedly. Exploring Josh's ranch today was amazing. His passion and love for his land was clear when he told me about the different facets of the ranch. It's successful because he loves it so much, and failure is not an option for him.

Our time by the pond was the most amazing experience, both physically and emotionally, that I've ever had.

My phone pings again.

Josh: **No worries, just drive safe. I'll worry.**

I smile and reply, **I'll be safe. Will text when I'm on the way.**

"Flight number 223, direct service from Salt Lake City, is arriving at gate C," a bored voice announces. Jill's flight is here at last. I tuck my phone away as sleepy-looking passengers begin to file through the gate door and through the glass security doors to the main room.

I smile as I see Jill come through the door. She and I are the same height, but she's on the petite side. Where I'm curvy, she's slender. Almost delicate. She has beautiful thick, dark hair, which she keeps long and typically back in a French braid. Her soft blue eyes find mine and she offers me a weary smile as she approaches me.

"Hey, Jillybean!" I wrap my arms around her and pull her in for a long, hard hug.

"Hey, Carebear," she replies with a laugh, and holds on tight. When I pull back and look at her, something feels off. She's smiling at me, but her eyes are sad.

"What's wrong?" I ask immediately.

Jill shakes her head and leads me to the baggage claim. "Not a thing."

"Okay, why the impromptu trip?" I watch as black bag after black bag passes before us on the conveyor belt.

"Missed you." She shrugs and chews on the inside of her lip.

"I've missed you too." I hug her again and kiss her cheek with a loud, hard smack, making her laugh.

"Are we going to the Fourth of July party at the lake?" she asks as she pulls the one and only bright red suitcase off the belt, lifts the handle, and rolls it alongside her as we walk out to the car.

"Of course. We've never missed a year yet."

"Good." She sighs and settles in the passenger seat of my car, leaning her head back and closing her eyes.

"Don't you dare go to sleep on me." I laugh as I pull out of the airport parking lot, pay the parking fee, and turn on the highway, heading back into town. "Are you staying with Ty?"

"No, Mountain Lodge," she murmurs, and I can feel her gaze on me. "I'm gonna surprise Ty. Stay with me at the lodge while I'm in town."

I shake my head slowly and grin over at her. "I can't."

"Things going well?" She closes her eyes again.

"They are going very well."

"Good." Jill yawns beside me and drifts, and I let her sleep. She seems exhausted, and I can't tell if it's because of her demanding job or something else, but she clearly doesn't want to talk about it.

Yet.

I'll get it out of her eventually.

I pull into the parking lot of her hotel. Jill checks in while I grab her bag and join her at the elevator.

"I'm in room four-twenty."

"Okay."

We link arms and ride the elevator in silence, then stroll down the hallway of the fourth floor. Jill unlocks her room and leads me inside.

"Home away from home," she mutters, and strips out of her hoodie and messenger-style handbag, tossing them both on the small round table by the sliding glass door that leads to the balcony.

I kick my shoes off and throw myself across one of the queen-size beds, hugging a pillow to me.

"Make yourself at home," Jill remarks dryly.

"Okay," I reply happily. "How's work?"

"Busy." She climbs onto the other bed and sits Indian-style, facing me. "As usual."

"So, why are you here?"

"What, a girl can't take some vacation days?"

"You didn't give me much warning that you were coming."

"It was a last-minute thing." She shrugs and pulls a pillow into her lap, holding it against her chest. "I'm fine." Her blue eyes are determined, and her mouth set in a line, and I know the subject is closed.

"Well, I'm glad you're here. I missed you."

"You've been banging Josh King. You haven't had time to miss me." She giggles and twists her body, lying flat on her stomach like me, facing me. "So, how is it?"

"How is what?" I ask innocently, and trace the pattern on the bedspread with my fingertip.

"The conversation," she replies dryly, and rolls her eyes at me. "The sex, Carolina! How is the sex?"

"Fine."

She narrows her eyes at me and tilts her head to the side. "I will punch you in the neck if you don't spill it."

"God, you're violent."

"Talk."

"It's fine."

"If it's 'fine' "—she uses the air quotes with *fine*— "then it's not going great."

"Maybe it's not all about the sex."

Jill laughs and shakes her head at me. "I'm sure it's not *all* about the sex. But a man doesn't look like that and not give good dick."

I giggle hysterically and roll onto my back. "You are so classy."

"Is it big?"

"Stop talking!" I can't breathe now, and tears are rolling down my cheeks.

"Is it one of those that has weird coloring, or is it a handsome dick?"

"Stop!" I grip my stomach in my hands and continue to laugh, my abs aching.

"Come on," she giggles, and flings her pillow at me, then grabs the other one to hug to her. "Spill it."

"The sex is the best I've ever had." I wipe the tears from under my eyes. "He's hung, and he knows how to use it. Is that what you wanted to know?"

"Fuck, I hate you." She buries her face in the pillow and screams.

"No, you don't."

"I haven't gotten laid since Todd," she mutters into the pillow.

"And we all know Todd is a shitty lay with a tiny dick," I murmur, and scowl. I hate that man with every fiber of my being. Jill's ex-husband is a first-class asshole.

"Yeah." Jill sighs and lifts her head, staring at me with those sad blue eyes.

"What's wrong, Jilly?" I whisper, but she just shakes her head and lays her cheek on her pillow just as my phone rings in my pocket.

Josh's name and photo are on the display.

"Hey," I greet him softly.

"Hey. Jill get here okay?"

"Yeah, we're at the hotel. She's staying at the lodge." I glance over at the clock and frown. "Wow, it's after midnight. What are you still doing awake?"

"Waiting to hear from you."

"I'm a grown-up, you know." I grin at his chuckle in my ear. "You don't have to wait up for me."

"It's late, and I need to make sure you're okay."

God, I love the sound of his voice. "I'm fine. I'll probably just crash here, since it's so late."

"That's a good idea, although this bed is too big and too cold without you."

Movement on the bed next to mine catches my attention, and Jill is using her hands, making obscene gestures.

I giggle again and slap my hand over my mouth.

"What's so funny?" Josh asks.

"Jill is being stupid." I glare at the laughing Jillian.

"Hi, Josh!" she calls.

"Tell her hi," he says with a smile in his voice.

"He says stop being disgusting."

"That's not what he said." She shakes her head and laughs.

"I'll see you in the morning," I murmur.

"Okay. You're at the lodge?"

"Yep."

"Okay, sweetheart, have fun with Jill. I'll see you tomorrow."

He hangs up and I sigh as I set my phone aside and curl up around my pillow.

"You love him," Jill whispers. My head snaps toward her. She's lying flat on her back, diagonally across her bed, her hands on her belly, and she's staring at the ceiling.

I watch her for a long minute, then I sigh.

"Yeah," I whisper.

"Have you told him?"

"No."

"Why not?" She turns her head and looks me in the eye, watching me.

"It's really soon."

"So?" She shrugs and continues to watch me.

"What if he doesn't say it back?" I whisper, and feel tears fill my eyes. "What if he doesn't feel the same?"

"Why wouldn't he feel the same?" Jill turns onto her side, tucks her arm under her head, and continues to watch me.

"I don't know." I turn on my back now and stare at the ceiling.

"Why wouldn't he feel the same, Cara?"

"Because I don't understand why he's interested in me in the first place." There. I said it out loud.

"God, you're dumb." Her voice is hard and almost angry.

I whip my head back toward her in surprise. "What?"

"You're an idiot if you don't understand why he's interested in you, Cara. I love you, but you have got to get over your insecurities. The frumpy, frizzy-haired, chubby girl from high school is long gone. Have you seen you lately?"

I frown at her and process what she just said. "But I am still that girl."

"No, you're not." She sighs and rubs her hands over her face. "You're beautiful, and Josh sees it. He sees *you*. Men who just want to fuck you don't call to check on you late at night just because they're worried about you."

You're more than just a fuck buddy.

She's right.

"Okay, fine, I'm fabulous." I look back up to the ceiling and feel myself smile. "And my boyfriend is fucking hot."

"Yeah, he is," she agrees with a sigh.

"And Jilly?"

"Yeah?"

"He's fucking awesome in bed."

"God, I hate you."

Knock, knock, knock.

A light tapping on the hotel door wakes me from a light sleep. I glance over at Jill, who is knocked out, still lying on top of the covers. Moving quickly and as quietly as possible, I peek through the peephole before opening the door wide.

"What are you doing here?" I whisper at Josh as he moves into the room and scoops me up into his arms.

"Couldn't sleep without you," he whispers into my

ear. He bends to pull the blankets back on the bed
and lays me down onto the sheets before disappearing into the darkness again. He reappears moments
later with a spare blanket from a small closet and
spreads it over Jillian before joining me in the bed,
both of us fully clothed.

"How did you know what room we're in?"

"I asked, baby," he replies dryly.

"You have to work in just a couple of hours," I
remind him softly, both of us on our sides looking
at each other in the darkness.

"Louie and the guys can handle it. Plus"—he leans
in and kisses my cheek—"Zack's back. He'll pick up
my slack today."

"You didn't have to come here."

"Yeah," he sighs, and pulls me to him, resting my
cheek against his chest, and kisses my head. "I did,
baby."

"If you two have sex with me lying three feet away
from you, I will cut you both in your sleep."

Josh laughs hard and loud and hugs me close.

"She's really violent," I inform him with a giggle.

"I mean it." Her voice is stern, but I can hear the
smile on her face.

"Can I talk you into a threesome?" Josh asks over
his shoulder, earning a punch in the arm from me
and a pillow in the head from Jill. "Can't blame a guy
for asking."

"Perv," I mutter with a laugh.

"I'm just kidding," he calls over his shoulder at Jill,

who just waves him off and turns on her other side. "You're the only one I want," he whispers in my ear for only me to hear. I burrow down deeper against his chest, wrap my arms around his waist, and fall asleep to the sound of his heartbeat.

"Holy shit, your house is a mess." Jill wrinkles her nose and holds her hand up to her brow, shielding her eyes from the sunshine as she gazes at my little white house, covered in plastic and lumber. We're walking through town, on our way to Ty's house to surprise him and to check on the progress of my own place.

"It looks so much better," I inform her. "They say it'll be done on Wednesday."

And then I'll have to leave him.

"Wow." I'm suddenly wrapped in one of Jill's superstrength hugs and I feel the air leave me in a whoosh.

"Can't breathe," I squeak.

"I'm so happy that you're safe." She loosens her grasp and rests her forehead on my cheek. "What would I do without you? What if you'd been seriously hurt?"

"I'm fine, Jill."

"I wanna kick that tree's ass."

"We really need to discuss these violent tendencies of yours. I don't remember you being this hostile."

"I must be PMSing." She smirks as we walk away

from my house and toward Ty's. It's the Fourth of July, so most of the town is closed to observe the holiday, and we're hoping to catch Ty at home.

Jill bounces up the stairs of his porch ahead of me and knocks on the door.

"You could just go in."

"Nah, it's better this way." She winks at me and waits patiently for Ty to answer his door. After thirty seconds she knocks again.

"I'm coming!" Ty yells, and swings the door open with a scowl. At the sight of his sister, his face transforms into a big, wide smile and he scoops her off her feet into a big bear hug, turning her in a circle. "Oh my God, Jillybean! When did you get here?"

"Last night." She laughs. "I wanted to surprise you."

"Best surprise ever." He smiles at her widely. "How long are you here for?"

"I go back Tuesday morning."

"Quick trip." He tugs on her braid.

"I'm here for the holiday."

"So we'll all be at the party at the lake?" he asks as we sit on his porch, Jill and I in the porch swing, and Ty on the railing, leaning his back against the pillar in the corner.

"Of course."

"When do you get your house back?" Ty asks me, and crosses his arms over his chest. He's in a T-shirt again today, a Van Halen one this time, with ripped jeans. The muscles under his sleeve tattoo bulge with the movement and I can't help but watch.

Any red-blooded American woman would take notice.

"Wednesday," I respond.

"Good." He nods and looks over toward my house. "It's coming along fast."

"It's a good crew," I agree, and cross my legs, enjoying the sway of the swing. Jill leans against me and rests her head on my shoulder.

"What's new with you, big brother?" she asks.

"Absolutely nothing." He pushes his hand through his raven hair and turns his eyes to Jill. Their eyes and hair match perfectly. No one would miss that they're siblings. But where Jill is petite and delicate, Ty is tall and broad. Not quite as tall and broad as the King brothers, but then, few are.

"Nothing at all?" she asks doubtfully.

"Nothing at all."

"You're boring."

"What's new with you?" He narrows his eyes on her, and I know he sees what I do: pale skin and sad blue eyes.

"Nothing."

"Now, I know for a fact that's a lie."

"I'm not in a courtroom," she snaps, her voice hard, and it surprises the hell out of me. "Back off."

He just tilts his head to the side and watches her for a moment, then nods. "Okay. For now."

"You're so pushy."

He shrugs unapologetically and grins. "Job hazard."

"No, you've always been pushy."

He nods and grins at her, then turns his gaze to me and I squirm in my seat.

"I'm not in a courtroom either," I remind him lightly.

"How are things with King?"

"Good."

"He's phenomenal in bed and he came to the hotel in the middle of the night just so he could snuggle with her," Jill smirks, and evades my punch to her leg.

"Shut up," I say.

"I really don't need to hear about Josh's sex skills," Ty responds dryly, a smile tickling the corners of his lips. Finally, he gives in and lets out a belly laugh.

"Jilly hasn't gotten lai—" Jill's hand covers my mouth hard, her eyes wide with panic.

"Mmmph mmph poph," I mutter against her hand.

"What?" she asks, and drops her hand.

"Don't fuck with me."

"Cara's a badass." Ty laughs. "If you're not good, she'll show you the jail."

"Yeah," I agree with a laugh. "I'm a badass."

"Let's go get ready for the party, badass."

CHAPTER

Eleven

I absolutely love the Fourth of July.

Cunningham Falls always does it up big. Most of the townspeople gather by the city beach, which is nothing more than about one hundred yards of sandy beach at the shore of a large lake at the edge of town. The kids swim, and adults bring coolers full of food and blankets to lounge on. Boats float in the lake or zoom around, pulling water-skiers swiftly about the lake.

It's a day of fun and sun, and even the tourists get into it.

This year is no different. We've spent the majority of the afternoon with our friends, enjoying each other's company, laughing and eating good food.

Josh and I are sitting in the shade, on a blanket, very much like the night at the movies. He's leaning against a tree, me between his legs, and I'm leaning against his chest.

"Are you comfortable?" he asks into my ear, making shivers dance down my body.

"I am," I sigh happily, and watch Zack and Jill chat with each other several yards away. She is telling a story about a mansion she sold in Bel Air, gesturing wildly with her arms, her pretty face expressive, and Zack is laughing with her.

Seth is sitting under another tree not too far away, clad only in his swim trunks, listening to his iPod.

"What time do the fireworks start?" I ask.

"At dusk, so around nine thirty, I guess." I rest my hands on Josh's bare thighs and grin when he inhales sharply. He never wears shorts, so to see him in his tan cargo shorts and sexy black T-shirt is a treat. His soft hair tickles my fingers as I rub them rhythmically against his muscular thighs. "But if you keep doing that, we'll put on a fireworks display of our own, for all of our nearest and dearest to see."

I laugh and look up into his soft chocolate eyes. "You wouldn't dare."

"I think I would." He removes my hands from his legs, kisses them both, then links his fingers through mine and rests them on my belly.

"I like touching you," I pout.

"You're killing me," he whispers. "I haven't been inside you in almost twenty-four hours," he growls against my ear.

"Oh, no! Whatever shall we do?"

"Smart-ass," he mutters, and tilts my chin up to plant a soft, wet kiss on me, and I forget that our friends are standing nearby. His lips glide over mine, once and then again, and then he kisses my cheek and my jawline before pulling away to smile down at me.

"Get a room!" Zack calls out.

"They had one last night," Jill responds dryly, also watching us closely. "Unfortunately, I was also in that room."

"Kinky." Zack grins and nods, earning a punch in the arm from Jill. "Ow! Easy there, killer."

"The King men are pervs," Jill complains as everyone laughs.

Ty grabs two beers out of the cooler nearby and hands one to Josh.

"Thanks, buddy."

Just then, I notice Zack allows his gaze to roam up and down Jill's body, paying special attention to her hips and her thick, lush dark hair. He takes a pull on his beer and turns away, looking for Seth.

I follow Zack's gaze and then feel my chest tighten when Seth's not still sitting at the base of the tree. His iPod is on the blanket, but he isn't.

"Where did Seth go?" I ask as I begin looking around frantically.

Everyone joins me, looking around the crowd. Zack takes off down to the water to see if Seth's decided to go for a swim.

"I saw him just a minute ago," I murmur, and pull my sunglasses down as I stand and begin to roam around the area. "He can't have gone far."

"He's in the water," Jill confirms, and points to where Zack is standing at the edge of the shore, hands on his hips, glaring at the boy, who is splashing happily in the lake.

I sigh and shake my head. Seth's swimming isn't an issue, but he'll get in trouble for disappearing without letting anyone know.

We're all watching as Seth glances toward shore and sees his dad at the edge of the water. Zack just raises one hand and makes a "come here" motion with his fingers, and Seth scowls deeply, not moving closer to shore.

"Get your ass over here, now." Zack's voice is deceptively calm, but hard as steel. He's in denim cargo shorts and a gray T-shirt, the cotton pulled tightly over his toned, muscular body, revealing ink on his biceps, and at over six feet tall he's intimidating.

Much more so than Josh, despite their being identical twins. Something in the way Zack holds himself warns anyone off.

"What?" Seth asks defiantly as he approaches the shore. "I can't swim?"

He juts his chin out and mirrors his father's stance, arms crossed, body tense.

When he grows up, he's going to look exactly like Zack.

"Why does he do that?" Josh murmurs from behind me, and wraps his arms around my middle.

"Because he's angry," I answer.

"You can swim just fine," Zack responds patiently.

"But you aren't allowed to come down to the water without letting one of us know. You know the rules."

"I'm right where you can see me."

"I believe the correct answer is 'Yes, sir.'"

"This isn't the army," Seth spits out defiantly.

Zack leans in to murmur in Seth's ear so he's the only one who can hear. His eyes go wide and he swallows hard, but when his dad backs away to look down at him, he scowls again.

"I don't care." Seth drops his arms to his sides and fists his hands. "Why are you such a jerk?"

Zack laughs and props his hands on his hips, shaking his head in exasperation. "I'm not a jerk, I'm a parent."

"Same thing," Seth mutters.

"I'm gonna beat him up," Josh whispers, and I chuckle.

"No, you're not. Look, he's softening." I gesture with a tilt of my chin, and sure enough, Seth gives his dad a half smile. Zack ruffles Seth's hair but drops his hand when Seth backs out of his reach.

"Can I swim some more?"

"No, it's getting dark. The fireworks are about to start."

Just as the words leave his lips, someone lets off a firework on the street, sending a screeching wail through the air followed by a loud *boom*.

Zack springs into action. He grips Seth by the shoulders and throws him to the sand, covering him with his big, strong body. His arms cover both their heads, and Seth's legs are tucked neatly between Zack's.

"Fuck!" Josh runs down to his brother, Ty close behind him, and squats next to Zack, carefully laying his hand on Zack's shoulder.

"Z, you're okay. It was just some fireworks."

Zack won't budge. He's holding on to Seth with all his might, every muscle in his body taut with fear and adrenaline.

"Z," Josh tries again. "Come on, man. You're safe. You're home."

Zack slowly raises his head and looks up at his brother, then down at the frightened boy in his arms.

"Damn it," Zack mutters, and slowly lifts himself off Seth. "I'm sorry, Son."

"It's okay." Seth's voice is small and shaky.

"I'm sorry," Zack repeats, sitting back on his heels as he helps Seth up.

"I'm okay," Seth says, but looks down at his dad with wide, sad eyes. "It's okay, Dad."

Josh and Ty step back, and we all watch in wonder as Seth starts to cry and falls into his dad's arms, burying his face in Zack's neck and holding on tightly.

"I believed her," Seth cries.

"Hey, it's okay," Zack murmurs, and holds Seth firmly against him.

"I believed her," Seth repeats, and I feel my own tears on my cheeks as Jill joins me and links her hand with mine.

"Seth," Zack begins, but Seth pulls back to look him in the eye and shakes his head, cutting him off.

"No, I believed her when she said you weren't doing anything over there, that you just stayed there because you didn't care about us." Seth's crying in earnest, his small hands braced on his dad's shoulders, and neither of them cares about the audience they have right here on the city beach.

"People keep thanking you today, and I thought it was dumb." Seth wipes his nose with his arm. "All these people saying thank you for going to war, but I thought it was stupid because you just left me and Mom, and I didn't think it was anything great."

"Hey," Zack tries again, but Seth is on a roll.

"But you didn't go because you don't love me."

It's not a question.

"No," Zack simply says.

"And she lied when she said that you didn't want to talk to me on the phone."

"She did. I suppose that's why you refused to take my calls all these months?"

Seth nods and sniffles again. "And just now, when you thought there was a bomb, you were trying to save me."

"Seth, I'll probably always react that way to loud noises. It's just habit." Zack shrugs uncomfortably, but Seth is shaking his head adamantly.

"You were trying to save me."

"I was," Zack whispers, still looking his boy in the eye.

"I'm sorry, Daddy." Seth wraps his arms around Zack's neck and holds on tight. Finally, Josh leans down and murmurs in both of their ears, and they stand and walk back to our group.

Zack sits on Seth's blanket and his son sits beside him, leaning his head on his shoulder. "Can I watch the fireworks with you?"

"Damn, that kid breaks my heart," Jill murmurs, and I nod in agreement.

"Yeah, we'll watch them from here," Zack replies.

"I didn't think Zack was going to stay for the fireworks." I look over to Josh for confirmation.

His face is grim. He sighs and watches his brother and nephew. "He wasn't. But I think he'd hang the moon if Seth asked right now."

The sun has begun to set, and from two pontoon boats out in the water, fireworks begin filling the night sky.

Josh pulls me back down on our blanket, but I know he's keeping a sharp eye on his brother. When I glance over, Zack has a firm grasp on Seth's shoulders, his jaw is clenched shut, and sweat is beaded on his brow. He glances over to me and winks, sending me a cocky smile, but I know he's panicked inside.

Seth is curled against Zack's side, his eyes wide with wonder as he watches the bright flashes across the sky.

"They're fine," Josh murmurs against my hair, and tightens his arms around me. I glance up at him and smile and then settle into his arms to watch the show.

I love to cook. I especially enjoy cooking in Josh's kitchen. It's big, providing me with plenty of space to dance around to the Top Forty station on the satellite radio. Pink is currently encouraging me to get up and try.

I love Pink.

Seth and Zack are gone for the day, having packed up early to go fishing. Seeing them joking and arguing over who would catch the most fish warmed my heart. I hope they have a great day together, getting to know each other again after so much time apart.

I shimmy to the fridge and pull out the eggs, bacon, and hash browns and set about the task at hand.

I'm making breakfast for my man.

Josh is out working on morning chores, but I called Louie and asked him to send Josh back to the house in about a half hour.

I glance at the clock on the microwave.

Make that twenty minutes.

I slide the bacon into the oven and move my body with the loud music, swinging my hips in time with the beat, switching gears to a Kelly Clarkson song.

"I don't think I've ever seen anything so sexy in all my life," Josh murmurs from behind me just as I'm pulling the bacon out of the oven. I turn to smile at him and take in the sight of him. He's leaning against the counter behind me, his ankles crossed and his hands gripping the countertop. He's sweaty and dirty from morning chores, but when he smiles at me in that way that says that I'm about to be rewarded handsomely for cooking this meal, I've never wanted anyone so badly in all my life.

"A barefoot woman cooking in your kitchen is the sexiest thing you've ever seen?" I ask dryly.

He laughs as he saunters over to me and kisses my forehead without touching me anywhere else. "*This* woman cooking in my kitchen is the sexiest thing I've ever seen. Do I have time to shower?"

"Yep." I grin up at him and then begin dancing about again as I move to the stove and put the hash browns in the skillet.

"Keep moving your hips like that and I'll take you right now," he growls.

"Go shower!" I laugh and throw a piece of potato at him. "I'm working here."

He returns to the kitchen twenty minutes later, clean and fresh and *hot*.

I toss his words back at him as I set the table: "Sexiest thing I've ever seen."

"You didn't have to cook." He pulls me into a tight hug and kisses my cheek and then slants his mouth over mine, kissing me slowly and thoroughly.

"I know, but I like to cook." I pull back and pat his cheek lightly. "Have a seat."

"How are you feeling this morning?" he asks, then sips his coffee.

"I'm good. I think my ears are finally recovered from the fireworks last night." I laugh and pass him the bacon.

"Zack and Seth seemed to be good this morning." Josh's tone is light, but I know he's relieved.

"They did." I nod and take a bite of my eggs. "I hope the worst is over."

"He's twelve. We haven't seen the worst yet."

"You know what I mean." I laugh and shake my head at him.

"This is delicious." His happy brown eyes meet mine as he takes a bite of his bacon. "I'm discovering all kinds of hidden talents."

"I wasn't hiding my cooking talents," I respond wryly.

"I was referring to your dancing-while-cooking talents." He grins widely.

"I need music to cook. It's a requirement."

"I'll remember that."

I take my last bite and lean back in the chair, full and happy.

"When will your house be done?" he asks without looking at me, finishing up his meal.

"The day after tomorrow." The thought of moving back home, of not being next to him every night, is like a knife to the chest, but I know it's too soon to suggest that we live together, and Josh hasn't said anything about my staying.

"I'm sure you'll be relieved to have it done."

"Mmm," I murmur noncommittally. "You'll probably be happy to have your house back to yourself."

He grows quiet and sits across the table from me, staring down at his plate, his hands fisted on the table.

"Josh?"

"Are you finished?" he asks quietly, his voice in direct opposition to his body language.

"Yes."

"Good." He stands, scoops me out of my chair, and heads straight to his bedroom.

"Aren't we supposed to wait thirty minutes after eating before we can do this?" I ask with a laugh, and bury my face in his neck as he carries me through the house.

"I think we'll be fine. I need you."

He kisses my temple gently and sets me on my feet at the edge of the bed.

"No kitchen sex today?"

"Maybe later. For now, I want you here, in my bed."

His eyes are intense as he steps to me and runs his knuckles down my cheek. I settle my hands on his hips, looping my middle fingers through his belt loops and brushing my thumbs on the warm, smooth skin beneath his T-shirt.

"I love the way you touch me," he whispers, and leans in to kiss my forehead, so gently that I can barely feel it. His lips move down to my cheeks, my nose, and finally settle over my own. His hands grip the hem of my shirt, and he lifts it over my head, making me back away for just a moment, and then his lips are on mine again.

He unfastens my denim shorts and lets them fall around my ankles.

"Fuck me, you're not wearing underwear." His wide eyes catch mine and I grin smugly.

"Nope."

"That's fucking hot."

"I'm glad you approve." I make quick work of his own jeans and shirt, anxious to feel his skin under my hands.

When his jeans and shorts slide down his hips, his erection springs free, and I immediately sit at the edge of the bed, wrap my hands around the length, and suck the tip into my mouth.

"Fuck," he whispers, and plunges his fingers into my hair, not pushing himself into me, but needing to have his hands on me.

I lick the length of him, down to the small patch of dark hair at the base, and then back up again, tracing the thick vein that runs up the underside of his beautiful cock.

"I love your cock," I murmur, and look up at him as I take him into my mouth, my tongue swirling around the tip, and sink down until I feel him at the back of my throat.

He growls as his head falls back and his hands clench in my hair. Now he does begin to guide me up and down on his length in a steady, even rhythm. I cup his ass in my hands, reveling in the clench of the muscles as he thrusts into my mouth.

I sink down again, and this time when the tip is

in the back of my throat, I swallow, massaging the tip of his cock.

"Son of a bitch!" He grips my hair roughly and pulls me off him, bends down to wrap an arm around my waist, and scoots me effortlessly back onto the bed.

"I wanted to make you come," I pout, batting my eyelashes at him playfully.

"I don't want to come in your mouth." He shakes his head and covers me with his body. "I want to come in your pussy."

"Well then, do it."

"I will." He flashes me a naughty grin that has my stomach muscles tightening and my legs flexing around his hips. "Eventually."

I rotate my hips, pushing my wet pussy against his full cock, and he moans, narrowing his eyes down at me playfully.

"You're trouble, you know that?"

"Me?" I roll my hips again and grin when he bites his lower lip. "I just want you inside me."

He suddenly reverses our positions, rolling us across the bed, and I'm now on top, straddling him. I grip his hands in mine, linking our fingers and holding them down at either side of his head, and kiss him deeply as I continue to grind on him, spreading my juices up and down his hard, thick cock.

"Jesus Christ, sweetheart, you're fucking with my head."

"I think I'll fuck with something else too," I murmur, and lift my hips, feeling the tip at my opening. I sink down until he's seated inside me. "God, you feel good."

He pulls his hands out of mine and grips my hips, raising and lowering me on him. I lean back and plant my hands on his thighs and ride him in earnest, hard and fast, glorying in the look of complete rapture on his face, the feel of his hands gripping so hard on my hips that they're sure to leave bruises, and the feel of his rock-hard cock thrusting mercilessly inside me.

Making him lose himself like this is my undoing.

He sits up and wraps his arms around my waist, takes my nipple into his mouth, and suckles hard, pulling me even harder and deeper onto him.

"Come," he commands, and sucks on the other nipple, and his harsh voice sends me over into an amazing orgasm. I push down and clamp on to him, grinding against him, riding the wave of the orgasm.

He suddenly lifts me off him and crawls quickly off the bed, turning me so my legs are dangling off the side and I'm facedown into the covers and pillows that have been scattered about.

"My feet can't reach the floor." My voice is breathless as he plants himself behind me and grips my hips roughly in his callused hands.

"Wrap your legs back around my thighs."

He slams inside me as my calves clench the backs of his thighs, and he grips one wrist behind my back and pulls my hair with his other hand, holding me down against the bed as he fucks me blind.

It's the most savage he's ever been with me, as though he's reminding me with every thrust just whom, exactly, I belong to.

After just a few thrusts, he slams into me and stills, coming hard. He groans my name and releases my wrist and hair and then bends over and plants wet, openmouthed kisses across my shoulders and on the back of my neck.

"Mine," he whispers before pulling out of me and helping me back onto the bed. He wraps himself around me. "I think we could both use a nap," he murmurs, and kisses my cheek.

"Okay."

He brushes my hair back off my neck and kisses that tender spot just under my ear.

I sigh deeply, and before I know what's happening, the words "I love you" leave my mouth.

Josh tenses up behind me, and my eyes go wide as I realize what I've said aloud, my body also stiffening.

Fuck, what do I say now?

Josh suddenly pulls me onto my back and leans up on his elbow to look down at me, watching my face carefully.

He's not saying it back.

He's not saying anything at all.

His eyes narrow on my face and he gently brushes a single strand of hair off my cheek.

"Say it again."

I feel tears fill my eyes; tears of frustration and embarrassment and love as I shake my head no.

He catches a tear with his thumb, and his eyes soften as he continues to watch me.

"Say it again, Carolina."

Oh, how I love the sound of my name on his tongue. That alone almost makes me cave, but I resolutely shake my head no.

He glides his hand down my face, down my neck to a breast, where he brushes his thumb across my already-puckered nipple, making me gasp. His lips twitch as his hand moves farther south, over my stomach to my center. But instead of sinking his fingers inside me or worrying my clit with his thumb, he just cups me in his hand and leans in to kiss my cheek in that soft way he does that makes me sigh.

"Cara," he whispers, and moves over me, his cock already hard once more, and slowly slips inside me. "Say it again."

"You say it," I whisper so softly I'm not even sure if he's heard me.

With his body filling mine, covering mine, his eyes holding mine, he leans on one elbow and grips my hand with the other, holding it between us.

"I love you, Carolina Donovan, more than I ever thought was possible." He nudges his nose against mine and then rests his forehead on my forehead, sighing deeply. "I don't remember what my life was like before you."

"I love you," I murmur, with more conviction this time, and sigh as he begins to make long, slow movements with his hips, building us both back up slowly.

"You're so beautiful." He kisses one cheek and then the other. "So damn smart." Kisses my jawline and down my neck, then over to the other side and back up again.

"Josh," I whisper, the sensations running through me making it hard for me to form coherent thought.

"Yes, love?"

"I need you."

"You have me, baby." His pace doesn't change, but the intensity of the thrusts do, and before I know it, I'm on the precipice of another amazing, teeth-numbing orgasm.

"Oh, God!" He plunges inside me and holds himself there, watching me as I shatter beneath him.

"I fucking love it when you massage my dick like that." And with that he comes again, loudly, shuddering over me.

I run my fingertips up and down his back, absorbing his weight as I kiss his neck and shoulder softly.

He pulls back, his dark hair falling over his forehead, and I brush it back with my fingers. "You're so handsome."

"You destroy me, Cara."

Just like that, I'm thrown. I can only stare up at him as he tries to pull his thoughts together.

"You. Destroy. Me." He swallows hard and cups my face gently in his hands. "I love you and respect you so much."

"Josh"—I lift my head and kiss him softly—"I love you too."

CHAPTER

Twelve

JOSH

She loves me.

I unconsciously rub my stomach, as if that will clear out the butterflies, while I lean on the doorframe of my large master bathroom and watch Cara dress for our night out with our friends. Since Jill's in town, we're all going downtown to play pool and dance.

Well, the guys will play pool and the girls will dance.

Cara pulls a sexy tank dress over her head and down her amazing, curvy body. It's black and hugs her breasts and hips, the hemline hitting her midthigh. Her honey-blond hair is down, falling in gentle waves down her back and around her sweet face. She's worked some magic with a few pieces of makeup, and her lips are pink and pouty.

Just like her pussy.

I was inside her an hour ago and damn if I don't want to boost her up onto that countertop and take her again. I don't know what the hell she's doing to me, but I hope she never stops.

"Hoops or studs?" She holds one of each earring up to her ears, asking my opinion. I move up behind her, wrap my arms around her middle, and bend down to bury my face in her neck, breathing her in. She is everything soft and gentle and *good*.

She's everything.

"They both look great," I murmur into her neck, and let my hands glide down her hips to her naked, smooth thighs and up under her dress.

"We don't have time for this," she mutters with a giggle.

"I love that sound."

"What sound?" She tilts her head farther to the side, giving me better access to her throat.

"Your giggle." Her dress is up around her waist now and my hands are roaming over her hips and ass, glorying in the warmth of her soft skin.

"Josh, we have to—" She can't complete the thought as she bites her lip and leans into my chest, widening her stance as my hand moves between her legs to fondle her pussy.

I fucking love her pussy.

"We have to what?" I ask, and chuckle when she swallows hard and opens those gorgeous green eyes to watch me in the mirror.

"Go."

"We will." I smile softly at her in the mirror and hold her gaze in mine as my hands drive her wild.

No one else is as responsive as Carolina is.

"When I touch you"—I kiss her shoulder and her neck—"you always give yourself to me so easily."

"Did you want me to put up a fight?" she asks dryly.

"No, it's fucking sexy as hell." I push her hair away from the back of her neck and kiss her there, push on her clit with my thumb and wrap my arm around her to pinch a nipple through her dress. "Come for me, Cara."

And she does, bending at the waist, holding on to the countertop and pushing her sexy ass back against me.

I pull my hands away, smooth her dress back into place, and grin at her.

"I like the hoop earrings."

She's panting as she grins back at me, her eyes glassy with lust. "Okay."

The bar is crowded, which is expected on a holiday weekend in the heart of summer. A mixture of tourists and locals are mingling in various stages of drunkenness. The band has been playing in this bar for the past twenty years. They play a mixture of classic rock and country, and they are badass.

Right now they're playing "Brown Eyed Girl."

The stage and the dance floor are adjacent to the pool room, with tall, round tables and stools scattered about. Ty secured one of the four pool tables before we got here.

"Good shot, man," Ty calls to Zack, who just sank his red ball in a corner pocket.

"I figured you'd have forgotten how to play over there in the sandbox." I take a pull on my beer and watch my brother circle the table, looking for his next shot.

"Fuck you," he retorts with a grin, and sinks his yellow ball in the side pocket.

"Nope, nothing's changed." Ty laughs and sips his gin and tonic.

"How can you drink that shit?" I ask him with a grimace. "It tastes like toilet water."

"How do you know what toilet water tastes like?" he asks with a raise of a brow.

Fucker. "You're an ass." I laugh and shake my head, looking out to the dance floor to watch my girl and her friends dancing and moving about.

"They're having fun," Zack comments without looking over to them, and sinks another ball.

"Are any of us going to get to play, Z?" I ask.

He shrugs and chalks his cue.

Cara rushes to me and grabs my hand. "Come dance with me. I love this song!"

How can I resist her?

I grin and pass my cue to Ty. "Take my turn, if we ever get a turn. I'll be back."

Cara pulls me out into the middle of the dance floor where the band is playing "Just a Kiss" by Lady Antebellum. When she's happy with our spot, she turns and presses her body against mine, loops her arms around my neck, and smiles up at me.

"You're too tall."

"You've had a few too many drinks," I respond with a laugh.

She's adorable.

"Here." She pulls her arms down around my waist and snuggles up against my chest. Her cheek rests perfectly against my heart.

Isn't that fucking appropriate?

I wrap my arms around her shoulders and we sway about the dance floor. Her hair smells of her usual strawberries and it's soft against my lips.

The lyrics of the song pull me in and I'm lost in the music and the feel of my girl in my arms.

When it's over, she pulls her head back and grins up at me happily. Leaning down, I kiss her lips hard and fast, then laugh when she pulls away and screams at the first few notes of the next song.

She's a Daughtry fan.

Jill joins her and they begin shaking their asses and singing along, and I make my way back to the pool tables.

"The girls are having fun." Ty sips his disgusting drink, his eyes on the dance floor.

If I didn't know better, I'd think he was checking out Cara, and I know he's not looking at Jill. I glance back and see that Lauren Cunningham has joined the girls, dancing and swaying with the music, laughing and enjoying herself.

Ty's eyes are glued to her.

"Dude, you know Lo's married."

He doesn't even spare me a glance, just takes another sip of his drink.

"Been separated for two years," he reminds me, and leans his elbow on the table, still watching her.

Lauren is beautiful. She's tall, almost as tall as Ty in her heels, with straight auburn hair and big blue eyes. She has an athlete's body, is lean, and when she raises her arms over her head, the short halter top she's wearing rides up to show off her abs, which are spectacularly defined.

The girl works out.

"Being separated doesn't mean she's any less married," I murmur, and take a pull on my beer.

Ty turns his attention to me, his face sober. "Hasn't stopped her soon-to-be-ex from fucking anything with two legs."

"True." I grimace as I think of that asshole, Jack. "Just watch yourself."

Ty's jaw tightens and I follow his gaze to see that Misty has joined Lauren on the floor, dancing and glaring at Cara and Jill.

"Why does Lo hang out with that bitch?" I ask aloud. "I don't get it."

"I don't either," Ty agrees softly.

At the end of the song, the band takes a break and the jukebox starts up. Cara and Jill join us, smiling and panting and not a little sweaty.

"Hey!" Cara greets me, and kisses me soundly.

"Hey yourself, baby."

Zack takes his shot and then stands, leaning on his cue, and shoots Jill a grin.

She was watching his ass.

"You have a nice ass, King," Jill remarks with a smirk, and picks up her beer bottle, then frowns when she discovers it's empty. "Well, shit."

"I'll go get more!" Cara offers, and kisses my cheek before sauntering happily to the bar. I watch her move across the room and climb onto a barstool, cross those spectacular legs, showing off her thighs in that short dress, and pull her debit card out of her bra.

"I love her storage system," Ty remarks, making me laugh.

"So do I."

"There you are!" Misty is suddenly at my side, and Ty quickly moves away from us, joining Zack and Jill on the other side of the pool table.

Traitor.

"Here I am," I confirm, and continue to watch Cara. A tourist sits down next to her and smiles at her brightly. My eyes immediately narrow.

The fucker better not touch her.

"I was just saying to Lauren the other day, I haven't seen you around much lately," Misty babbles.

"Been busy," I respond absently, my fists clenching when the asshole tourist drops his arm behind Cara's back. From this angle I can't tell if he's touching her back or just resting his arm on the back of the stool, but it's too close for comfort.

Cara smiles politely at him and shakes her head no to whatever he's said.

Good girl.

She places her order and gestures over to me, talking to the stranger, whose smile slips for a second before he winks down at her.

That's right, asshole, she has a boyfriend.

"And then she said, 'Well, that's just silly!'" Misty gives me her fake laugh and lays her hand on my forearm, pulling my attention away from Cara.

I quickly grip her wrist in my hand and pull it away from me, dropping it at her side.

"I'm only going to say this one time, Misty." Her eyes go wide at the hard edge in my voice. "I am not available, and even if I was, I'm not interested. Don't ever touch me again."

I dismiss her, not caring that she's glaring at me as the crowd around us laughs, and seek out Cara once again. She's still sitting at the bar, the tourist is grinning down at her, and they're holding shot glasses in the air, toasting.

Cara pounds her shot back and slams the glass on the bar, and I've seen enough.

I stomp across the bar and move up beside Cara, glaring at the short, slender man to her left, who is laughing and trying to order them another shot. When he sees me, his face sobers and he grabs his beer and joins his friends.

Cara turns to me, a smile spreading over her face when she sees me. "Hi, babe!"

I cage her in, one hand on the bar and my other arm draped across the back of her stool. I'm not touching her as I lean in and press my lips to her ear so she's sure to hear every word coming out of my goddamn mouth.

"Let's get something straight, Carolina. You. Are. Mine. I'm the only man who will be buying you drinks."

I hear her gasp and see the pulse in her neck speed up.

"Josh, you're being ridiculous. He was just a nice guy, and it was just one shot."

"I'm sorry, do I have this wrong?" I back slightly away so she can see my eyes. "Would you rather flirt with and get hit on by other men? Am I wrong to stake a claim? Because just a few hours ago you claimed to love me while I was buried deep inside you."

She frowns and swallows again, and I know I should feel like a dick for that, but I can't bring myself to. I need to know the score now.

"You're not wrong," she replies softly, and covers my hand with her own. "It felt innocent, Josh. It was just a shot."

"It was innocent on your part, but not on his, sweetheart. He wants in your pants. Not that I blame him."

"Just because he wants in my pants doesn't mean I'd let him go there. Besides"—she smiles up at me and bites her lip, and I know she's about to be a smart-ass—"I'm not wearing any pants."

I laugh and shake my head, pull her small hand up to my lips, and kiss her knuckles.

"It made you uncomfortable?" she asks sweetly.

"It pissed me the fuck off," I reply calmly, and watch her face as I kiss her knuckles again. "I'd rather not repeat it."

"Caveman much?" she asks dryly, but her hazel eyes smile at me as she leans in to kiss my cheek. "I love you, babe. No creepy tourist with a shot of tequila is going to change that."

"Good to know," I respond wryly, and help her gather the beer bottles and Ty's gin and tonic off the bar, then follow her back to our pool table.

Jill and Zack are gone, and Ty is working the table by himself, frowning and brooding.

"What's wrong with you?" Cara asks him. "We're having fun."

"I'm having fun." He shoots a ball in the side pocket.

"You're frowning."

"No, I'm not."

"Yes, you are." Cara props her hands on her hips and watches Ty.

"No, I'm not," he repeats with a half grin.

"Why are you lying to me?"

"Josh, do something about your girl. She's harassing me." He laughs and runs around the table as Cara chases him.

"I'll show you harassment, Sullivan!"

"Don't make me sue you!" he taunts her, barely evading a punch to the arm.

"You don't scare me!"

"Harassment and assault!"

As I laugh at their antics, I spy Zack and Jill out on the dance floor, slowly moving in each other's arms. The song is slow and sexy and they are all over each other, completely wrapped up in each other.

Jill has had a good amount to drink tonight, but Zack hasn't had a drop.

He leans down and murmurs something in her ear. She smiles and nods, and he clasps her hand in his as he leads her off the dance floor. As they pass by us, Z doesn't look our way, but Jill catches Cara's gaze and waves at her with a wink.

Cara stands perfectly still, watching with wide eyes as her best friend leaves the bar with my brother.

I hope he knows what he's doing.

"What the fuck?" Ty steps forward, as if to follow them, but Cara grabs his arm and holds him back.

"Zack's not an asshole," she reminds him calmly. "And Jilly's a grown woman. She's fine."

Ty glares down at her and then sighs deeply and pulls his hand down his face. "If he hurts her, I'll skin him alive."

"No, you won't." Cara grins at him and pats his arm soothingly. "Don't be such a worrywart."

But she glances back at the door they just left from, worry of her own evident in her hazel eyes.

"You always were a pain in the ass," Ty mutters.

"Yep." Cara saunters back to me and her beer. She winks at me and takes a drink from the bottle. "Are you gonna teach me to play pool, or what?"

My dick immediately comes to attention at the thought of Cara bending over this table and me bending over behind her.

"Sure, you wanna learn how to play?"

"Sure." She shrugs and grins.

"I'm out, guys." Ty passes Cara his cue and gives her a hug before clapping me on the shoulder and waving good-bye.

"Don't go," Cara pouts, her lips pursed.

"No, do go." I wave him off, ready to spend some time with my girl.

"Rude." She glares at me.

I shrug and laugh. "Now I have you to myself."

"Okay, then teach me how to do this." She positions the white ball on the green felt of the table, lining it up to hit a green stripe in the corner. I lean back against my stool and watch her lean over the table, her ass pulling the cotton of her dress tight, and she shoots, completely missing.

"Josh?" She looks back at me over her shoulder.

"Yes, baby?"

"Help."

"Put the cue down, Cara."

She frowns and lays the cue on the table and turns to me.

"Come here."

My arms are crossed over my chest, hands tucked firmly under my biceps as I lean on the chair, my feet shoulder-width apart.

"What is it?" She comes to stand directly in front of me.

I stare down at her for a moment, taking in her wide amber eyes, glassy from a little too much beer, and her long blond hair, tucked behind her ears now, showing off the hoops in her ears.

"You don't want to play pool?" she asks with a raised brow.

I shake my head no, my face perfectly calm.

"What do you want to do?"

I lean in, still not touching her, and whisper directly into her ear, "I want to take you home and fuck the hell out of you all night long."

I pull back in time to see her mouth drop in surprise, and then she sends me a sassy smile. "What are we waiting for?"

With a laugh, I bend down and lift her onto my shoulder, my forearm looped over the back of her thighs, careful to make sure the hem of her dress is covering all the necessary parts so I don't have to kill anyone for looking up her skirt, and carry her out, to the delight of the patrons still in the bar.

"Hey!" She slaps my ass and then braces herself on my hips as I slap hers back.

"Stay still, baby."

"I was right, you are a caveman."

"At least I'm not dragging you by your hair."

"No, but can you still pull it later?" She giggles, earning another slap on her ass.

"Absolutely."

"You sure slap my ass a lot, caveman."

"I fucking love your ass, baby."

"What the hell are you doing?" I ask, and come to a stop in my bedroom.

"Packing?" She glances back at me over her shoulder and offers me a small smile. "Did you get your morning chores done?"

"Yeah," I automatically respond, surprised the sound came out over the lump in my throat.

She's leaving me.

"I took Jill to the airport this morning. Just got back a bit ago." She's calmly folding her clothes and placing them in a box, and I can barely wrap my mind around the words coming out of her mouth.

"Okay." I shove my hands in my pockets and rock back on my heels. What do I say? There's no way in hell that I want her to go, but it's too soon to suggest we live together.

Although, I love having her here, in my home, in my bed.

She belongs here.

"Cara!"

We both turn toward the door at Zack's calling Cara's name from down the hallway.

"In the bedroom!" she calls back.

He stomps into the bedroom, his jaw tight and hands in fists, but otherwise not showing any emotion. "Where is Jillian?"

Cara frowns at him in confusion and tilts her head to the side. "On an airplane."

"She left?"

"Yeah, her flight was this morning. She said you left before she woke up this morning." Cara raises an eyebrow at him, clearly wanting to know more.

"I had to be home when Seth woke up," he mutters, and runs a hand over his head, scrubbing his scalp with his fingertips. "She didn't mention that she was leaving today."

"I'm sorry, I figured you knew."

"Thanks." He turns and leaves the room, and a few seconds later we hear the front door shut as well.

"Well"—she cringes and offers me an apologetic smile—"that didn't go well. Jill wasn't very forthcoming about what happened last night."

"You can't figure it out on your own?" I pull her against me, her stomach against my pelvis. "I could show you."

"Ew." She wrinkles up her nose and then laughs.

"That's not what you said last night." I slap her ass. "In fact, I believe your exact words were 'Harder.' "

"Those were my *exact words*?" She laughs and leans her forehead against my chest.

"Well, it might have been something more like

'Harder, Josh, you're the best I've ever had and I can't believe what a sex god you are.'"

She's laughing in earnest now, shaking her head and slapping my chest gently. "I know I didn't say that!"

"You were drunk, it's okay." I nuzzle her neck and laugh with her. "I love it when you laugh."

She pulls back to smile up at me, and my gut clenches just as it does every damn time she smiles at me like that, as if she can't get enough of me and I hung the moon especially for her.

She takes my breath away.

I lean down and rest my forehead against hers and take a deep breath. She cups my face in her hand and I lean into it. "Love the way you touch me."

"Love to touch you," she murmurs, and pushes her hand up into my hair, combing it through her fingers.

"When are you leaving?" I ask softly, watching her face carefully.

She frowns and clears her throat, almost as though it's hard for her to get the words out. "Tomorrow after my lesson with Seth."

Tomorrow?

"Why?" I ask bluntly.

"Because my house is done, Josh. Thank you for letting me stay here, and everything you've done for me. I don't know what I would have done without you." The last few words are said in a soft whisper, and her thanking me pisses me off.

"You don't need to thank me. I wouldn't have had it any other way, Carolina."

She smiles sadly and kisses my cheek. "I know."

She pulls away from me and returns to folding her clothes and placing them in that damn box.

"I'll be back every morning for Seth's lessons. I won't be able to stay for lunch this week though because I'm helping out downtown with the Huckleberry Festival. I'll be serving ice cream."

"I love huckleberry ice cream," I murmur, and watch her pretty hands fold her underwear. I have to ball my fists to refrain from plucking the underwear out of her hands and unpacking the rest of her things and making her stay here with me.

"I hate it," she responds with a wrinkle to her nose. "It's disgusting. I'm a chocolate-ice-cream girl, so I figure I'm safe serving the ice cream. I won't be tempted to eat it and gain a million pounds."

Just tell her, you idiot. Tell her to stay. Tell her you don't want her to go, that she is your world and you can't imagine going one day without waking up with her by your side.

"Cara . . ."

She stops what she's doing and turns to me, her hazel eyes big and smiling, biting her lower lip, and I can't get the words out. Instead I pull her to me again and bury my face in her hair, gliding my hands up and down her back, hugging her close.

"Josh? What's wrong?"

"I love you."

She pulls back and narrows her eyes as she watches me, looking for what, I don't know. She finally drops her shoulders and sighs in defeat, but offers me a wobbly smile.

"I love you too."

CHAPTER

Thirteen

CARA

I'm sitting in my favorite chair, a cup of hot tea in my hands and Daughtry singing "Tennessee Line" over my sound system. It's late in the evening, and my home is cool, thanks to the air-conditioning unit my parents had installed ten years ago when the summer heat was becoming too much for them.

It's everything that I love about my house, and I hate it.

I glare at the cell phone in my hand and wish for the fortieth time in the past fifteen minutes that it would ring. I haven't seen Josh since this morning when he came in the house to wake me up and say good morning before he was called back out again because of an emergency. Louie called, frantic, having found several calves killed in the pasture by what they think are wolves.

I already miss him.

Finally my phone beeps, and my heart jumps into my throat, hoping and praying that it's a message from Josh.

Jill: **Hey! How does it feel to be home?**

Me: **Fine.**

I take a sip of my tea and lean my head back against the cushion just as another text comes through.

Josh: **Being in my bed without you just feels wrong.**

I grin and set my mug aside, settling in to text him back, although I can't help but be a little peeved that he's texting and not calling.

Although everything he does right now pisses me off because he didn't ask me to stay, and even that is ridiculous because I know it's too soon and I'm being an idiot.

Me: **I miss you too.**

Josh: **I love you.**

I want to text back with **Then call me! Come see me!** but I just set my phone aside and lean my head back again with a deep breath.

Yes, it's irrational to want Josh to ask me to move in with him, and it *is* too soon, but I love him and I enjoy being with him.

God, I'm needy.

I'm dozing in my chair when the doorbell rings, startling me. Maybe Josh is surprising me?

I hurry to the door and fling it open with a big grin on my face, then feel my shoulders fall.

"Oh, it's you."

"Gee, it's great to see you too," Ty mutters with a chuckle.

"Sorry, come on in." I stand back and let him inside before shutting and locking the door. "Have a seat."

"Thanks, I will." He flashes me his cocky grin and plops down on my couch, crosses his ankles on my ottoman, and makes himself comfortable.

He's still in his black slacks and white button-down from work today, but his sleeves are rolled up, showing off the bright colors of his ink.

"No suit today?" I reclaim my chair.

"Naw, no court today."

I nod and take a sip of my tea.

"Why are you here?" I ask with a raise of my brow.

"Saw your light on." He shrugs and leans his head back on the cushion of the couch, looking at the ceiling. "Thought I'd come by and see how you are, since it's your first night home and all."

"I'm good." I shrug and take another sip of tea. "It's good to be home."

"Why do you look like someone just killed your puppy?" He turns his head on the cushion so he can look at me.

"I'm tired. I'm helping Mrs. Baker get ready for the Huckleberry Festival this weekend."

"I loved her in school. Did you have her?" he asks with a grin.

"I did. She hasn't changed a bit."

"Are you serving the ice cream again this year?"

"Yes. I'll give you two scoops, just like every year."

"You're so good to me," he mutters with a sleepy smile. "If Josh hadn't snatched you up, I might have tried to lure you in."

I frown at the mention of Josh's name and take another sip of tea.

"I knew that he's why you're unhappy," he murmurs.

"I don't know what you're talking about."

"Come on, tell Uncle Ty all about it." He smiles again as I throw my head back and laugh.

"You are anything but my uncle, Ty."

"Big brother, then." He blinks sleepily, his blue eyes tired and lined with stress, but he's here for me, and he's absolutely right.

He's the only brother I've ever had.

"It's stupid."

"Probably." He links his fingers on his flat stomach. "Tell me anyway."

"He didn't ask me to stay." My voice is soft, and I just stare down at my empty mug, avoiding Ty's stare.

"Seriously? Did you tell him you wanted to stay?"

"No."

Ty laughs and scrubs his face with his hands. "So, he didn't ask you to stay, as in, move in with him?"

"Yeah," I whisper. "I know it's too soon."

"Have you done the 'I love you' thing yet?"

I can't help but meet his eyes and grin.

"I take that as a yes." He smirks and watches me

for a long minute, blinking sleepily, but not breaking eye contact. "I'm not surprised, you know."

"Why?" I ask, taken aback.

"He's always had a soft spot for you. Not to mention, you're hot."

"Shut up." I wave him off as he smirks.

"You are, Cara. It doesn't surprise me that he's finally noticed."

"He's a good guy," I whisper, and close my eyes.

"One of the best. So you didn't tell him you wanted to stay?"

"Of course not."

"Cara." Ty pinches the bridge of his nose between his finger and thumb and shakes his head ruefully.

"Why would I say that? It's like inviting yourself to someone's party or something. It's his house, he should say it first."

"Says the girl who has clearly never been in a relationship."

Ouch. "Eff off, Ty."

"I'm sorry, hon, but how is he supposed to know that you want to stay if you don't tell him? Josh has many talents, but being psychic isn't one of them."

"You're psychotic," I mutter, and glare at him, making him laugh.

"You need to communicate if you want it to work, you know. That's just Relationships 101."

"Are you a lawyer or a couples counselor?"

"A little of both." He smiles softly, his blue eyes full of humor.

"I have to pee. I'll be right back." I jump up and head for the bathroom, needing a minute to gather my thoughts.

Could it be that simple?

Is that why Josh looked so torn yesterday when he watched me pack? Maybe he wanted to ask me to stay, but didn't think I wanted to.

Yep, I'm an idiot.

I wash my hands and walk back to the living room, surprised to see Ty with my phone pressed to his ear.

"Dude, seriously? Don't be an ass. Cara's back. Here she is." He hands the phone to me, his face sober.

"Hello?"

"What the fuck is Ty doing at your house this late in the evening?" Josh's voice is deceptively quiet.

"He came over to say hi. My lights were on."

"How long has he been there?"

"Why?"

"I'm just asking a question, Cara."

"Long enough for us to get naked and have wild and crazy sex in every room of my house. Is that what you want to hear?"

"Watch yourself, Carolina."

"No, you watch yourself! Who do you think you are to call me and question me about having my friends over? I've known Ty my whole fucking life, Josh, just like you. What exactly are you accusing me of?"

"Cara, stop." Ty is standing with his hands on his hips, shaking his head. "You're not helping."

I shake my head in return and listen to silence on the other end of the line.

"Well?" I ask Josh.

"I'm not accusing you of anything," he murmurs, his voice resigned and tired. "I'm sorry. I hope you sleep well, baby." He hangs up.

I throw my phone across the room. "What the fuck, Ty?"

"Cara . . ."

"Why is he acting like this? I just saw him this morning, and he has the balls to be jealous because you are over here *talking with me*?"

"Cara, he's in love with you. He'd be jealous of fucking Santa Claus right now."

"Bullshit." I'm panting, my hands are in fists at my side, and I'm just fucking pissed.

"No, it's not bullshit. If the roles were reversed, I'd kick his ass. It was inappropriate for me to come over. It just didn't occur to me because you're my sister in my head, but not in *his* head."

Ty sits at the edge of the couch, his elbows on his knees, and watches me calmly as I process what he's said.

Well, shit.

"I fucked up," I whisper, and sit dejectedly in my chair.

"It happens. He'll get over it."

"He was so mad." My voice is shaky, and I feel the tears welling in my eyes.

"Whoa." Ty raises his hands in surrender, his blue eyes wide. "Whoa, whoa, whoa. It's time to call Jill."

He finds my phone across the room, pops the battery back in it, and as soon as it's rebooted, he finds Jill's number and calls her.

"No, I'm not fucking Josh right now, thanks for asking." He swears under his breath about what girls talk about on the phone and pushes his hand through his hair. "You need to talk to Cara. She's crying, and tears are so not my department."

Ty walks back to me and kisses my forehead gently. "You'll be fine. I'm gonna go home and call Josh. Talk it out with Jilly."

He hands me the phone and lets himself out of my house.

JOSH

I'll fucking kill him.

And spank the shit out of her.

What the fuck?

I'm never going to sleep now, so I get dressed and head out to the barn to get a head start on chores. With a wolf out there killing some of my cattle, I have more on my plate than I can handle.

This week is going to be hell. I don't know when I'll see Cara again, and I *need* to see her, like I need to breathe.

Apparently I need to remind her that she's mine.

As I walk up to the barn, I'm surprised to see my mom coming from the chicken coop, a basket looped in her arm.

"Mom?" I hurry over to her. "Is everything okay?"

"Of course." She smiles at me and kisses my cheek when I bend down and offer it to her. "Couldn't sleep, so I figured I'd come out and see if there were any fresh eggs for breakfast."

"Any luck?"

"Yep. Come inside, I'll fix you something."

"You should go back to bed," I mutter, secretly longing for some bacon and eggs.

"Nonsense, come inside and talk to me." She smiles and leads me to the house, dressed in her usual yoga pants and oversize T-shirt.

At sixty-eight, my mom is in great shape and is active in our community, serving on the board at the credit union and on the town council, and she still helps with fund-raisers for the school.

I take a seat at the table as she pulls out a skillet to cook the eggs.

I immediately begin to help, pulling the bacon from the fridge and washing my hands.

This is what I needed.

"So, why are you awake, Son?"

"Just worried about the wolf killing the cattle," I reply, and pull the bacon apart.

"Bullshit."

I raise my head in surprise to find her glaring at me, her hands on her hips. Her salt-and-pepper hair is up in a bun, and her face is clean of makeup, but she's no less forbidding.

"What?" I ask.

"You heard me. Is this about Cara?"

Just the mention of her name is both a stab to the heart and causes butterflies to explode in my stomach.

"She left."

"She just moved back home, Joshua."

"I know." I shrug and turn away, making coffee.

"If you want her to stay, why didn't you ask her?"

"Because it's too soon to live together. Going home was right for her; I just got used to having her around."

"Mmm . . ." she murmurs noncommittally. "She's a sweet girl."

"Yes. She is." When the coffee has brewed, I pour both my mom and myself a cup, and she slips the bacon in the oven, sets the timer, and we sit at the kitchen table until it's time to scramble the eggs.

"I always liked her parents."

I nod and grip the mug in the palms of my hands, thinking about Cara and her kindness, her gentleness.

Fuck, I miss her.

"Gram would have loved her," I whisper, and take a sip of coffee.

Mom smiles and nods. "Absolutely." She sits back and narrows her brown eyes at me, deep in thought. Z and I get our features from Mom.

"Dad still in bed?" I ask, trying to change the subject.

"You're in love with her," Mom responds instead, and I know she won't let me off the hook.

"Yeah, I'm in love with her. It's got me all messed up." I sigh and push my hands into my hair.

"Love will do that." She smiles softly. "I'm so happy for you, my sweet boy."

"Well, don't get too happy. I pissed her off last night."

"Love will do that too." She laughs and takes a sip of her coffee. "Are you thinking marriage?"

Marriage?

I swallow hard and scowl down into my mug. "It's entirely too soon to go down that road," I mutter softly.

"Don't be ridiculous." She shakes her head adamantly and rises from the table to refill our coffees. "Your dad and I got married after dating for four weeks and we'll be celebrating forty years next month."

"But you knew each other all your lives."

She turns to me with a raised eyebrow and a small, knowing smile on her lips.

Point taken.

"Yes, I'm going to marry her." I sigh and close my eyes as calm settles over me. "If she'll have me."

"She'd be stupid to pass you up. You're brilliant and funny, not to mention the handsomest man I've ever seen."

"Zack will be happy to hear that," I reply with a grin.

"He looks just like you, so it works for me." She chuckles and then gets that gleam in her eye that says she has a great idea. "I'll be right back."

She leaves the kitchen just as the timer for the bacon dings, so I take it out and put it on paper towels to drain. Just as I set the pan aside, she's back with a small black box.

"If you'd like, give this to her when you propose." She hands me the box and I open it to find Gram's diamond-and-sapphire engagement ring nestled inside.

"Mom, I can't take this."

"It's an heirloom, of course you can."

"Why didn't you give it to Zack?" I ask, and take it from her.

"Because your grandmother might have had a problem with that, given that it was still on her finger when he married that woman. Besides," she sniffs, and crosses her arms over her chest, "that little bitch was never going to get any of my jewelry."

"Good girl." I smile and kiss her on the forehead. "Thanks, Mom."

"You're welcome."

CARA

"Who's that?" Seth asks, and points out the window to the men and one woman standing in the back pasture. Josh is with them, and it's like drinking water after being in the desert for months. I haven't spoken to him since our angry phone call on Wednesday night.

I know he's irritated about Ty being at my house, but is he punishing me for it? Because it sure feels like it.

"Have you seen them before?" I ask.

Seth twists his mouth in thought. "Yeah, they've been around off and on all week."

"I bet they're the Fish and Wildlife people," I mutter, watching Josh wipe his forehead on the sleeve of his white T-shirt. His biceps flex with the motion, and my stomach clenches as I remember how it feels to have those arms tighten around me.

God, he's gorgeous.

"Are we done?" Seth asks, interrupting my thoughts.

"Yeah, I'll see you Monday. You get tomorrow off since I'll be at the festival all day."

"Yes!" He pumps his fist and grins.

"I'll miss you too," I mutter sarcastically, and he grins wider.

"I'll miss you, but I won't miss those worksheets."

He waves as he leaves the house, and I'm disappointed to see that Josh and the others are gone when I look back outside.

I miss him so much.

I gather my things and head for my car, surprised to find Josh standing in his driveway with the others.

"Hey."

"Cara." Josh's head snaps around, his brown eyes wide, taking me in from head to toe as if he has missed me too.

Thank God.

He quickly walks to me and pulls me in for a long hug. I blink, keeping tears at bay, relieved that he's holding me.

"We need to talk," he whispers in my ear.

"I know."

"I don't have time now." He backs away and brushes the backs of his fingers down my cheek and offers me a small smile, his dimple winking at me.

"Is everything okay?"

He sighs and shakes his head. "No. These guys"— he gestures and leads me over to where they're standing—"are from the Fish and Wildlife department. The one wolf I thought I had killing my cattle is actually a pack of about eight."

I gasp in surprise and take in everyone's grim faces. "Eight?"

"Yeah," Josh confirms as the others nod.

"We're tracking them, but they're sneaky bastards. We didn't meet the last time I was here. I'm Erica." She shakes my hand and smiles kindly.

"What will you do to them?" I ask.

"Kill them," one of the other men replies matter-of-factly.

"Kill them?" I ask, surprised. "I thought they were endangered."

"Not anymore." Josh shakes his head and wipes his forehead on his sleeve again. "They're overpopulated here now and can bankrupt a rancher or farmer if they're not taken care of."

"A small pack of wolves killed an entire flock of sheep east of the mountains last month," the taller man agrees. "They don't hunt to eat, they kill because they can. We've been tracking this particular pack. We didn't realize they'd moved so close to the Lazy K."

"I had no idea." I slide my hands in my back pockets to keep from reaching out to Josh. "How many cattle have they killed?"

"Five calves since Monday," Josh replies grimly.

"Oh my God, I'm sorry."

"We're pretty sure we know where they are. We're heading out now to go track them."

I stare longingly at Josh, wanting nothing more than a few minutes alone with him.

"Be safe," I whisper instead.

"I'll be fine, baby." He kisses me quickly and turns to the others.

"I told you earlier, Josh," Erica begins, "you don't have to go with us."

"My land, my problem." His face is set in determined lines. "Let's go."

*   *   *

I lean my head back into the stream of hot water in my new and improved master bathroom and moan as it hits the tight muscles in my shoulders. I'm worried. I still haven't heard from Josh, and now I don't think I will today. It's almost midnight.

I turn off the shower, twist my hair up in a towel, and when I begin drying off, I hear pounding. Loud, incessant pounding.

I secure the towel around me and hurry into the living room, toward the *bam bam bam* on my front door.

What the hell?

I fling the door wide, shocked to see Josh standing there, his jaw set and eyes intensely . . . *fierce.*

"I miss you," he says, his voice strong, as his eyes roam over my face. "I miss you so damn much."

I step back, allowing him to come inside, and once I shut the door, he gently cups my face in his palms and backs me against the wall.

"I'm so sorry about the other night, Cara." He rests his lips on my forehead and takes a long, deep breath.

"You don't have any reason not to trust me," I remind him firmly, absorbing his heat, reveling in the strength of him against me.

"I know." His lips glide softly down my temple to my cheek. "I do trust you. I wasn't expecting Ty to answer your phone."

I rest my hands on his hips. "Did you get the wolves?"

"We got them," he confirms grimly.

His eyes are tired, and he has dark circles under them. I brush my thumbs over the dark smudges. "What else is bothering you?" I whisper.

"I miss you so much." He closes his eyes, tightening his arms around me. "With everything happening at the Lazy K, not seeing you, not having you in my bed, I'm going crazy." I start to answer, but he covers my lips with his finger. "I need you, Carolina. Please don't send me away."

"Oh, sweetheart." Looping my arms around his neck, I pull him down to me as he tightens his arms around me again, and we hug each other close. "Stay with me."

"Those are the words I should have said to you on Tuesday," he murmurs softly against my forehead.

I kiss his chin and comb his hair soothingly in my fingers, my chest bursting with relief and love for this amazing man in my arms.

He hoists me against the wall, just like that night so many weeks ago, and kisses me aggressively, his mouth hot and demanding on mine, his tongue sliding against my own. He supports my center against his hips, wrapping my legs around his waist, and cups my face in his hands, never taking his lips away.

I open my eyes to find his on mine, hot and urgent.

He kisses his way across my cheek and to my ear, sucks the lobe in his mouth, making me moan.

He boosts me higher and sinks two fingers inside me.

"So wet," he murmurs, and kisses down my neck, licking water droplets from the shower. His fingers begin to move, his thumb worrying my clit, driving me crazy.

This man makes me crazy.

He suddenly wraps both his arms around my torso and allows me to slide down his body until my bare feet hit the floor. He drops to his knees, pulls my right leg up over his shoulder, and buries his face in my core.

"Ah, fuck!" I exclaim, sink my hands in his hair, and hold on. "I'm going to fall."

"Won't let you," he mutters, and licks from my labia up over my clit and kisses the crease between my pussy and my thigh. "I've got you."

He latches on to my lips, hollows his cheeks, and pulls deeply, rubs his nose against my clit, and I swear to God I see stars. I come fast and hard, electricity zinging along every nerve, glorying in this man.

My man.

Before I can recover, he stands with my leg still on his shoulder, lifting me easily in his arms, the towels falling away from both my hair and my body.

"You're so fucking sexy," he groans, and bites my neck, hard enough to leave a mark. He lowers me to the couch and steps back long enough to shuck off his own clothes. While he's stripping, I sit up, and when he sits, I straddle him, lift my hips, and sink down onto him.

"Josh." My voice is raspy with lust and need, and I begin to ride him, hard. He grips my hips and guides me up and down on him, thrusting his hips up to meet me.

One hand glides up my side to plump my breast as he leans in and sucks the nipple, tugs it with his teeth, and sucks it some more. He finds my clit with his other hand and drives me over the edge a second time.

"Not yet," I rasp.

"Yes," he growls. "Come. Now, Cara."

I can't help it. I clench down on him, my pussy convulsing around him as I come again and scream his name.

Before the contractions slow, he cups my ass in his palms and begins a hard, fast rhythm again, pushing into me forcefully and steadily.

"I have a weakness for you." His teeth are clenched and the muscle at his jaw flexes as he speaks. "You are mine, do you understand?"

"Yes," I whimper, and lean my forehead down to rest on his.

"Look at me."

I pull back and meet his brown eyes.

"Mine."

"Yours."

His face contorts in a mixture of ecstasy and agony as he comes, pulling me down against him and grinding against me hard, making me come again as well.

"Josh!"

"Fuck." As his body calms, he leans his head back against the cushion, panting and stroking my skin with those amazing hands of his.

I lean in and kiss him, softly, tenderly, cupping his face in my hands as he continues to gently stroke my back, sides, and thighs. I sweep my lips over his, nuzzle his nose with my own, and kiss each of his cheeks.

"Love you so much," I murmur against his mouth.

"I can't be without you, Carolina."

"Back at you, Joshua."

I wake to soft sunlight and a cold bed. Without opening my eyes, I know that Josh has already left to go back to the ranch to take care of his responsibilities.

And that's okay.

Because he loves me and he wants me.

I turn onto my side and feel something crinkle under my cheek. Opening my eyes, I pull the piece of notebook paper out from under my head and grin when I see Josh's handwriting.

Baby,

I didn't want to wake you. I have to go back and handle a few things, but I'll see you later today at the festival. Save some ice cream for me.

Love you,

J

With a wide grin, I hug the note to me and sigh happily as I snatch up my phone and send him a quick text.

I love you too. Will have huckleberry ice cream waiting for you. xo

CHAPTER

Fourteen

"How are things going?" Mrs. Baker asks as she ties her pink polka-dotted apron and joins me behind the ice cream counter.

"Good. I've already sold three five-gallon tubs' worth. My arms are going to hurt tomorrow." I smile over at her as she grabs a scoop and motions for the next person in line. The weather is perfect. The sun is shining brightly, and the crowds are thick and loud. The scent of grilled hamburgers drifts over to me from the vendor next to us, and my stomach growls, reminding me that I'm hungry.

"You should squeeze a tennis ball," she informs me. "Builds those muscles right up."

"I'll remember that for next year." I laugh. Despite her age, Mrs. Baker has kept herself in excellent shape. She's petite with short, salt-and-pepper hair and a wide smile.

"Cara!" Seth and his grandma Nancy King are next in line.

"Hi, guys." I grin at Seth. "Let me guess. You're here for crab legs?"

"Dude, we want ice cream." He shakes his head and frowns at me.

"Right." I wink at him and begin rolling the soft, purple ice cream. "One scoop or two?"

"Two!" Seth crows at the same time Josh's mom says, "One."

"I tried," Seth mutters, and grins.

I hand him his cone and smile at his grandma. "The same?"

"Please." She nods happily. "How are you, Cara?"

"I'm great, thanks for asking." The Kings have always been nothing but kind to me. "And you?"

"I'm staying busy and out of trouble."

"Sounds boring." I wink at her as she throws her head back and laughs, taking the cone from me.

"I like you, Cara. I'm glad Josh has found you."

I feel my cheeks burn as I look down at the ice cream before I meet her gaze and offer her a small smile.

"Me too."

"Come on, Seth, Cara has work to do." She leads Seth away and I watch them go, happy that Josh's mom approves of me.

"She's a nice woman," Mrs. Baker remarks beside me.

"She is." I nod and smile down at her just as she glares at the next customer in line.

"*She*, however, is not."

I follow her gaze to find Misty next in line, take a deep breath, and mentally prepare myself for her nastiness.

"Misty."

"Cara, how nice to see you." She throws me a sharp, fake smile from beneath her pink baseball cap. She's wearing short denim cutoffs and a white sleeveless button-down top, tied above her navel to show off her flat stomach.

"What do you want?"

"Just one scoop. I have to watch the calories." Her eyes move up and down my body, then she smirks at me. "You know how that is. How's Josh?"

"Fine." *Do not react to her. She wants to piss you off.*

"Well, that I know." She chuckles and tosses her long ponytail over her shoulder. "Is he going to be here today? Maybe I'll try to catch up with him."

"Why?" I ask bluntly.

"Oh, honey." She tilts her head to the side and gives me a sympathetic smile. "You still think he's got a thing for you, don't you?"

"No," I respond calmly, proud of myself for not scratching her eyes out. "I don't think he has a 'thing' for me."

"Good." She takes the cone from me and leans forward, as if she's about to tell me a secret. "Because he's been with me for over a year now. He was fucking me when your tree fell, and he'll come back to me after he tosses your fat ass aside and moves on, just like he always does with the girls he fucks around with. You don't scare me. You're just a bump in the road."

I have had it up to my eyeballs with Misty's bitchiness. Before she can turn away, I lean back and smirk, announcing loud enough for everyone to hear, "Well, if that's true, which I know for a fact it isn't, you must be a horrific lay for Josh to jump from bed to bed, trying to find something better than you."

Misty's mouth drops and her cheeks redden in fury and embarrassment.

"You've got your ice cream. You can go now." I glare at her as she turns and stomps away, marching toward her own booth.

"You don't believe that bull, do you?" Mrs. Baker asks, her eyes narrowed and voice sharp as a blade.

"Of course not," I sigh, and wipe my forehead with the back of my hand. "She's just a hateful, horrible person."

"Good. She's the most evil thing I've ever seen."

I silently agree and take a drink of water, enjoying the brief lull from people demanding ice cream.

The rest of the afternoon moves quickly as we serve many more customers, chat with locals, and explain just what, exactly, a huckleberry is to the tourists.

At around three, Josh walks around the counter, wraps his arms around me, and plants a big kiss on me, not giving a rat's ass who's watching.

"Hey there, handsome."

"Hey, beautiful." He kisses my cheek and grins happily. The circles are gone from beneath his eyes and he looks calmer today.

"You look good," I tell him as I cup his face in my hand.

"You always look good."

"I wish Misty had been here to see this," Mrs. Baker comments, and hands a customer his change.

"What?" Josh's body stills, and he narrows his eyes at me. "What happened?"

"Misty showed up earlier." I wave him off as though it's no big deal, but he grips my shoulders in his hands, keeping me in place.

"What did she say?"

"She just wanted to remind me that you'll be tossing me aside anytime now and go back to sleeping with her, as you were doing when my tree fell—"

Before I can finish my story, he grips my hand in his, pivots, and pulls me through the crowded park, between tents and tables, through the crowd of people toward Misty's booth, where she has her home-based cosmetics business on display.

Zack is standing nearby and sees us walk past. "What's going on?"

"I need to rectify something," Josh replies, his voice low and measured.

Zack falls into step behind us. "I wouldn't miss this for the world."

As we approach Misty's booth, Misty is applying makeup to Lauren, a potential customer, and startles when she sees Josh headed straight for her. Josh releases my hand and I hang back, watching my angry man stomp up to Misty, who is sitting behind her table with Lauren seated before her, holding samples of lip gloss.

I feel Zack step up beside me, but I don't take my eyes off Josh's back as he slaps his hands down on the table, toppling pink tubes and jars in his anger, and leans into Misty's shocked face.

"Who the fuck do you think you are"—his voice is like steel, low and measured—"to tell my girlfriend that I was fucking you when the tree fell on her house?"

Misty swallows hard, her eyes widen, and she licks her lips nervously.

Before she can say a word, Josh continues, "I am sick to death of you trying to ruin the best thing that's ever happened to me. I don't know what your problem is, whether you're jealous or just plain mean, but I do know one thing: you're fucking pathetic." He stands tall and looks down at her, and from behind him I can't see his face, but I do see his hands fisting at his sides. "I never had sex with you."

Misty's eyes shift left and right, looking at all the people watching the scene unfold, her cheeks pink and mouth agape as she pants in embarrassment.

"I never fucking touched you, and I regret the two dates I was stupid enough to take you out on before I realized what a toxic woman you are. Leave. My woman. Alone. Do you understand me?"

She finally finds her voice, sneers at Josh, and tosses her hair over her shoulder in Misty fashion. "Best thing that ever happened to you?" she asks incredulously. "Bullshit. Look at her. She's nothing but a fat, ugly bitch!"

"Ignore her," Zack whispers in my ear as he wraps his arm around my shoulders. "You're gorgeous."

Before Josh can respond, Lauren stands, sending her chair crashing behind her, her eyes flashing in anger.

"Shut the fuck up, Misty! The only ugly bitch here is you. I'm so done with your bullshit. Give it a damn rest!"

Misty's mouth opens and closes in shock, and she watches in horror as Lo marches from behind the table and over to me, pulls me into a hug that shocks the shit out of me, and smiles down at me before stalking away from the scene. As I watch her go, I spy Ty leaning against a tree, watching her go as well, his eyes narrowed and jaw clenched. He looks back over at me and raises his eyebrows, and I just shrug back at him.

"Well, I never!" Misty exclaims, but is drowned out as people begin to clap and whoop and holler.

It seems everyone is sick of Misty's shit.

Josh turns back to me as Zack lets his arm drop and backs away. Josh cups my face in his hands and kisses me long and slow, his lips soft, claiming me in front of all of these people.

"You're staying with me this weekend."

"I can't. I have to be here all weekend."

"I'll cover for you, dear." Mrs. Baker winks at me, her eyes sparkling with humor. "You should be with your man."

Josh kisses my cheek and then whispers into my ear, "You're staying with me."

He scoops me into his arms and carries me off, garnering more applause and whistles.

I smile up at him and shake my head. "Caveman."

His eyes grow serious and he shakes his head sharply. "I love you. It's about time everyone knows it and respects it. I won't have anyone telling you lies about me, or about what I feel for you."

"I knew it was all lies, babe." I kiss his cheek and then rest my head on his shoulder. "But you can carry me around whenever you'd like."

"Get used to it."

"Wake up, baby."

I'm pleasantly warm, cocooned in Josh's blankets. And in Josh.

My brain clears enough to realize that I'm waking up with Josh still in bed, naked, wrapped around me.

"Carolina," he croons to me, kissing my neck and shoulder, his hand roaming up and down my side. "Wake up."

"You're here," I murmur, and turn to face him.

"Where else would I be?" he asks with a grin and drags his fingertips down my cheek to my neck.

"I've never woken up with you before." He brushes

his thumb over my chin and then leans in to plant a soft kiss on my lips. "This feels so good."

"You have to wake up." He kisses me softly again, pushes his fingers into my hair at the nape of my neck, rubbing rhythmically.

"Why? What time is it?"

"Five." He winces as my eyes widen.

"Are you waking me up to say good-bye before you go do your morning work?" I sigh as he continues to massage my neck.

"No, I took the weekend off." He smiles softly, his dimple winking at me, as he leisurely rubs the tip of his nose over mine.

"How is that possible?"

"I need some time with you."

"Okay," I whisper.

"Good." He smiles down at me. "Because I have something to show you." He kisses my shoulder.

"I've seen that before," I remind him with a laugh.

"Not that." He laughs. "Let's go."

"But this is so nice," I pout, and tighten my arms, trying to keep him still, but he easily pulls away and rolls out of bed. "We should stay here and take advantage of this soft bed and our lack of clothing."

"Come on, up. It'll be worth it." He grins again and winks. "We'll finish this later."

"Promise?" I yawn, sit up, and let the covers fall around me.

"I promise." He pulls his jeans up over his hips. "Hurry, or we'll miss it."

"What is it?" I ask, curious now, and pull on my own clothes.

"You'll see. Come on."

He pulls me out of the house and to the barn, where Magic is waiting with Louie, wearing a bridle and a blanket draped over her back.

"Mornin'," Louie murmurs, and smiles down at me.

"Do you people *ever* sleep?" I ask incredulously, earning laughs from both men.

"Not much." Louie hands the reins over to Josh. "See you on Monday, boss."

"Up you go." Josh lifts me easily onto Magic's back, then swings himself up effortlessly.

"That was kind of hot." I lean my head back so I can look up at him and smile.

"You're easy to please, honey." He kisses my cheek and urges Magic along, out of the barn and across the pasture.

The air is cool in the early morning and dew covers the tall grass brushing my feet. It smells clean, woodsy, as I take a deep breath and inhale it all, the forest ahead, the horse, and the sexy man curved behind me.

"Lean on me, baby. We have about a thirty-minute ride ahead of us."

"Can I nap?"

"You do enjoy your sleep, don't you?" he asks wryly.

"Doesn't everyone?" I ask with a frown.

"Mmm."

I lean back, my head resting on his shoulder, and he kisses my cheek, his arms wrapped loosely around my waist, the reins in his fists.

The rhythm of the horse soothes me, but I don't sleep. We ride in silence, and as twilight breaks over-head, casting everything in gray and blue, Josh stops Magic near a tall maple tree in the middle of a field. The mountains are ahead, dark in shadow, and as we sit on the horse, Josh wrapped around me, the sun begins to rise, sending a riot of color down over the mountains.

Red, orange, and yellow bleed through the sky, interrupted only by a few white clouds.

"My grandmother," Josh begins in a hushed voice, "used to bring me here very early in the morning, just like this. After my grandfather died, she brought me more often. I think she was lonely."

I tilt my head back and watch him speak, enjoying the way he feels behind me.

"This is the best view of the sunrise in the world." His eyes are trained on the mountains, watching as the whole world wakes up.

"But the best part"—he smiles down at me and guides Magic closer to the tree—"is right here. Look closely."

He points to the trunk of the tree, where there are carvings. Three sets of old-fashioned hearts and initials are carved in the tree. At various heights.

"My great-grandparents"—he points to the set of

initials highest on the tree. "My grandparents, and my parents."

"No Zack and she-who-shall-not-be-named?" I ask sarcastically.

"No." Josh shakes his head and glances down at me. "Z signed on with the army and they left pretty quickly after they got married."

"It's beautiful," I murmur, looking at the weathered letters and hearts, and then back over at the sunrise. "This is amazing."

"You are amazing," he corrects me, and cups my cheek, pulling my lips to his. "I want to spend every sunrise with you, Carolina. Don't go back to your house next week. Stay with me."

"We've moved fast from the beginning," I begin, but he shakes his head and frowns down at me.

"Tell me you were fine with sleeping alone last week."

"I can't do that."

"Tell me you didn't miss me."

"I can't do that either."

"I need you here, baby." He pushes my hair over my shoulder, his eyes soft and gentle. "I shouldn't have let you go in the first place."

"You didn't let me go . . ."

"Yeah, I did. I'm not going to let it happen again."

"I'm right here." I snuggle against him and smile contentedly. "Let's go home."

"My pleasure."

*   *   *

"Okay, I'll say a word, and you say the first word that comes to mind." We are sitting on Josh's couch on Sunday afternoon, him in his sexy gray sweats that hang low on his hips, showing off his sexy V and defined abs and dark skin.

I want to lick him.

I'm in a tight tank and his short boxer-briefs, lying on the opposite side of the couch from him, my feet in his lap.

Those glorious hands of his are kneading the sole of my foot. I want to purr like a kitten.

"Uh, why?" he asks skeptically.

"We're getting to know each other better." I switch feet.

"I know you pretty well." He offers me a playful smile and runs his hand up my calf.

"My head, not my body, perv," I mutter dryly, making him laugh.

"Okay, shoot."

"All right." I settle back into the cushion, my hands on my belly, and watch him happily. "Tractor."

"Field." He's watching his hands on my foot.

"Picture."

"Frame," he responds absently.

"Horse."

"Friend." I tilt my head and watch him carefully. He's still looking down at my feet and legs, and enjoying giving me the massage. His voice is soft and relaxed, and his body is loose and stress-free.

"Cara."

"Love." I grin at him as he raises his eyes to mine before turning his gaze back down to my legs.

"Sex."

"Cara." His eyes find mine again, heating up now, and his hands tighten around my ankle. "My turn."

"Okay."

His hands glide up the side of my leg to my knee and back down again in long, fluid strokes. "Tree."

"Fall," I murmur with a smile.

"School."

"Work."

"Jillian." He tilts his head slightly.

"Crazy." I laugh.

He grips my leg and pulls me easily down the couch and moves over me, bracing himself on his elbows beside my head and nestling his pelvis against mine. He gently brushes my hair back from my face.

"Cock." He grins widely.

"Hard." I wrinkle my nose and circle my hips against him, feeling his hard cock pressed against me.

He sits back on his heels and pulls my shorts off quickly, tugs his sweats down to his knees and returns to me, not filling me yet, just rubbing that hard, long cock through my lips and against my clit.

"Mmm . . ." I moan.

"Shhh, this is my turn." He brushes his lips over mine softly. "Kiss."

"Sexy," I gasp as he moves his hips back and forth, tormenting me.

"Clit," he whispers, and pushes his hand between us, circling my clit with his middle finger.

"Happy." I smile up at him and brush my hands down his side.

He sinks into me then, slowly filling me, and then pulls back, only to push inside again, setting a beautiful rhythm of push and pull, setting my core on fire. He kisses down my throat to my breast, sucking my nipple gently into his mouth, worrying it with his teeth and then brushing his tongue back and forth over the hard nub.

"Oh my," I murmur, running my fingertips up and down his back.

"Shhh." He pulls the other nipple into his mouth and pays it the same attention as he did its twin, then pushes up to kiss me deeply.

"Josh." His eyes are hot as he says his own name, thrusting in and out of me quickly now.

I gaze up at him and push my hands through his soft, dark hair. How do I come up with one word to describe him?

"Everything."

"Ah, baby," he murmurs, and kisses me again, pushing his tongue inside me to rub and coax my own tongue in a sensual rhythm that matches that of his hips.

I wrap my arms tightly around him, holding him flush against me, and feel my pussy begin to contract around his hard length. He pushes inside and holds himself there, grinding his pubis against my clit. I come undone, shuddering beneath him as the orgasm rolls through me.

He groans and cups my face in his hands as he comes, his hips pulsating against me as he empties inside me.

"I love you, Carolina. Don't ever forget that."

"I want to watch something romantic," I inform him smugly.

"I don't have anything romantic," he replies, looking exasperated.

"It's okay, I came prepared." I jump up off the couch and run to the bedroom where my suitcase is, grab the Blu-ray case from my bag, and run back to the living room, where Josh is kneeling by the television.

"Did you seriously bring a Nicholas Sparks movie into my home?" He glares at me.

"Yes." I smile sweetly and bat my eyelashes, making Josh laugh. "It's the newest one. The lead actor's real name is Josh too, so you should love it."

"That's pure girl-logic." He shakes his head and takes the disc from me, slides it into the player, and flops onto the couch with me. "I get sexual favors for this later, right?"

"I can't confirm or deny that." I take a sip of my Diet Coke. "If I start spoiling you like that, you'll expect it all the time and it'll be anarchy around here."

"I'm going to spank you later," he whispers playfully in my ear, and despite having had a mind-numbing orgasm less than thirty minutes ago, my stomach clenches and electricity shoots through my fingertips.

"Don't make promises you can't keep," I warn him.

"God, you're sassy." He laughs and shakes some Skittles into the palm of his hand. He feeds me a green one and pops a purple one into his own mouth as the movie begins.

"Um, do we have to watch a chick flick, Dad?"

We are suddenly joined by a bouncing, slobbering puppy who wants in on the wrestling fun. Thor jumps up on both of us, tail wagging furiously and trying to lick us both at once. He happily slurps an orange candy from Josh's fingers.

"Whoa, I don't think you're supposed to eat Skittles, buddy." Josh scratches Thor's head and pushes him onto the floor. "Hey, guys."

I sit up to see Seth and Zack standing just inside the doorway, both of them watching us as if we've just sprouted wings.

"Hi." I wave.

Seth glances at his dad and then back over at us. "They're weird."

Zack smirks and pats Seth on his shoulder. "They're in love, Son."

"That's dumb." Seth scowls and crosses his arms.

"I hope you still feel that way in five years," Zack

mutters, then looks at the television. His face falls in shock and he pins Josh with a glare. "Wait. You really are watching chick flicks."

"It was my turn to pick." I glare at Zack defensively and snuggle Seth's sweet, soft puppy, who has jumped back up onto my lap. "Thor would watch it with me, wouldn't you, baby? Yes, you would."

Thor licks my face happily.

"Thor was licking his butt earlier," Seth informs me with a giggle.

"Yuck!" I push the pup onto the floor and wipe my mouth with my hand as the three men laugh at me. "Are you guys going to join us?"

"Hell no." Zack shakes his head and backs toward the door. "We don't do chick flicks."

"No way," Seth agrees, and motions for Thor to join them. "Dad, can we go fishing?"

"Not today, the water is running too fast and too high. We'll have to wait a few weeks for it to recede." Zack pats Seth's shoulder.

"So, does this movie even have a plot?" Josh asks, and pulls me against him tightly.

"Don't be an ass. Of course it does."

"Are there guns? Car chases? Aliens?" he asks hopefully.

"No." I laugh and kiss his cheek. "You're going to survive it, I promise."

"And I don't even know for sure that I'll get sexual favors out of this deal?" He sends me a mock glare and I laugh, holding my stomach.

"You probably will."

"What do I have to do to get a 'definitely'?" He eats an orange Skittles.

"Go pop me some popcorn."

"Done."

CHAPTER
Fifteen

JOSH

"Hey, man, wait up," Zack calls to me as I walk from the barn toward my house. He jogs up to join me, matching my pace.

"What's up?"

"How are things going?" he asks casually, but I know my brother.

"Fine." I eye him suspiciously. "What's going on with you and Jilly?"

"None of your fucking business."

"Come on, Bro." I smirk at him and shake my head. "Cara and Jill are as close to sisters as they can be. You're my brother. Talk to me."

"There's nothing to tell. She went back to LA."

"Have you heard from her?"

He slowly shakes his head no.

"Have you tried to call her?" I push my hands in my pockets.

"No."

"Fuck," I mutter under my breath, and shake my head at him. "One-night stands aren't usually your style."

His jaw tightens as he looks away, and I want to punch him in the chin, but I keep my hands in my pockets and my eyes trained on his face.

He laughs humorlessly and scrubs his hands over his face. "We are a fucked-up pair."

"No, we're not. I know who I want, man. She's right inside with your kid. You'll figure it out too. You always were the slow learner of the two of us."

"You're a dick."

"Yeah, I can be." I grin at him. "Cara will fit in here. Hell, she already does."

"Just be careful, and for God's sake, don't knock her up."

My eyes widen in surprise. "Are you saying that if you could do it all over again, you wouldn't have had Seth?"

"No, I love my kid. I just wish I'd had him with someone else." He brushes his hand through his hair and sighs.

"Well, maybe now you can have more kids with someone else."

"Fuck that."

"What did you really want to talk about, Z?"

"I can't ask you how you are?" He grins when I

glance over at him with a raised brow. "Okay, how are things with Cara?"

"Good."

He nods and looks ahead to the house where Cara is getting her day started tutoring Seth. "She moving in here?"

"That's the plan."

We stop by my truck and I lean my arm against the bed, watching my brother. He won't look me in the eye, and I know it's because he has something to say and doesn't want to piss me off.

"Just say it, Z."

"Is that smart?" he asks quietly, and looks me in the eye.

"She's not *her*," I remind him, and sigh when his eyes harden. "Dude, what were you supposed to do? Your wife was miserable. You tried to give her what you thought she needed."

"Yeah, and where did that get me, J? She fucked anyone who looked at her sideways and abandoned my kid."

I flinch and roughly rub the back of my neck.

"Why didn't you say anything to me about her?"

I don't even pretend to not understand him. "What was I supposed to say, Z? 'She doesn't belong here'? It's not like it was gonna be a forever thing anyway. I have a habit of putting my foot in my mouth, I didn't want to hurt anyone's feelings by telling her she was not welcome here."

Zack shrugs and looks over the pasture to the

mountains and takes a deep breath. "She never would have fit in here. City girls rarely do."

"That didn't have anything to do with it," I murmur. He looks back at me, then shakes his head ruefully. "Besides," I chuckle, "it's not like she's from the big city."

"No, but she grew up in town. What could she possibly know about this life? It's hard for us and it's in our blood."

"True." I nod. "Well, it's just a good thing it didn't turn out to be forever."

"We're all better off without her. I have so much to make up for with Seth. I had no idea things were so bad when I was gone. I don't think it was always the case. I hope it wasn't."

"You'll work it out, man. Seth will be fine. The change in him from the day he arrived to now is like night and day."

CARA

"But I really, really want to go fishing." Seth has folded his hands as if he were praying and is begging to play hooky from today's lesson.

"Seth, we took Friday off for the Huckleberry Festival. We don't want to get too far behind." I smile softly at the handsome boy. He's in his usual long jeans, T-shirt, and sneakers. He's in desperate need of a haircut.

I'll have to take him to town for one this week.

"Cara, you know I already know this stuff. I'll ace the tests. Pleeeeeeease?"

"I don't think so. Where is Thor today?"

I watch as Seth slumps dejectedly in his chair. "He's at the vet. He has to get fixed." He wrinkles his nose and then turns his big hazel eyes on me again. "Please, Cara? I really want to show you how good I am at casting. Dad showed me a really funner way to do it."

"Showed you a *more fun* way to do it," I correct him, and chuckle when he rolls his eyes at me.

"A *more fun* way. It's awesome, and the creek isn't very far away. We can totally walk to it in just a few minutes." He can see I'm softening because he goes in for the kill with "I really want to spend some time with you at the creek. It's my most specialest place ever."

"We really need to work on your grammar," I murmur.

"You're gonna love it, I swear. The poles are still outside by the back door." He points to the back door, his face is happy and hopeful, and I cave.

"Why not?" I ask, and he lets out a whoop. "Come on."

We head out back, and as he gathers the poles and a bucket of worms—gross—I pull my phone out of my pocket.

"Who are you calling?"

"Josh. I need to let him know where we're going. It's not safe to walk about the ranch and not let someone know where we are."

"I think I hear him talking out front."

I stop and listen, and sure enough, I hear voices at the front of the house. "Oh, cool. Okay, I'll run around and let them know we're going, and I'll be right back."

I saunter around the house, and as I get closer, I hear both Josh's and Zack's voices, and what I hear has me stopping in my tracks, right out of their sight.

"What was I supposed to say, Z? 'She doesn't belong here'? It's not like it was gonna be a forever thing anyway. I have a habit of putting my foot in my mouth, I didn't want to hurt anyone's feelings by telling her she was not welcome here."

Josh's words are hard and hit me like a punch to the gut.

"She never would have fit in here. City girls rarely do." I hear the disgust in Zack's voice.

"That didn't have anything to do with it," Josh murmurs. "Besides"—he chuckles humorlessly—"it's not like she's from the big city."

"No, but she grew up in town. What could she possibly know about this life? It's hard for us and it's in our blood."

"True. Well, it's just a good thing it didn't turn out to be forever."

I've heard enough.

Before I hear another word, I turn silently and walk back around the house where Seth is waiting for me.

What the hell was that?

"There you are!" Seth exclaims as I join him on the back deck. "What took you so long?"

"Nothing." I shake my head and force a smile for him. "Ready?"

"Let's do it!" He lifts the poles and pulls them out of my reach when I try to take them from him. "No way, the girl doesn't carry the poles."

"That's very chivalrous of you," I praise him, and ruffle his hair.

"The girl carries the worms!" He laughs and dances out of my reach as I try to tickle him.

"No way!" I cringe and stick my tongue out in disgust. "You get the poles *and* the worms, kid."

Seth laughs, grabs the bucket, and we take off through the pasture to the creek.

"What's *chivelrist*?"

"*Chivalrous*," I correct him.

"Yeah, that."

"It means 'gentlemanly.'"

"Dad says that you should open doors for girls and carry stuff for them and crap like that."

"Yes, your dad is very chivalrous."

"Is Uncle Josh?" Seth swings the bucket back and forth.

"If those worms come flying at me," I warn him sternly, "I will beat you with that fishing pole."

He just laughs hard and continues to swing the bucket. "You will not."

"Will too. Anyway, yes, Josh is chivalrous."

When he's not regretting asking me to move in with him.

"You really like him, huh?" Seth watches me out of the corner of his eye.

"I do."

"Are you gonna marry him and have babies and all that other gross stuff?"

"It's early days yet," I murmur, evading the question. Until about ten minutes ago those things seemed to be a reality, and now I'm not so sure.

"You shouldn't." Seth shakes his head firmly.

"Why?"

"Because getting married sucks. It makes you mean and then you fight all the time, and you mess around with strange men who like to beat your kids."

I stop in my tracks and stare at the boy who is almost the same height as me and is the spitting image of his dad and his uncle.

"Come on!" he urges impatiently, and I fall back into step beside him as we walk past the edge of the pasture and into the brush. I can hear the rush of the creek now, and as we walk just about ten yards farther, I can see and smell it too.

"It's pretty back here," I murmur, and take a deep breath. "Damn, Seth, your dad was right. The water is really high." The water is rushing past us at an alarming rate, deeper than usual because it's crested the banks, due to the snow in higher elevations still melting.

"It's not too bad," he disagrees, and turns pleading eyes to me.

"You stay on the bank, understand? No wading in. This water is too high and running too fast."

He flashes me his grin and my chest tightens. This poor kid has seen so much more than he ever should have.

He strips out of his socks and shoes, rolls his pants up, and I follow suit. I'm in shorts today, so I don't have to worry about getting my pants wet, but I tuck my phone in my bra, just in case.

Seth baits the hooks and hands me a pole. "Okay, I'll show you how to cast." He sounds so mature and sure of himself as he steps into the edge of the water, just close enough to get his toes wet, pulls his pole back over his shoulder, and flings the line smoothly into the water.

"Your dad is a good teacher," I mutter with a smile.

"Yeah, he's not as bad as I thought he was." Seth shrugs as I also cast my line, and we stand in companionable silence for a long minute until I just can't stand it anymore and I have to ask some questions. He's finally talking, it's private and quiet here, and he's doing what he loves.

"So, you know that not all marriages are like your mom and dad's was, right?" I ask nonchalantly.

"I guess," he mutters, and I can tell he's not convinced.

"Did a lot of your mom's boyfriends hurt you?" I cast again.

"Some." I look back at him to find that he's looking down into the water, not paying attention to his pole. He suddenly looks over at me with wide hazel eyes. "Why did she let them do that?"

I sigh deeply and blink the tears away, determined to keep this conversation comfortable and safe for him. "I don't know, buddy." I shake my head and reel my line in. "Some women just shouldn't be moms."

"Yeah." He reels in his own line and casts it out again. "So, my mom is a bad mom."

"It sounds like she won't be winning any mother-of-the-year awards."

"But not all moms are bad."

"Nope, they're not."

He's chewing on the inside of his cheek, watching the spot in the water where his line is sunk. "I hope she never comes back. I love it here, with Dad and Gram and Gramps and Uncle Josh." He looks up at me. "I don't ever have to go back with her, right?"

"No, sweetheart, you don't."

He nods and grins at me. "Maybe someday you'll be my Aunt Cara."

And there goes the wind right out of me.

"Maybe."

The conversation ends there and we cast and reel, cast and reel, for a long while without catching anything. I find my mind wandering as I settle into the rhythm of casting, listening to the wild rush of water and the wind through the trees.

Just what did Josh mean when he said he didn't

want to hurt my feelings by telling me that I am not welcome to live here? If I'm not welcome here, why did he ask me to stay?

I don't get it, but one thing is certain, I'll be damned if I'll move in now.

I suddenly hear an abundance of splashing and glance over at Seth, skipping through the water gleefully.

"Seth, I told you not to go in the water! Those rocks are slippery!"

"It's not so slippery." He jumps deftly from one river rock to the next. "See?"

"Keep splashing like that, and you'll scare all the fish away!" I laugh at him as he plays in the water, then suddenly, to my horror, he slips.

He lets go of his pole and waves his arms frantically, trying to regain his balance, but it's no use. He falls hard, and I can see by the angle that he's hurt his leg.

"Ahhhh!" he cries as he falls into the water.

"Seth!" I throw my pole onto the bank and run as fast as I can through the rushing water to the boy, who is now sitting on his butt.

The water is cold, biting my legs as I scramble to get to Seth. Before he can slip off the rock into the dangerous current, I grip his arm and guide him to a rock on the shoreline.

"Ow!" He holds his ankle up out of the water, and I can see, even from here, that it's broken.

Oh, shit! "Stay where you are!"

His eyes are wide and he's staring at his ankle, clearly in shock. "It hurts, Cara."

"I know, buddy." I grip his calf gently in my palm and hold his leg up, examining it. "I think it's broken, kiddo."

"No!" He starts to cry and leans his forehead against my arm.

"Let me call Josh." With my free hand, I pull my phone from my bra and call Josh's number, praying he picks up.

"Hey, baby."

"I need you." I hear the near panic in my voice, but I can't stop it. "Seth fell in the creek. I think his ankle is broken."

"Where are you?" Josh's voice is bewildered and I can hear Zack in the background.

"I don't know," I choke out, full panic setting in.

"Cara." Josh's voice has hardened. "Listen to me. Where are you, baby? I hear water. Are you at the creek?"

"Yes." I swallow hard. "Seth and I are down at the creek behind the house."

"We'll be there in two minutes."

The line goes dead and I stuff the phone back in my bra.

"Okay, your dad and Uncle Josh will be here in just a few minutes. I'm going to put your ankle in the water to keep it cold, okay?"

He's sobbing now, bracing himself back on his hands on the rock. I lower his ankle into the water, keeping his toes above the waterline.

"You're going to be okay, sweetie. I promise."

"I'm sorry," he sobs. "I didn't mean to."

"It's not your fault."

"You told me not to go into the water."

"Seth, it's okay. You're not in trouble. We'll get you fixed up." I cup his sweet young face in my hand and smile at him, ignoring the fast beat of my heart.

Where are they?

"It hurts," he cries again.

"Okay, focus on my voice. Seth, do you hear me?" He nods and sniffs. "Okay. I'm right here, Seth. You're going to be okay." I make my voice low and steady, willing him to just listen to me and not focus on the pain in his ankle. "Think about how happy Thor is going to be to see you tomorrow. You and Thor can get well together. He'll need extra cuddles too, you know."

"Yeah," Seth mutters, and takes a deep breath.

"Yeah, so just think about how great it'll be to hang out with Thor tomorrow." I hear the roar of the ATVs approaching and thank the good Lord above that help is almost here.

"Your dad is almost here, buddy. Do you hear them?"

He nods and grimaces.

"Okay, you're being really brave, Seth. I'm so proud of you."

"Will you come with me to the hospital?"

"Of course," I tell him firmly. "Do you think I'll let you out of my sight? We're in this together, kid."

"Okay."

"Seth!" Zack calls from behind the bushes at the shoreline.

"Over here!" I call out, careful to keep Seth's leg immobile. My arm is singing in protest at the icy water, but I ignore it and focus on Seth's face.

"Seth!" Zack cries again as he sees us and runs straight into the water, not even caring that he's in jeans and work boots. Josh follows and I've never seen such a welcome sight in all my life.

"What happened?" Zack asks as they approach.

"I fell. I was jumping even though Cara told me not to." Seth starts to cry again, but I brush his hair off his forehead.

"Stop, Seth. It's not your fault." I look up into Zack's and Josh's concerned faces. "I'm holding the ankle elevated and in the cold water. Closest thing I had to ice." I shrug. "I couldn't lift him."

"Excellent." Zack nods. "Okay, Uncle Josh and I are going to get on either side of you and lift you to take you to the ATV, okay?"

Seth nods.

"I'm not gonna lie, Son, it's gonna hurt."

"Okay." Seth nods.

"What can I do?" I ask, and watch as the guys move to Seth's sides.

"You can move out of my way," Josh snaps as he squats next to me. Zack shoots him a hard look, but Josh ignores him. "What were you thinking, Cara? You know better than to leave the house without telling someone where you're going."

"I'm sorry," I reply, shame washing through me.

"I begged her to come," Seth interjects.

"Let me steady his ankle for you," I say.

"Zack and I have this, Cara."

Josh doesn't spare me a glance as I do my best to scoot toward the bank. Seth cries out as I let go of his leg, but when I immediately reach back to grab it, Josh yells, "Back away!"

"Josh." Zack's voice is quiet. "Calm down."

"Mom called the ambulance," Josh says without acknowledging Zack's comment.

"On three," Zack mutters. "One, two, three." They stand in unison, lifting the boy out of the water.

"Ow!"

"I know, Son, I know," Zack croons to him as they walk briskly to the shoreline and up the bank to the four-wheelers.

"Seth, think about Thor," I remind him. "I'm so sorry, you guys," I begin, but Zack cuts me off.

"Accidents happen, honey. We'll get him patched up."

They settle Seth on the back of one of the ATVs. Zack hops on and takes off toward the house.

Josh hops on the other one and glances back at me. "Get on."

"Why are you so angry?" I ask as I swing my leg over and wrap my arms around his waist.

"Because you know better than this, Cara. You knew the creek was too high, you know to never venture out on your own without someone else knowing where you are. Fuck." he shakes his head. "We could be pulling both your bodies out of the water two miles downstream, if we ever found you at all!"

He takes off at top speed toward the house, and I have to hold on tightly to him or fall off the back.

He's right.

He comes to an abrupt stop in his driveway, right behind Zack and Seth. The ambulance is just pulling in.

"Good timing, boys." Josh's mom and dad meet us as well, worry etched in their faces.

"I'm okay," Seth assures them.

"You'll be fine," his grandma agrees, and kisses his head.

"How bad?" Josh's dad asks.

"It's broken," Josh confirms. "But he'll be okay."

Sam Waters and his partner jump out of the ambulance and approach us. "Hey, guys."

"Hey, Sam." I offer him a shaky smile.

"We have to stop meeting under these circumstances, beautiful." He winks at me and I flush.

"Thanks for all you did when the tree fell."

"That's my job." Sam unfastens the straps on the stretcher that they've pulled out of the back of the ambulance. "Ready, Seth?"

"It's gonna hurt again, huh?"

"Yeah, it is, but only for a minute. We'll get you to the hospital fast, okay?"

"Okay."

The guys lift Seth onto the stretcher, strap him in,

and load him into the ambulance. Zack climbs in with Sam as Sam's partner climbs behind the driver's seat.

"Are you coming, Josh?" Sam asks before he pulls the doors closed.

"Absolutely."

"Josh"—I grab his arm—"what do you need me to do?"

"You've done enough." He still doesn't look me in the eye. "I have to go take care of my family."

And you're not a part of it.

His response is a slap to the face. He climbs into the ambulance and they race out of the driveway to the highway.

"Cara," Nancy murmurs, and takes my hand in hers, but I just stand and numbly watch the ambulance drive away.

"It's not your fault, honey." Jeff wraps his arm around me and hugs me to his side. He's tall and broad like his sons, but he has fair hair and blue, kind eyes.

"I know," I whisper.

"Come on, you can ride to the hospital with us," Nancy offers.

I shake my head and back away toward my car. "That's okay. I'll meet you there. I need to change my clothes. Go on ahead and I'll be right behind you."

"Are you sure?" Jeff asks, his voice and face worried. "We'll wait."

"No." I shake my head again and offer them a wobbly smile. "I'll see you soon."

I turn away and hurry into the house, grabbing my things and stuffing them into the suitcase I brought over Friday night when Josh asked me to spend the weekend with him.

An incredible, sexy, fun weekend.

And now, I've learned that he didn't mean to invite me to live here and he blames me for his nephew's being hurt.

I carry my things to the car and pull out. Josh's parents' car is gone.

I hit the highway and head to town, but when I get there, I turn toward my house rather than the hospital.

I told Seth I'd be there for him, but I'll be damned if I'm going to show up where I'm not welcome. I'll call Seth and check in on him later. I need a break from all this drama. I need some distance, and there is only one person I need to be with right now.

I pull up to my house, and as I pull my bag out of the car, I call Ty.

"Bob's Pizza."

"I need a favor."

"Shoot," he says with a chuckle.

"I need a ride to the airport." I unlock the front door and step inside, toss my keys in their bowl, and stride quickly to my bedroom.

"Are you okay?" His voice has lost its humor.

"No. Can you give me a ride?"

"What time?"

"I don't know. I haven't bought the ticket yet." I pull the dirty clothes from my suitcase and throw them in the hamper, then randomly pull clean ones from my drawers and closet and replace them.

"Text me when you know what time."

"Okay, thanks."

I hang up, zip my bag shut, and open my laptop, thankful that I just deposited my insurance check on Thursday, because this is going to be expensive.

Finding a flight out tonight, and feeling nauseous at the amount of money it costs me as I enter my credit card number, I text Ty with the info.

I need to leave in fifteen minutes.

Ty rings my doorbell in ten.

"Thank you," I murmur earnestly as he takes my suitcase from me, watching me carefully.

"What's wrong?" he asks softly.

I just shake my head, tears in my eyes. *I have to hold it together until I get to Jilly.*

He nods once and sighs. "Got it."

CHAPTER

Sixteen

JOSH

"Where is Cara?" Seth cries, his eyes wild and afraid as he looks around the small emergency room at the hospital. "She said she'd be here."

"Seth, I need you to calm down," Dr. Anderson tells him firmly as he examines Seth's ankle. "Order X-ray, stat," he instructs his nurse. "We're going to have X-ray come see you to see what's happening in there, Seth. I'll be back with the results in a bit." The doctor smiles at all of us and hurries out of the room.

"I want Cara," Seth repeats, crossing his arms over his chest and scowling.

"Where is she?" I ask my mom, who is standing in the opposite corner of the room, leaning against my dad's chest.

"She said she would meet us here." She shrugs and frowns. "She should be here soon."

I pull my phone out of my pocket and dial Cara's number, only to have it go straight to voice mail. I redial, just in case she was trying to call me at exactly the same moment, but it again goes to voice mail.

"Her phone is turned off," I mutter.

"Hopefully it didn't get ruined in the creek when she was holding Seth's leg," Zack responds, glaring at me.

What the hell?

Before I can respond, the X-ray techs bustle into the room.

"We need everyone out, please." A young woman with blond hair, dressed in blue scrubs, pulls a high-tech X-ray machine into the room and positions Seth for the images.

"What the hell, man?" I mutter to Zack, out of our parents' earshot. He simply shakes his head and hurries back into Seth's room when the tech leaves.

I try Cara's cell again, and my stomach clenches in fear when it goes straight to voice mail.

Where the fuck is she?

Long minutes later, the doctor returns with a grim look on his face and dark gray X-ray films in his hands. He pushes them against a backlit frame on the wall and turns to face us.

"I'm afraid I don't have fantastic news. You did a good job on that ankle, Seth." The doctor points to the anklebone on the film. I'm no doctor, and even I can see that it's severely broken. "See here where the bone is completely separated from itself? This isn't something that can heal with just a cast. I'm afraid you're going to need surgery, buddy."

"Can you do that here?" Zack asks with a frown.

"Yes, we have an excellent orthopedic team. We'll get him into surgery in about twenty minutes."

"That's fast," Mom mutters with surprise.

"We have an OR available, and I want to get this set as soon as possible." The doctor smiles reassuringly at a shocked Seth. "Don't worry, you're going to be fine."

The nurse bustles in to prepare Seth for surgery, and before we know it, the anesthesiologist arrives.

"I want Cara," Seth whimpers. "She said we were in this together."

"I know, buddy. She'll be here when you wake up."

Seth is whisked to surgery, and Zack, Mom and Dad, and I are led to the surgical waiting room, where we pour horrible coffee and wait.

I dial Cara's number again and curse when I get voice mail.

"Where the hell is she?" I ask the room at large.

"I wouldn't have followed you here either," Zack replies calmly, and grimaces when he takes a sip of his coffee.

"What the hell, man? What is your problem?"

"You were a dick to her today, Bro."

"I was not."

"What happened?" Dad asks as I scowl at all of them.

"You should have seen him at the creek." Zack

shakes his head and throws his untouched coffee into the trash. "She was doing everything right, and he snapped at her to get the hell out of his way."

"I didn't snap at her, and she wasn't doing everything right. She put herself and Seth in danger, and she knew she was wrong."

"Yeah, she screwed up. Who hasn't? But she was doing everything right with Seth."

I cross my arms over my chest to suppress the need to punch my brother and break his nose all over again.

"I get that you were panicked, but so was she, and you were a dick," Zack repeats. "Before you got in the ambulance you told her you needed to go take care of your family. You made it pretty clear that Cara wasn't included in that."

"She was devastated," Mom chimes in. "I didn't want her to drive herself, but she insisted."

"Fuck." I push my hands through my hair and pace across the small space. "I didn't mean that."

"I know." Mom smiles at me and pats my arm reassuringly. "You were worried about our boy. But you hurt your girl today."

"Where is she?" I ask again, fear and anger growing in me. "If she promised Seth she'd be here, she should be here."

"Go find her," Zack suggests, lounging back in his chair and watching me calmly.

"I'll wait until Seth is out of surgery."

I pull my cell out and send Cara a text, just in case she turns her phone back on.

I just need to know that you're safe, baby. Seth is in surgery. Please call me.

The following three hours drag in a blur of more bad coffee, pacing and sitting, and more pacing.

I continue to call Cara's phone, getting more and more angry each time I hear her voice mail.

When I find her, I'm going to take her over my knee and spank her spectacular ass until it glows.

The surgeon finally walks into the room and smiles. "Mr. King?"

"There are three of us," Dad tells him with a grin. "Zack is Seth's father."

"Seth is doing great. The surgery went well, and he'll be moved to his room in about half an hour. He's already coming out of the anesthetic. He'll be in a cast for a while, and there won't be any more swimming this summer, but he should be recovered by the time school starts."

"Can I see him?" Zack asks anxiously.

"The nurse will come get you when he's in his room."

"Thank you," we all murmur.

"Okay, go find your girl." Mom grins at me and leans her head on Dad's shoulder. "We've got things handled here."

Her car is in the driveway, and my anger spikes again. She's home, rather than at the hospital as she promised.

She belongs with us.

I pound on her front door after ringing the doorbell.

No answer.

I peek in her windows, but don't see any movement, so I make my way around her small house to the back door and pound there for a good five minutes, still not getting an answer.

I'm really fucking sick of not having Cara answer me.

I pull my phone out and call her number again and curse a blue streak when I get her voice mail.

Returning to her front door, I continue to pound until my fist is sore.

"She's not there."

I twirl at the sound of Ty's angry voice behind me. He's standing a good five yards away on Cara's sidewalk, his hands shoved in his pockets and his face as angry as I've ever seen it.

"Where the fuck is she?"

He smirks and shakes his head. "I can't tell you that."

My feet carry me down the steps and to my best friend of nearly thirty years without any thought, and I grip his shirt in my fists, pushing my nose an inch away from his.

"Where. The. Fuck. Is. She?"

"She's not home. I don't know what the hell happened, but she couldn't even talk to me, Josh." Ty narrows his eyes on me. "I should kick your ass. Cara is as much my sister as Jilly is, and she was shattered when I saw her."

"Tell me where she is." I drop my hands and step back, panting. My heart is racing, and for the first time, true fear joins the anger in my gut.

"No." He shakes his head and pushes his hands through his hair. "I can't. The women in my life have taken too much shit from assholes."

"Goddamn it, Ty, you know that's not me!" I yell, and pace away, frustration rolling off me.

"You didn't see her face." He shakes his head. "She won't see you now. How is Seth?"

"He'll be fine." I swallow as I remember the scene at the creek. Seth crying and sitting in the frigid water, and Cara standing with him, holding his leg, reassuring him.

I fucked up.

"Please." I meet Ty's gaze with mine. "This was a misunderstanding. C'mon, Ty, you know I love her."

"Go be with your family. Keep me updated."

"Damn, Ty."

"You didn't see her, man. You'd do the same. Go be with Seth and give Cara a few days to calm down."

With that, he turns, hands still in his pockets, and walks toward his house without looking back.

"Ty knows where she is," I inform my parents, and slump in a chair as they eat chicken from a bucket in a hospital waiting room.

I've never before seen my mom eat chicken that she herself didn't fry.

"He's right," Mom mutters, and frowns at the mashed potatoes and gravy. "She'll come around. Give her some breathing room."

"I need to apologize and shake some sense into her." I stand and pace around the room. "Is Seth awake?"

"He is. Zack is with him," Dad confirms. "Your chicken is so much better than this," he mutters to Mom, who smiles lovingly at him.

Zack saunters in and sinks in a chair, grabbing a piece of chicken as he does.

"How is he?" Mom asks.

"Pretty good, actually. A bit sleepy, but he's not in any pain."

"Good."

I call Cara's phone, elated when it rings, but curse when it goes to voice mail yet again.

"That horrible language isn't going to make her answer the phone," Mom says matter-of-factly.

"I just wish I knew where she is." The adrenaline is gone now, replaced by worry. Regret.

Fear.

"You could go ask Seth," Zack mentions casually, as if my world weren't falling apart around me. "He's talking to her right now."

I immediately hurry out of the waiting room, down the hall to Seth's room, and push my way inside. He glances up with Zack's cell pressed to his ear and says, "I won't."

"Please hand me the phone, Seth," I murmur calmly, not wanting to scare the boy. He hands it to me and I immediately stalk out to the hallway, almost running headfirst into Zack.

"Where the hell are you?"

The line goes dead.

"Where is she?" I demand.

"I don't know," Zack insists. "She wouldn't tell me when I asked. She just wanted to talk to Seth, to make sure he's okay."

"I wonder if she told Seth."

"If you're going in that room," Zack warns me with narrowed eyes, "you'd better damn well be calm, J. I don't need you scaring the shit out of my kid."

"Jesus, man, I'm not going to scare Seth."

We both open Seth's door and walk in calmly. Seth is sleepy, but smiles at us when we approach his bedside.

"Hey, buddy, did Cara tell you where she went?" I ask as I push my hand over his soft hair.

"Yeah."

"Can you tell me?"

He shakes his head and frowns. "I promised I wouldn't."

"Seth." Zack sits on the edge of Seth's bed and cups Seth's face in his hand. "Uncle Josh is really worried about Cara."

"You hurt her feelings," Seth whispers.

"I know," I reply. "I just want to make sure she's safe, Seth." I brush his hair off his forehead and offer him a small smile. "I love you, buddy. I'm glad Cara called you to make sure you're okay."

"She loves all of us, Uncle Josh. She didn't mean to put me in danger."

"I know." I sigh. "Please tell me where she is so I can tell her I'm sorry."

"I can't. I promised." He shakes his head resolutely. "I trust her and she trusts me."

"Seth," Zack says, catching his attention. "Do you remember how you felt when you thought that I didn't love you and I didn't want to be with you?"

"Yeah," he whispers.

"Cara and Josh both feel like that now. Josh needs to find her so he can make it right."

Seth twists his lips, his face pale from his ordeal, and grips the blanket in his fingers.

"She's with Jill."

Zack curses under his breath and pushes his hands through his hair.

"She left the *state*?" I ask incredulously.

"Well, she was calling from some other city where she's waiting for another plane to take her to LA." Seth's voice is small and shaky. "Are you mad at her?"

"I'm furious." I nod. "But don't worry, I'll figure it out."

"There aren't any more flights out tonight," Zack reminds me softly. "You'll have to catch one in the morning."

"I'm going back to the house." I look up into Zack's face. "I need to pack and book my flight."

"Go. We're fine."

"I want regular calls with updates." I look back over at Seth and wince. "I'm sorry, buddy."

"It's okay. Dad and Gram and Gramps are here. Go find Aunt Cara." He slips into sleep before he can see the stunned look on my face.

Hell yes, she's your Aunt Cara.

"Call me when you get there." Zack grins at me and claps his hand on my shoulder. "Go grovel for forgiveness. I recommend having chocolate with you." He frowns as his phone pings and scowls when he reads the message.

"Who is it?"

"Jillian." His eyes find mine and then he reads the message again. "She's just checking on Seth. Cara must have filled her in."

"You look surprised."

"I haven't heard from her since the Fourth," Zack murmurs as he types a response with his thumbs and shoves his phone back in his pocket.

"Maybe you should do some groveling of your own?"

He sighs and shakes his head. "What is up with women today?"

"Full moon?"

He chuckles. "I think they're like this every day."

"Like what, difficult?"

"No, maddening."

He's probably right.

*   *   *

"Attention please. All flights are now delayed indefinitely due to severe weather. Flight information will be updated as we have it. Repeat . . ."

"Son of a bitch," I mutter, and lean back in the hard, black airport seat. I dial Zack's number and sigh.

"Did you get there?"

"No, I'm stranded in Salt Lake City. All of the flights are grounded."

"It can't be snowing," he mutters incredulously.

"No, thunderstorms." I stand and pace to the window to watch long streaks of lightning touch down in the distance. "It's a killer storm. Great timing."

"I'm sorry, man. How long have you been there?"

"All day."

"Dude, it's ten o'clock at night."

"I know, it's been a shitty day."

"Have you slept?"

"A little on the flight down here."

"Maybe you should go get a hotel room and rest and then fly down tomorrow."

"Is that what you would do?" I ask.

He laughs. "Fuck no."

"Exactly." I return to my seat and sigh. "I'll text you when I get there."

"Be safe."

He hangs up and I decide to take a chance that Cara has turned her phone back on and dial her number.

My heart stutters when it rings.

On the third ring, I hear Jill's voice. "You're an ass." She slurs the last part of *ass*, making it *ash*.

"Excuse me?"

"No, let me tell him!" I hear Cara's panicked voice in the background and I cross my arms, interested to hear where this is going.

At least she's safe.

"You're a jerk, King," Jill resumes.

"I know."

"Good. He knows," she informs Cara, making me smile for the first time in more than twenty-four hours. "It wasn't cool to say that Cara isn't welcome to move to the Lazy K after you already asked her."

"Wait. What?" I'm stunned. I know I never told her that.

"You said that you didn't want to put your foot in your mouth the way you always do and hurt her feelings, and it's not a forever thing anyway."

"I didn't say that."

"She heard you with her own ears."

"Jill, stop!" I hear Cara shriek, as I rack my brain.

"And then you had to drive the nail even deeper in her heart and make it clear that she's not part of your family."

My heart climbs up in my throat. *Jesus, she heard my conversation with Z.* "Jill—"

"No, you listen to me, pal. You had no problem fucking her brains out with that impressive cock of yours—"

"*Jillian!*" Cara yells.

"—but if you didn't want to live with her, you should have just manned up and been honest. Grow a pair, King. If I was in Montana right now, I'd hunt you down and shove my foot so far up your ass you'd have toes for teeth!"

"Ouch," I mutter, and grimace. "Listen to me. Cara misunderstood."

"No, she didn't!"

"I was talking about Kensie, Jill. Not Cara. She didn't hear the whole conversation." Jill grows quiet, and I can hear Cara in the background.

"What is he saying? Hang up, Jillian."

"Do not hang up this phone." My voice is hard, and I've never been so pissed in my life. "She ran because she misunderstood a conversation that didn't include her and because I was a dick when Seth got hurt. I'm on my way, Jill."

"What?" She sounds perfectly sober now, and I hear her stand and move away from Cara.

"Seth told me that she was on her way to you. I'm stuck in Salt Lake, but I should be there later tonight."

She doesn't answer for a long minute and I'm afraid she's hung up.

"Jill?"

"I'm here. If you're lying to me . . ."

"I'm not. Leave the front door unlocked. I'll be there late. And, Jill?"

"Yeah?"

"Tell her—"

"No, tell her yourself. Hurry up, loverboy."

She hangs up and I grin as I push my phone in my pocket and check the flight status on the large television screen above the windows ahead.

Delayed.

"Damn," I murmur.

"You're trying to get to your girl." An older woman sitting opposite me is knitting a red scarf and smiles at me.

"Yeah."

"Must be pretty important." She pushes the yarn down the needle.

"It is."

"My daughter had a baby yesterday, and I'm on my way to spend time with her and her family." I'm surprised. She doesn't look old enough to be a grandmother. She smiles again, and I take a deep breath and sit back, giving her my attention.

"Congratulations."

"Thank you." She leans down and rifles through her large yellow carry-on and comes out with two candy bars. "Snickers?"

"Thanks." I accept the candy and take a big bite, realizing how hungry I am.

"I wish my Richard were here to see our first grandbaby," she murmurs quietly, her eyes on her candy bar. "He passed away a few months ago."

"I'm sorry to hear that."

She nods and then meets my gaze again. "Time goes so fast. I know you probably hear that all the time, but it's true. There isn't anything I wouldn't give to have my Richard here to fight with me again." Her smile is sad as she watches me, and I just don't know what to say. "Do you know what would always work to soften me up when I was mad at him?" she asks with a grin.

"Chocolate?" I hold up my candy wrapper.

"No." She laughs and shakes her head. "Just an honest apology. It's surprising how hard it is to say the words *I'm sorry*. When we were young, he was so damn stubborn. But he finally learned that all he had to do was say he was sorry."

"I was a jerk yesterday."

"It happens." She shrugs and returns to her knitting.

"But I'm pissed at her too." I clench my hands into fists.

"Well, you wouldn't love her if you weren't."

"I wish the weather would break." I scowl and watch the rain outside.

"You'll get there when you're supposed to get there."

I just pray I'm not too late.

CHAPTER

Seventeen

CARA

"What the hell did you just do?" I demand as Jill stumbles back into her living room, weaving through the plethora of shopping bags scattered about from today's shopping trip.

According to Jill, all worries can be solved with retail therapy.

"I told him off." She refills both our wineglasses.

"You had to leave the room to do it?" I sip the sweet white Moscato.

"I had to pee."

"So you peed while you told him off?" I giggle.

"He didn't know." She waves me off and takes a long drink. "I know it's shitty circumstances, but I'm glad you're here."

"Me too. I miss you. When are you moving home?"

Jill bites her lip and stares down into her glass.

"Jilly?"

"I'm thinking about moving home soon, actually."

"Really?" I screech, and jump up and down on the cushions of her couch. "Why? When?"

"In the next few weeks." She shrugs and pulls her legs up under her.

"Spill."

"Todd and his new wife are pregnant," she whispers, and blinks tears away as she drinks her wine, stunning me into silence. "Five years," she murmurs. "We tried to have a baby for five years, Cara."

"I know." I take her hand in mine and squeeze.

"All those medications and hormones and trips to the doctors." She sighs and clenches her eyes shut. "I don't know how many times I was on my back, feet in stirrups, for all of LA County to see. And not once could anyone tell me *why* I couldn't get pregnant."

"Is that why he left you?" I ask quietly. "You never would tell anyone."

"No." She shakes her head and refills her glass. I consider suggesting she slow down, but what's the harm? "I left him because I came home early from work one afternoon to find him fucking Sheila in our bed."

"Sheila the new wife?" My voice is an octave higher than normal, my eyes wide in alarm.

"The same one." She toasts me with her glass. "He said that it was my fault. I was too preoccupied with getting pregnant, only wanting to have sex when I was ovulating, blah, blah, blah. At the end of the day, he fucked around because he's an asshole."

I nod, shocked. "And then he married her?"

"Oh, honey"—Jill laughs humorlessly—"he married her two days after our divorce was final."

"No fucking way!" I can't feel my lips now as I fill my glass again. "What an asshole!"

"First-class asshole, for sure." She bites her lip and looks at me with big tears in her eyes. "Why couldn't I give him a baby, Cara? What's wrong with me?"

"Oh, sweetie, nothing is wrong with you. Maybe you just weren't supposed to have babies with *him* because he's a first-class asshole."

"I guess."

"Is that why you came home for the holiday?"

"Yeah, I had just found out and I needed to be home to clear my head. And I realized that home is where I need to be. The only thing holding me here is my job, and I can sell houses back home just as easily as I can here."

"Yes, you can." I smile widely.

"Can I crash with you?"

"Of course. Like you even have to ask." My phone beeps with an incoming text. "You didn't turn it off?"

Josh: **I miss you.**

"No, what's the point?" She leans her head against the couch and sighs.

"I don't want to be nice to him." I frown at the phone as the letters blur together. "I mean, I know I screwed up, but he wasn't very nice to me."

"Don't be."

"Okay." I grin as I begin to text him back.

Meat me above.

"What did you say?"

"I told him to leave me alone," I smirk. "Okay, now let's talk about Zack."

"He's so sexy," Jill purrs. "Like, so, so, so, so sssssssexy."

"God, you're so drunk." I laugh and take another sip of wine, dribbling some down my blouse. My phone beeps again.

Josh: **Huh?**

"He's not the brightest lightbulb in the box, is he?" I ask Jill, and try again.

Go Adam.

"There, I told him to go away." I lay the phone on the coffee table and settle back with my wine. "Okay, tell me about Zack. Is he hung?"

"Are you paying me back for when I was home and hounded you about Josh?"

"Hell to the yes!"

"They're identical-twin brothers, Cara. What do you think?"

"Oh, I hadn't thought of that." I take a sip and think about Josh's beautiful body. "Does he have a freckle right here?" I point to my pelvis, just to the left of my pubis.

"Yes! How funny." She giggles and takes a sip of wine, also thinking. "Does Josh have dimples above his ass?"

"Yes, and, oh my God, they are so fucking lickable." I fall back against the cushions as if in the middle of an orgasm, making Jill laugh.

"I know! And their shoulders? Hello, hot muscles!"

We're laughing in earnest now, our wine set aside.

"When he kisses, is it, like, hot and intense, or soft and sweet?" I ask, daydreaming about Josh kissing me.

"Zack is super intense. Like, he grips on to my neck, not like he's choking me, just, you know, holding on to me, and kisses like he never wants to stop. Damn, he's really good at it."

"Josh is too."

"Does Josh do this thing where he hooks your legs up over his shoulders—"

"And pushes down on the backs of your thighs?"

"Yes! Oh my God, that makes me hot." Jill fans herself.

"I wonder if they ever compare notes."

We just stare at each other for a few seconds, then burst into giggles again.

"So what happened?" I ask. "Why didn't you tell him you were leaving in the morning? The sex didn't suck."

"The sex was ah-mazing, like with a capital *A*." She frowns, pursing her pretty pink lips. "I didn't expect him to fuck me and then slip out in the middle of the night without saying good-bye."

"I don't think it was a one-night-stand thing, Jill." My eyes won't stay open now. "Jesus, how much wine did we have?"

"Three bottles. Why don't you think it was a one-nighter?"

"Because the next day he was freaked-out, asking me where you were."

"What?" she screeches, and pulls on my arm. "You never told me that!"

"I figured he would have called you."

"He hasn't." She sighs and lays her head on my lap. I sink my fingers in her thick dark hair and comb my fingers through it, over and over.

"Maybe he doesn't know what to say," I offer.

"Maybe the sex really wasn't very good, and he just didn't know how to tell me." She sighs deeply and then sits straight up. "Shit!"

"What?"

"If I move home, I'm gonna hafta see him all the time." She squishes up her nose. "That'll be 'barrassing."

"Nah, you'll be fine."

"We'll see, I guess." She stares at me through glassy eyes. "Don't be mad at me tomorrow, okay?"

"Why would I be mad?" I ask with a frown.

"You just might. So don't. Because I love you."

"I love you too." I hug her close and then stand and pause to get my balance as the room spins around me. "I'm going to bed."

"Me too."

"Good night, Jillybean."

"Good night, Carebear."

*   *   *

Dear God, it's too bright in here. I throw my arm over my face and groan as I turn over onto my side and pray that I won't throw up.

Jill fed me way too much wine last night.

I scrub my hand over my face and down my body, frowning when I discover that I'm naked.

Damn, I didn't even pull on my pajamas before I fell into bed last night.

My mouth is dry and my head hurts, so I sit up, still not opening my eyes, and try to boost my energy up enough to get out of bed and hunt down some Advil and a glass of water.

The covers fall around my waist and my nipples pucker in the air-conditioned air. I take a deep breath and open my eyes and squeal in alarm.

"Holy shit!"

"Good morning."

Josh is sitting in a chair on the other side of the room. He's leaning forward, his elbows resting on his knees. His fingers are threaded together and dangling between his knees.

He's in jeans and a rumpled button-down, and his hair is a mess from pushing his hands through it over and over.

Despite his casual appearance, his face is hard, and his brown eyes are the angriest that I've ever seen them.

"What are you doing here?" I whisper, my hangover instantly forgotten.

"There's water and Advil on the table next to you." His voice is calm.

Too calm.

With my eyes still on his, I take a long drink of water and toss back the Advil.

"What are you doing here?"

He doesn't answer, he just watches me, unblinking, until I frown and cover my nakedness.

"If you're not speaking to me, why did you come?" I ask, my voice rising. "And how did you get in?"

"Jill let me in. Watch yourself with me, Carolina. It took me a very long time to get here."

"Why are you here?"

"Because I told you once before, if you run, I'll find you. I meant it. Why did you run, Cara?"

God, I hate his voice right now. It's cold, and he's way across the room, and he hasn't made a move to touch me.

I so want him to touch me.

"Do you want the long or the short list?" I ask sarcastically, and hate myself when I see a flash of hurt cross his face before he schools his features.

"I want the truth."

"I left because I overheard you tell Zack that you regretted asking me to move in with you, and I left because you made me feel like a piece of shit about what happened to Seth."

"I am so fucking pissed at you right now," he mutters, his voice low.

"Yeah? Well, I'm fucking pissed too, Joshua." I push my hair off my face and glare at him.

"First of all"—he leans back and crosses his arms over his chest, watching me intently—"that conversation you heard wasn't about you at all. If you'd come by a few seconds earlier, you would have heard that we were talking about Zack's ex-wife."

My jaw drops and eyes widen. "Are you fucking kidding me?"

"Oh, I'm pretty serious right now, Cara. Let me finish."

I frown and close my mouth, waiting for him to continue.

"I apologize for the way I acted when Seth was hurt. I was worried about both of you, and when I saw that you were safe, I was just worried about getting help for Seth. I don't even remember what I said, but Zack filled me in and busted my ass for it."

"How can you say you were worried about me? You didn't spare me a glance. You didn't even ask me if I was okay! You just made it perfectly clear that I fucked up!"

"I'm sorry! I was panicked."

"And you think I wasn't? I had your nephew's broken ankle in my hand and I was standing in ice-cold water!" My adrenaline has kicked in now, and if he thinks he's going to get off easy with a simple *I'm sorry*, he's sorely wrong.

"Fucking A," he spits out, and scratches his scalp vigorously in agitation.

I sit and glare at him, wanting nothing more than to wrap him in my arms and soothe us both.

"What *I'm* most fucking pissed about," he continues, noticeably calming his voice, making me meet his gaze again, "is the fact that you didn't trust me. You assumed that I would betray you, even after everything I've said and done with you."

My eyes widen.

"You doubted my love for you, Carolina, and that cut me deeper than anything else you could have ever done."

"You weren't showing me love—" I begin, but he cuts me off.

He sighs and rests his face in his hands. "You shredded me."

"Back at you." I fling the covers off me and jerk the dress I was wearing last night over my head in quick, angry movements.

"If you try to run from me right now, Cara, so help me . . ."

"I'm just getting dressed! I can't fight with you naked!" Satisfied that I'm now covered, I quickly pull my hair up into a knot to keep it out of my way.

"I'm not a part of your family. I get it. But the way you spoke to me before you got in that ambulance—"

"I did not tell you that you aren't a part of my family!" His voice rises as he stands and paces around the room. "Jesus, Cara, I asked you to move in with me. If I didn't think of you as a part of my family, I never would have done that."

"You were cold and heartless, and not the man I'd fallen in love with. I saw a side to you that scared the fuck out of me, Josh."

He stops before the window, staring outside, and braces his hands on his hips.

"I'm sorry," he murmurs, and then turns to look at me again. "I'm very sorry for that. I'm excellent in dealing with emergencies when it comes to the animals on the ranch, but seeing Seth hurt, and that rushing water, knowing you could have both been killed, it just destroyed me, and then . . ."

His hands shake as he pushes them through his hair. "I couldn't find you." He swallows, his voice quiet and rough. "I've never been that scared in my life. I didn't know if something had happened to you. I couldn't find you."

His voice catches and he stops talking, swallows again, and shakes his head in disbelief as he leans his hips against the windowsill, and in this moment, my resolve disappears and I'll do anything to make this right.

"I couldn't find you. You own me, Carolina. Body and soul. I promise this will never happen again."

I stay still, watching him carefully, taking in the handsome man who possesses my heart.

"I'm sorry too. I shouldn't have handled it like that."

"I need to know that you're not going to run again. If you get scared, come *to* me, baby."

"And I need to know that when we're in a crisis again

that I can depend on you to be the strong man that took care of me when the tree fell through my roof."

"Who the fuck is Adam?" he suddenly asks.

"What?" I'm struck dumb, frowning at him. "I don't know an Adam."

He pulls his phone out of his pocket, wakes it up and brings up my text messages, and holds the phone out, showing them to me.

Cara: **Meat me above.**

Cara: **Go Adam.**

"Fucking autocorrect," I mutter, and then start to giggle. I clap my hand over my mouth, my eyes wide and glued to his phone, and then I can't stand it anymore, the dam bursts, and I begin laughing and laughing, holding my belly and falling back on the bed.

I let out a most unladylike snort, and that makes me laugh even harder.

"I don't even remember," I gasp, "what the fuck I was trying to say."

The laughter begins to calm and I sit up and push my hair off my face, panting and wiping the tears from my eyes. When I glance at Josh, he's grinning at me, his eyes soft and loving, and I think the storm is almost over.

He tosses the phone on the nearby dresser, pins me in his gaze, and sighs. "Come here, Cara."

Staying where I am, I slowly shake my head back and forth and take a long, deep breath.

"No?" he asks quietly, and again I shake my head.

He crosses his arms over his chest and narrows his eyes. "Come. Here."

"Why?"

He raises his eyebrows and doesn't answer, the dimple in his cheek still winking at me, waiting for me to do as he asks.

Finally, I stand, walk around the bed, and stop a few feet in front of him. "Now what?"

His eyes travel leisurely down my body and back up again, taking in my hair and eyes. No part of me goes untouched by his eyes.

"I can't stay mad at you when you laugh like that," he murmurs. "I love it when you laugh."

"Josh?"

"Yes."

"I love you."

He doesn't move.

"I really need . . ." I hate how my voice quivers as my emotions surge to the surface.

"What?"

"I really need you to hug me."

He watches me for a long moment, then closes his eyes and exhales deeply and folds me into his arms, holding me hard and close, and I begin to cry in earnest, relieved that he's here.

"I love you too, Cara," he whispers in my ear.

"I'm so sorry," I cry.

"Me too." He kisses my head and runs his hands up and down my back.

"I thought you didn't want me."

"Cara, how could you think that?" His arms tighten more, as though he's afraid I'll run again. "After everything we've been though?"

"I know it's stupid now, but it just sounded so horrible and I didn't think to ask you who you were talking about."

He swoops down and lifts my dress over my head and me into his arms, lays me gently against the soft sheets, and then stands up.

"You're entirely overdressed," I inform him with a shaky smile.

He yanks his shirt out of his jeans and strips out of it, giving me an awesome view of his muscular torso. He unfastens his belt buckle and jeans and hastily shoves them down his legs, along with his shorts, and comes back to me, completely naked.

"That's better."

I reach out to take his beautiful cock in my hand, but he pulls back and takes my hand in his, kissing my knuckles as he joins me on the bed.

"I'm gonna have to take a rain check on having your sweet hands on me, sweetheart. I want you too much right now."

He covers me and pushes his forearms under my shoulders, cradles my head in his hands. His face is just inches from mine, his body flush against my own from our chests all the way down to our feet. His erection is pressed against my belly.

"Love the way you feel," I murmur, and brush my fingertips up and down his back.

"Cara," he whispers, and sweeps his lips over mine softly. "I love everything about you." He nibbles the corners of my lips before kissing me again, just as softly. "You take my breath away."

"Josh—"

"Let me finish," he whispers, and drags his lips down my jawline to my ear. "I love everything about you." He tugs my earlobe between his teeth, making me squirm beneath him. "I love your sexy curves." He kisses down my neck to my collarbone. "I love how your eyes are amber when you're pissed, hazel when you're happy, and bright green when you're turned on, like you are right now."

He lifts up onto his elbows so he can smile down at me, his dimple winks at me, and I kiss it gently.

"I can't get enough of your sweet smile." He nibbles my lips again and grins at me. "You take me to a place that no one else can. You own me."

I pull my fingers down his face, not noticing the tears falling down my temples, and frown up at him. "You said that before."

"I don't think you understand, baby. I'm yours. Always. You are it for me." He rests his forehead against mine. "You destroy me."

"You are everything I've ever wanted," I whisper. "You make me a better woman."

"Baby," he whispers, and brushes his thumbs over my cheeks. He pulls his hips back and sinks completely inside me. He rests there and gazes lovingly down at me. "No more running."

"No more." I cup his ass in my hands as he begins to move, slowly and reverently, sending goose bumps all along my body. The head of his cock drags along my pussy. I clench around him, moving my hips with his.

"You always feel amazing."

"Mmm." I grin. "I was just telling Jill last night about how amazing it is to make love with you."

He stills and stares down at me and then throws his head back and laughs. "How much did you guys have to drink?"

"Three bottles." I shrug, then giggle again.

"Ah, baby, when you giggle, your pussy clenches on my dick in the most crazy way."

"I don't think we're supposed to laugh when we make love," I inform him haughtily.

"No?"

"Nuh-uh."

"Okay." He kisses me deeply and pulls his hands down my shoulders, my sides, and up to my breasts, brushing his thumbs over my nipples.

"Oh, God."

"You like that?" He does it again.

"Yeah," I gasp.

He leans in and kisses me deeply, his hips pick up speed, and he continues to worry my nipples, sending a straight line of electricity from my nipples to my core, and I feel myself begin to shudder around him. His hands glide down to cup my ass, and he tilts my hips up, sinking even farther into me.

"That's it, my love. Come for me."

"Oh, sweet Jesus," I mutter, and fall apart in his arms, circling my hips and pulsing against him as he pushes as far inside me as he can go and cries out as he comes with me.

"I love you, Carolina," he gasps.

"I love you too, Joshua."

"Thank you." I smile at Jill and give her a big hug as Josh pulls our bags out of her car.

"For what?" She hugs me tight.

"For always being here." I grin at her and feel tears well up in my eyes.

"Stop! No crying. I'll see you in, like, two weeks." She strolls over to Josh, who pulls her in for a hug and whispers something in her ear, making her grin.

"Hurt her again and I'll be your worst nightmare."

"Right," he smirks. "You're a tiny little thing."

She raises her eyebrows and mutters, "Toes for teeth."

"Point taken." He laughs and nods. "Don't worry, Jilly."

"I always worry." She shrugs and waves as she saunters back to the driver's side of her car, ready to pull away from the departures lane at LAX.

"See you soon!" I wave and follow Josh into the airport.

"You know I hate to fly, right?"

"You do?" I ask, surprised, and join him in line.

"Yeah, I do." He drapes his arm over my shoulders, pulling me against his chest.

"I miss Jill already."

"So she's moving home?" He kisses my hair.

"In a couple weeks, yeah."

"It'll be here before you know it." He kisses my head again. "Your hair always smells so good."

I smile softly, enjoying the feel of his hard chest against my cheek. "I'm glad you like it."

We move quickly through the line, check our bags, and make our way through security. We finally make it to our gate and sit as we wait for boarding to begin.

"Are you ready to go home?" I ask.

"Very ready." He pulls me against him again. He has barely stopped touching me since he showed up in my bedroom at Jill's condo yesterday.

"How is Seth doing?" I trace my finger up and down his thigh, content to lie against his chest for as long as he'll have me.

"He's good. They're home now. He just has to take it easy."

"Poor kid. I feel so bad." I sigh deeply. "If I hadn't let him talk me into going fishing . . ."

"Stop that." Josh pulls me back to look him in the eye and grips my chin between his thumb and fingers. "It was an accident, Cara. I'm sorry if I ever gave you the impression that I thought otherwise."

"I know it was an accident, but I still feel badly about it. Poor guy." I frown as I recall the conversation Seth and I were having right before he fell.

"Josh, I need to tell you something."

"What is it?"

"With everything that happened, it completely slipped my mind." I recap my conversation with Seth and watch Josh's eyes grow colder and harder with every word. "I wouldn't normally betray a confidence, but as a teacher, it's my job to tell you. I think you should talk to Zack about putting him in some sort of counseling. There are a few I can recommend."

"I'll tell him." Josh sighs deeply and pulls me against him again. "That poor kid."

"I know. My heart breaks for him. Thank God he's not with her anymore."

"Never again," Josh agrees with conviction.

"Cara." Josh's soothing voice wakes me up. I fell asleep in his truck on the way home. "We're home."

I blink and frown as I realize that we're at the ranch.

"But we didn't stop at my house so I could get my things."

"You have your suitcase. I'm sure you can make do for a little while."

He grins happily and pulls himself out of his truck, strides around to open my door, and helps me down from the cab.

We grab our bags, and just as we get to the front door, he leans down and whispers in my ear, "Welcome home, baby."

We move through the front door and I stop in my tracks. "You invited your family?" I whisper to him in shock.

"We wanted to welcome you home, sweet girl." Nancy smiles from the kitchen as she mixes up what looks like a pasta salad. "Besides, you've got to be hungry."

Zack and Jeff and even Ty are sitting on barstools at the kitchen island, grinning at me.

"We're about to put some steaks on the grill," Zack announces.

"Cara!" Seth calls from the couch. I abandon my suitcase and hurry over to him. His leg is propped up on pillows. He has soda and snacks, the remote, and comic books nearby on the coffee table and his dog lying on the floor by his side.

"Hey, buddy!" I hug him close and kiss his hair. "How are you feeling?"

"I'm okay. Did Uncle Josh apologize for being a jerk?"

"Yeah." I laugh and ruffle Seth's hair. "He did."

"Good." Seth smiles and then something on the TV catches his attention. "Holy crap, the Undertaker is gonna kill the Miz!"

I laugh as I leave him to watch television and join everyone else in the kitchen.

"Wrestling?" I ask dryly.

"The kid has good taste." Ty laughs and steals a black olive out of the pasta salad, earning a slap on the hand from Nancy.

"Welcome home." Zack stands and hugs me to him, rocking back and forth. "And thank you," he whispers in my ear.

"Hey, get your own girl," Josh growls, and pulls me out of Zack's arms, making us all laugh.

"Hi," Ty murmurs, and kisses my forehead.

"Hi." I offer him a smile and pat his arm gently.

"Better?" he asks.

"Much."

"Okay, he can live then."

"Are you done?" Josh asks with a scowl. "You also need to get your own girl."

"Hey, why didn't you tell me that Jilly was planning to move home?" I ask Ty, and glare at him as Josh passes me a Diet Coke.

"Jilly's moving home?" Ty asks, surprised.

"Yeah, in a few weeks."

"Awesome." He grins.

Josh and Zack exchange a look, and Ty notices.

"Are we going to have a problem?" Ty asks Zack.

"Only if you make it a problem," Zack responds, his face perfectly serious.

"She's gonna live with me for a while," I inform them all, trying to lighten the mood, then take a long sip of my soda.

"So she's gonna live—"

"At Cara's house in town," Josh cuts Seth off quickly.

The men and Nancy exchange small smiles.

I'm lost. "Am I missing something?"

"Nope." Josh shakes his head, grabs a large platter of steaks, and takes my hand. "Let's go throw these on the grill."

"Oh, hell no!" Zack objects. "You always overcook the steaks."

"I know how to cook a damn good steak," Ty announces.

"Actually, I'm going to let you guys fight over the steaks and go freshen up a bit." I tug on Josh's hand, pulling him down so I can kiss him quickly, but he passes the steaks off to Ty and folds me into his arms, bending me back and kissing the living hell out of me in front of his entire family.

"Wow," I mutter, breathless, when he lets me back up. "What was that for?"

"I just love you." He winks and smacks my ass as I turn to walk back to his bedroom.

"Love you back. I'll just be a minute."

"No hurry," he assures me happily as I saunter down the hallway, pulling my suitcase behind me.

I plop the heavy case on the bed and unzip it, pulling my toiletries out so I can brush my teeth and my hair and reapply deodorant.

Feeling marginally better, I grab a few things that need to be hung and move to the closet, coming to an abrupt halt at the open doorway.

There in the closet are all of my clothes from home, hanging side by side with Josh's things.

I'm struck speechless. I can't move. A dress falls

from my hands to the floor and my hand covers my mouth.

"I called in a favor," Josh says from behind me. I can't make myself turn around to look at him.

"What does that mean?" I whisper.

"You already agreed to move in here," he reminds me, and comes up behind me, wraps his arms around my waist, and kisses my cheek. "So while I was gone, I had Ty bring your clothes and personal things over. We can move the rest later."

"Kind of presumptuous, aren't you?" I ask dryly.

"Maybe." He turns me in his arms and tilts my chin back to look me in the eye. "I need to wake up next to you every morning, Carolina, starting now. Tell me this is okay."

"Are you gonna start wearing cowboy hats and belt buckles?" I ask with a half smile.

"I hadn't planned on it, no." He chuckles and nuzzles my nose with his, tucking my hair behind my ear.

"Maybe I'll start wearing cowboy hats," I giggle, and kiss him playfully.

"You can wear anything you like, sweetheart, as long as you do it while living here with me." He's grinning, but his eyes are watching me closely.

I sigh and drag my fingertips down his cheek. "There's nowhere else I'd rather be, my love."

Epilogue

— TWO MONTHS LATER —

"Wake up, my love."

"Hmph." I bury my face in the pillow.

I hear Josh chuckle as he sweeps my hair off my back to plant a kiss between my shoulder blades. "Carolina."

"I mope mom poo."

"What?" He laughs and pulls me over onto my back. "English, please."

"I don't want to," I pout. "Time is it?"

He brushes my hair off my face and cups my face in his hand, running his thumb over my bottom lip. "Just before five."

"I'm going to kill you." I don't open my eyes. Instead, I stay still, enjoying Josh's hands roaming over my naked body. "After you make love to me one last time."

"God, you're sexy," he whispers, and kisses my cheek. "Open those gorgeous eyes."

I comply and glare at him. "Why am I awake?"

"Why are your eyes so green?" He glides his hand from my face to my breast.

"Because you're touching me and I'm naked."

"Well, we can't stay in bed."

"We can do it in the shower." I smile when he tosses his head back and lets out his big belly laugh.

"Later. We have something to do first."

"You're right." I nod and settle down into the covers. "We need a couple more hours' sleep."

"No." He stands and yanks the covers off me.

"It's cold!" I squeal.

"So get up and get dressed." He winks and crosses his arms over his chest and I notice for the first time that he's already dressed.

"What's in it for me?" I ask suspiciously.

"Just do it, Carolina." He shakes his head and chuckles.

"Fine," I grumble, and stalk to the bathroom to pee, then past him to the closet to pull on my underwear, jeans, and a T-shirt. "Is it cold out this morning?" I call out to him.

"Don't worry about it, I have it covered."

As I pull on socks and shoes, I continue to grumble about the downside of living with a morning person and then follow him out of the bedroom and out to the barn.

"Good morning." Louie smiles widely at me, earning a small grin from me.

"Mornin'."

"Thanks, Louie." Josh lifts me up onto Magic and does that sexy leap-up thing behind me, then accepts a thermos from Louie. "We'll see you in a while."

"Have fun." Louie waves us off as Magic walks out of the barn and through the pasture, heading toward the special sunrise spot with the large maple tree.

"Here," Josh murmurs, and reaches down into a saddlebag, pulls out a thick down blanket, and wraps it around us to ward off the early-morning chill that has settled in the air.

Fall is approaching.

"Summer never lasts long enough," I complain.

"Not in Montana. I can already feel fall in the air."

"Me too."

"Do you want coffee?"

"Sure." I smile back at him.

"Okay, take the reins." He slips the leather straps into my hands and pours us one large cup of coffee to share, slips the thermos into a saddlebag, and comes back out with a red-and-white-checkered linen napkin wrapped around something that smells amazing.

He takes the reins from me after handing me the mug of coffee.

"What's in there?"

"Huckleberry muffins," he responds casually, knowing that the sweet treats are my favorite.

"Did your mom make these?"

"Yep."

"God, I love you." I open the fabric and pull out a muffin, still warm from the oven. "Oh, sweet Moses," I moan, and chew the muffin.

"Can I have a bite?" He chuckles as I hold the muffin up for him to bite. "Mmm . . . good."

"They are." I settle my back against his chest. "You're sure spoiling me this morning. A girl could get used to this."

"I hope so," he whispers, and kisses my head. "You deserve to be spoiled."

"You're sweet." I lean my head back and kiss his chin.

"Has Jill settled into your old place?" Josh takes a sip of our coffee.

"Yep, she's all settled. She got her Montana real estate license, so she's getting back to work and into the swing of things."

"Good. It's good having her home."

"It is." I take a deep breath. "It smells good out here."

We settle into comfortable silence as Magic takes us to our special place. Twilight begins to spread through the sky, casting the trees and mountains around us into gray shadow.

"Look," Josh whispers, and points to our right.

"Oh, wow!"

Five deer are grazing in the field and stop, their heads rising in the air and ears perking up at the sight of us.

"They're so beautiful. I never get tired of them."

"You're going to have to be extra careful this winter when you drive in to work every day," he reminds me. "I don't want you to hit a deer and have an accident."

"I'll be careful," I whisper, still watching the majestic animals.

We finally arrive at the big maple tree, just as the sun is about to rise over the mountain peaks ahead.

"So, could you maybe show me a sunset or two, rather than pull me out of bed at the butt crack of dawn?" I ask sarcastically, secretly relishing the warmth of Josh's arms around me, his solid chest against my back, and the treat of coffee and muffins on our way out here.

"I could"—he nods and tugs on a piece of my hair—"but then we'd miss out on this."

The very top of the sun peeks over the mountain and I sigh. "It's beautiful."

"You're beautiful." He kisses my neck and then my cheek before resting his lips on my head, breathing me in.

"You're sweet."

"Are you waking up?"

"I think so." I yawn and then giggle. "Maybe."

"Hmm."

"I want to see the tree again."

I feel him stiffen behind me. *Did I say something wrong?*

"Okay," he whispers, and guides Magic over to the tall, thick-trunked maple. The leaves are just beginning to turn orange.

I gaze lazily at the initials carved in the trunk, then my heart stops in my chest.

"Um, baby?"

"Yes."

"Am I still half-asleep and dreaming?"

He chuckles and kisses my hair. "I don't think so."

There in the tree is a new, fresh carving. In the center of a large heart are the initials C.D. + J.K.

I whip my head around and gaze up at Josh with wide eyes. He's smiling gently down at me, his brown gaze soft and happy.

"This tree"—he looks up into the thick branches— "has been a part of this land for a few hundred years. It has deep roots here, just like my family does."

His gaze finds mine again and he brushes the backs of his knuckles down my cheek. "Are you still with me?"

I nod numbly and watch him carefully.

"These couples"—he points at the tree and I follow his gaze, taking in each set of initials separately—"all had a deep love for one another and this ranch. They made their homes here, raised their children here, and loved each other here."

He tips my chin up with his fingers and smiles as he holds up a ring, gripped between his finger and thumb.

No box.

I swallow hard, feeling tears flood my eyes, and listen.

"This belonged to my grandmother. The one who always brought me here."

The ring is gorgeous. The center stone is a large blue sapphire, and round diamonds surround it.

"No measure of time with you will ever be long enough, Cara. I need you with me to make a home, raise our children, and love me. I want us to be part of this legacy."

He cradles my face in his hand and stares deeply into my eyes. "Marry me, Carolina. I promise you, I will spend every day making you happy."

Tears run unchecked down my face, and I'm shocked to see tears in his eyes. I glance back at the tree, the initials there, and take in the land around me.

He's offering me so much more than I ever dreamed possible.

"You do make me happy," I whisper, and smile up at him.

"You're killing me," he whispers, and leans his forehead on mine.

"Of course I'll marry you." I grip his face in my hand and wipe a tear with my thumb.

He takes my hand, kisses my knuckles, and then slips the ring on my finger. Light dances in the stones in the early-morning sunshine.

"I love you so much." He kisses my lips softly and

wraps his arms around me, pulling me against him tightly.

"I love you too," I whisper.

Cupping my face in his hands, he says with a grin, "Welcome to the family."

Want more steamy romance
on the Montana plains?

Read on for a sneak peek of Kristen Proby's

SEDUCING LAUREN

Book Two in the
Love Under the Big Sky Series

Coming soon from Pocket Books

"Hey, Lauren."

"Hi, Jacob, what can I do for you?" I ask with a smile, opening my front door wider for the friendly county sheriff deputy.

"Well, I'm serving you." He offers me an embarrassed smile and hands me a large envelope, then backs away. "Have a good day."

Without moving back inside or shutting the door, I stare down at the envelope in surprise.

Served?

I rip open the envelope and see bright, flaming, inferno red as I read the court document.

"The fucker is *suing me*?" I exclaim to an empty room and read the letter clutched in my now trembling hands for the third time. "Hell no!"

I grab my handbag and slide my feet into flip-flops,

barely managing not to fall down the porch steps as I tear out of my house to my Mercedes and pull out of my circular driveway.

I live at the edge of Cunningham Falls, Montana. The small town was named after my great-grandfather, Albert Cunningham. Ours is a tourist town that boasts a five-star ski resort and a plethora of outdoor activities for any season. Thankfully, summer tourist season is over and ski season is still a few months away, so traffic into town is light.

I zoom past the post office and into the heart of downtown, where my lawyer's office is. Without paying any attention to the yellow curb, I park quickly and march into the old building.

The receptionist's head jerks up in surprise as I approach her and slam the letter still clutched in my hand on her desk.

"*This*," I say between clenched teeth, "isn't going to happen."

"Ms. Cunningham, do you have an appointment with Mr. Turner?"

"No, I don't have an appointment, but someone in this firm had better find time to see me." I am seething, my breath coming in harsh pants.

"Lauren." My head whips up at the sound of my name and I see Ty Sullivan frowning at me from his office doorway. "I can see you. Come in."

I turn my narrowed eyes on Ty and follow him into his office. I am too agitated to sit while I wait for him to shut the door and walk behind his desk.

"What's going on?"

"I need a new lawyer."

"What's going on?" He asks again and leans back against the windowsill behind his desk. He crosses his arms over his chest. The sleeves of his white button-down are rolled up, giving me a great view of the sleeve tattoo on his right arm.

"This is what's going on." I walk to his desk and thrust the letter at him. "Jack is trying to sue me for half of a trust fund that he has no right to."

Ty's handsome face frowns as he skims the letter. "You came into the trust while you were still married?"

"Yes," I confirm warily.

"And you didn't tell him about it?" he asks with raised brows.

"I didn't even know the damn thing existed until after my parents died, Ty. Until *after* I kicked Jack out." I pace furious circles in front of his desk, breathing deeply, trying to calm down. "He doesn't deserve a dime of my inheritance. This isn't about money, it's about principle."

"I agree." Ty shrugs. "Have you talked with Cary?"

"I was just served with the letter," I mumble and sink into the leather chair in defeat. "Cary's a nice guy, but I just don't think he's the right lawyer for this job." I glance up at Ty and my heart skips a beat as I take him in now that I'm calming down. He's tall—much taller than me, which is saying something given that I stand higher than five foot eight. He has broad shoulders and lean hips, and holy hell, the things this man does to a suit should be illegal in all fifty states.

But more than that, he's kind and funny, and has a bit of a bad boy side to him too—hence the tattoos.

He's been front and center in my fantasies for most of my life.

I bite my lips and glance down as his eyes narrow on my face.

"Why do you say that?" he asks calmly.

"It took two freaking years for the divorce to be final, Ty. I don't want Cary to drag this out too."

"It wasn't necessarily Cary's fault that the divorce took so long, Lauren. Jack had a good lawyer and your divorce was a mess."

That's the fucking understatement of the year.

"Will you take my case?" I ask.

"No," he replies quickly.

"What?" I ask, my dazed eyes returning to his. "Why?"

He shakes his head and sighs as he takes a seat behind his desk. "I have a full load as it is, Lo."

"You're more aggressive than Cary," I begin to say but halt when he scowls.

"I really don't think I can help you."

Stunned, I sit back and stare at him. "You mean you won't." I hate the hurt I hear in my voice, but I can't hide it. I know Ty and I aren't super close, but I considered him a friend. I can't believe he's shooting me down.

He folds the letter and hands it back to me, his mouth set in a firm line and his gray eyes sober. "No, I won't. Make an appointment with Cary and talk it over with him."

My hand automatically reaches out and takes the letter from Ty, and I'm suddenly just embarrassed.

"Of course," I whisper and rise quickly, ready to escape this office. "I'm sorry for intruding."

"Lo . . ."

"No, you're right. It was unprofessional for me to just show up like this. I apologize." I clear my throat and offer him a bright, fake smile, then beeline it for the door. "Thanks anyway."

"Did you want to make an appointment, Lauren?" Sylvia the receptionist asks as I hurry past her desk.

"No, I'll call. Thanks."

I can't get to my car fast enough. Why did I think Ty would help me? *No one will help me!*

All the connections I have in this town, all the money I have, and that asshole is still making my life a living hell.

I drive home in a daze, and when I pull up behind a shiny black Jaguar, my heart sinks further.

Today fucking sucks.

Prepared to call for help if need be, I pull my cell phone out of my bag and climb out of my car. I walk briskly past him and up the steps to the front door.

"Hey, gorgeous."

"I told you not to come here, Jack. I don't want to see you."

"Aw, don't be like that, baby. You're making this so much harder than it needs to be."

Shocked and pissed all over again, I round on him.

"I'm the one making this hard?" I shake my head and laugh at the lunacy of this situation. "I don't want you here. The divorce has been final for weeks now, and you have no business being here. And now you're trying to fucking *sue me*?"

He loses his smug smile and his mouth tightens as

his brown eyes narrow. "No, I'll tell you what will make it easy, Lauren. You paying me what's rightfully mine is what will make it easy. You hid that money from me, and I'm entitled to half."

"I'll never pay you off, you son of a bitch." I'm panting and glaring, so fucking angry.

"Oh, honey, I think you will." He moves in close and drags his knuckles down my cheek. I jerk my head away, but he grabs my chin in his hand, squeezing until there's just a bit of pain. "Or maybe I'll just come back here and claim what's mine. You are still mine, you know."

My stomach rolls as he runs his nose up my neck and sniffs deeply. Every part of me stills. *What the fuck is this?*

"A man has the right to fuck his wife whenever he pleases."

"I'm not your wife," I grind out, glaring at him as he pulls back and stares me in the face.

He flashes an evil grin and presses harder against me. "You'll always be mine. No piece of paper can change that."

I don't answer, but instead just continue to glare at him in hatred.

"Maybe you should just go ahead and write that check."

He pushes away from me and backs down the stairs toward his flashy car, a car he bought with my parents' money, and snickers as he looks me up and down. "You've kept that hot body of yours in shape, Lo. Maybe I'll come back sometime and take a sample. Remind you of how much you loved it when I fucked your brains out."

I swear I'm going to throw up.

I can't answer him. I can only stand here and glower, shaking in rage and fear, as he winks again and hops in his Jag and drives away.

Jesus Christ, he just threatened to rape me.

I let myself into the house and reset the alarm with shaking fingers. I take off in a sprint to the back of the house and heave into the toilet, over and over again until there's nothing left and my body shivers and jerks in revulsion.

How can someone who once claimed to love me be so damn evil?

When the vomiting has passed, I rinse my mouth and head over to the indoor pool that my parents had built when I was on the swim team in high school. I shuck my clothes, but before I pull my swim cap on, I dial a familiar number on my phone and wait for an answer.

"Hull," he answers. Brad is a police detective in town, and someone I trust implicitly.

"It's Lauren."

"Hey, sugar, what's up?"

"Jack just left."

"What did that son of a bitch want?" His voice is steel.

"He threatened me." My voice is shaky and I hate myself for sounding so vulnerable. "I want it documented that he was here."

"Did you record it, Lo?"

"No. I wasn't expecting it. He's been an asshole in the past, but this is the first time he's come out and threatened me since he . . ." I pace beside the pool, unable to finish the sentence.

"That's because I put the fear of God and jail time in him." He's quiet for a moment. "Is there anything you need?"

I laugh humorlessly and shake my head. "Yeah, I need my asshole ex to go away. But for now I'll settle for a swim."

"Keep your alarm on. Call me if you need me."

"I will. Thanks, Brad."

"Anytime, sugar."

We hang up and I tuck my long auburn hair into my swim cap and then dive into the Olympic-size pool. The warm water glides over my naked skin and I begin the first of countless laps, back and forth across the pool. Swimming is one of two things in this world I do really well, and it clears my head.

I do some of my best thinking in the pool.

Is all of this worth it? I ask myself. When I married Jack almost five years ago, I was convinced that he was in love with me and that we'd be together forever. He'd been on my swim team in college. He was handsome and charming.

And unbeknownst to me, he'd been after my money all along.

My parents were still alive then, and even they had fallen for his charm. My father had been a brilliant businessman, and had done all he could to convince me to have Jack sign a prenuptial agreement so Jack couldn't stake any claim to my inheritance.

But blind with love and promises of forever, I had stood my ground and insisted that a prenup was unnecessary.

My dad would lose his mind if he knew what was happening now. If only I'd listened to him!

I tuck and roll, then push off the wall, turning into a backstroke.

The small amount of money that Jack is trying to lay claim to is nothing compared to the money I have that Jack knows nothing about. Since our legal separation, I've become very successful in my career as an author, but I wasn't lying when I told Ty that it's not about the money.

This is my heritage. My family worked hard for this land, for the wealth they amassed, and Jack doesn't deserve a fucking dime of it. That's why the divorce took so long. I fought him with everything in me to ensure that he didn't get his greedy hands on my family's money.

In the end he won a small settlement that all of the lawyers talked me into.

Jack wasn't happy.

I push off the edge of the pool and glide underwater until I reach the surface and then move into a front crawl.

After my parents died in a car accident just over two years ago, Jack made it clear that he didn't love me, had been sleeping around since we were dating, but expected me to keep him in his comfortable lifestyle.

And when I threw a fit and kicked him out, he slammed me against the wall and landed a punch to my stomach, certain to avoid bruising me, before he left.

Thanks to threats from Brad, and Jack knowing how well-known I am in this town, he hadn't bothered me since.

And now he's threatening to rape me.

Rape me!

It's not worth it. Living in constant fear and embarrassment of seeing Jack around town. Seeing the pity in the eyes of people I've known my whole life when I see them on the street.

And now coming home to an ambush because he's feeling desperate.

I'm done.

Exhausted and panting, I pull myself out of the water and resign to go see Cary in the morning to agree to a settlement.

It's time to move on.

It's early when I leave the house and drive to the lawyer's office. I don't have an appointment, and I don't even know for sure if anyone is there yet, but I couldn't sleep last night. I couldn't lose myself in work.

I need to get this over with.

When I stride to the front door, I'm surprised to find it unlocked. Sylvia isn't in yet, but I hear voices back in Cary's office.

I stride through his door like I belong there, and both Cary's and Ty's faces register surprise when they see me in the doorway.

"You know, Lo, we have these things called phones. You use them to call and make what's known as an appointment." Ty's gray eyes are narrowed, but his lips are quirked in a smile. He's in a power suit today, which makes my mouth water immediately. His shoulders look even broader in the black jacket, and the blue tie makes his eyes shine.

"Ha-ha," I respond and sit heavily in the seat before Cary's desk. "I'm sick of this shit."

"Ty told me you came by yesterday," Cary informs me as he leans back in his chair.

"I was fucking served papers," I mutter and push my hands though my hair. "But I think I want to settle."

Ty raises his eyebrows. "I'll leave you two alone."

"You can stay," I mutter. "I could use both of your opinions. I'll pay double for the hour."

"That's not necessary." Ty's voice is clipped and he frowns as he gazes at me. "Why the change of heart?"

I lean back in the chair, tilt my head, and look at the tin tiles on the ceiling.

"Because Jack's an asshole. Because now he's decided to threaten me." I shake my head and look Cary in the eye. "But no payments. It's going to be in one lump sum and he needs to sign a contract stating that he'll never ask for another dime."

"Wait, back up." Ty pushes away from the desk and glowers down at me. "What do you mean he threatened you?"

"It doesn't matter."

"Lauren," Cary interrupts, "it does matter. What the hell happened?"

"When I returned home, Jack was at the house."

"Does he still have a key?" Ty asks.

"No." I shake my head adamantly. "I changed all the locks and installed a new alarm system the day he left."

"So he was waiting outside," Cary clarifies.

"Yes. I told him to leave, that I didn't want to see him and he isn't welcome at the house. He said I was making things harder than they need to be." I laugh humorlessly as Cary's eyebrows climb toward his blond hairline.

"I reminded him that there's nothing difficult about this at all. We're divorced. It's over, and he can just go away." I shrug and look away, not wanting to continue.

"What did he threaten you with?" Ty asks softly.

I raise my eyes to his and suddenly my stomach rolls.

"I'm going to be sick." I bolt from the room and run to the restroom in the hallway, barely making it in time to lose the half-gallon of coffee I consumed this morning. When the dry-heaving stops, I rinse my mouth and open the door to find Ty on the other side.

"Are you okay?" he asks quietly.

I nod, embarrassed. He reaches up and gently tucks a stray piece of my hair behind my ear.

"What did he threaten you with?" He asks as he leads me back to Cary's office.

I swallow and cross my arms over my chest. I don't want to say it aloud. "He just threatened to be a dick."

"Bullshit," Cary responds, leaning forward in his chair. "Lo, the man wasn't afraid to put his hands on you when you told him to leave . . ."

"What?" Ty exclaims, but Cary continues.

"So you need to tell me what he threatened to do to you if you don't give him what he wants."

I shake my head and close my eyes, remembering the feel of Jack's nose pressed to my neck and the crazy look in his eyes when he wasn't getting what he wanted.

"Excuse us for a minute, Cary."

Ty takes my hand in his and leads me toward the door.

"Uh, my client, Ty, remember?"

"We'll be right back," Ty assures him and leads me into his office and shuts the door behind us.

"What did the asshole threaten to do to you, Lauren?"

"You said no yesterday, Ty. This isn't your case."

He shrugs, as if what I just said is of no consequence. "Answer me."

I simply shake my head. "It doesn't matter. Cary and I will figure it out. You don't have to stay in there with us."

I try to walk past him but he catches my hand in his, keeping me in place.

"Lauren . . ."

"Stop, Ty. You don't want me—I get it."

"Are you fucking kidding me?" he asks, his voice deceptively calm. "Do you know why I turned you down yesterday, Lauren?"

I shake my head, my eyes wide and pinned to his.

"Because it would be a conflict of interest. I can't be your lawyer because I'm your friend, and I want to be a whole lot more than that."

If I thought I was stunned before, it's nothing compared to this. My jaw drops as he closes the gap between us. He doesn't touch me, but his face is mere inches from mine. His eyes are on my lips as I bite them and watch him. I'm completely thrown by this turn of events.

"You have the most beautiful lips, Lo."

"What?" I whisper.

He takes a deep breath as he lays his thumb gently on my lower lip and pulls it from my teeth. "I want to taste these lips."

It's whispered so softly, I can barely hear the words. I can't tear my gaze away from his mouth and I take a deep breath, inhaling the musky scent of him.

I've forgotten Jack and his threats, the lawsuit.

Everything.

Ty clears his throat and backs away, watching me carefully. "Cary will remain your lawyer, but I want to know what the hell is going on, Lo. I can help."

I blink and continue to stare at him, completely dumbstruck.

He wants me?

"And another thing, Lauren. You're not settling. Fuck Jack and his lawyer."

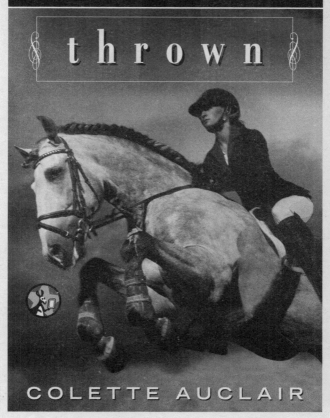